"What do y

D0709024

"I don't want a _____ _____ _____ed to the stairs. "But there's a little girl down there who thinks of you as her world. As her everything. As her—"

"Don't say it." Sophie lunged forward and pressed her palm over his mouth. "I'm better as Ella's aunt."

Brad pulled her hand off his mouth, anchoring her with their linked fingers. She searched his face, watched the emotions in his gaze and the words backing up against his closed lips. Maybe he finally understood.

"I lied." His voice was low. "I do want something from you."

Sophie waited. The attic seemed to be closing in on her. She shivered. "What?"

Brad tugged her close. "This."

Sophie stopped fighting, stopped running and stopped hiding. There was so much she couldn't be. Couldn't have. But this moment, she'd take this.

Dear Reader,

As a child, our family hopscotched across the US for my father's job. Living in Pittsburgh meant begging to be allowed into my brother's backyard snow huts and cheering on the Steelers. Houston brought rodeos and the largest flying cockroaches I've ever seen. Northern California introduced us to towering redwood trees and Lake Tahoe. And Hawaii gave us Christmas Day at the beach and a sense of aloha that remains with me today. My parents' relocations continued after my brothers and I moved out and I've been fortunate to experience even more new cities on my trips to visit them.

But one place has been a longtime favorite: San Francisco. I loved to visit the city as a child and I still cherish the time I lived there after college—ever grateful for the lasting friendships I made. Friends who today I consider family. I fell in love in the city and seventeen years later, my husband and I still talk about our first date to the Orpheum Theatre followed by a toast at The Fairmont Hotel.

I'm so thrilled to be able to write a series set in San Francisco with characters who discover all they've ever needed can be found in the City by the Bay, if they only open their hearts.

I love to connect with readers. Check my website to learn more about my upcoming books and sign up for email book announcements, or chat with me on Facebook (carilynnwebb) or Twitter (@carilynnwebb). Let me know what your favorite city is and I'll add it to my ever-expanding places-to-visit list.

Happy reading!

Cari Lynn Webb

www.CariLynnWebb.com

HEARTWARMING

The Charm Offensive

USA TODAY Bestselling Author

Cari Lynn Webb

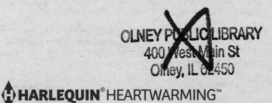 **HARLEQUIN**® HEARTWARMING™

Recycling programs
for this product may
not exist in your area.

ISBN-13: 978-0-373-36846-4

The Charm Offensive

This edition published by arrangement with Harlequin Books S.A.

For questions and comments about the quality of this book, please contact us at CustomerService@Harlequin.com.

Printed in U.S.A.

Cari Lynn Webb lives in South Carolina with her husband, daughters and assorted four-legged family members. She's been blessed to see the power of true love in her grandparents' seventy-year marriage and her parents' marriage of over fifty years. She knows love isn't always sweet and perfect—it can be challenging, complicated and risky. But she believes happily-ever-afters are worth fighting for.

Books by Cari Lynn Webb

Harlequin Heartwarming

Make Me a Match
"The Matchmaker Wore Skates"

To my daughter, Emma, whose laughter brightens every day. I love you more than you know. Don't ever stop laughing.

Special thanks to Melinda Curtis and Anna J. Stewart for answering every plotting SOS whether it was a late-night text, early morning email or last-minute Skype session. And thanks to my husband and family for their continuous encouragement and inspiration.

CHAPTER ONE

"THE WIRE TRANSFER was completed yesterday at the request of George Callahan." The financial advisor for Pacific Bank and Trust in San Francisco watched Sophie Callahan over a bland manila file folder. "The account is empty."

Empty. Sophie shifted sideways in the leather chair and crossed her legs as if that might minimize the impact of the woman's firm yet unapologetic voice. An ache wrapped around Sophie's throat and squeezed. "You're certain?"

"Yes. The funds have been withdrawn." She slid a floral tissue box closer to Sophie as if on cue. As if the efficient financial advisor had played out this scenario many times before and the tissues were standard procedure.

Sophie straightened her shoulders, refusing to slide back into the supple leather chair. The leather was pliant, not because it was expensive but rather from all the customers who'd collapsed after Beth Perkins, senior financial advisor, personally delivered their nightmares. "George Callahan is my father."

"According to our paperwork, he's joint owner of the savings account." Beth opened the manila folder and spun the documents to face Sophie.

Sophie recognized the flourish of her grandmother's signature in black ink on the bottom of the top page. Sophie's grandmother had added Sophie to her savings account seven years ago, the very same day her grandmother had told Sophie about her terminal cancer. Her grandmother had never mentioned that her son, George Callahan, was also listed on the savings account. And Sophie had been too busy, first caring for her grandmother those final months, then building her pet-store business and watching her three-year-old niece, to worry about who had access to the bank account.

She struggled now to make herself heard. "All of the money has been moved, then?"

And by all of the money, Sophie referred to the funds her grandmother's trust had released into the savings account at the first of the year with specific instructions to use for the purchase of the property where Sophie and her niece, Ella, lived. Sophie also referred to the additional money from the Pampered Pooch that she'd deposited at the end of every week so that one day, one day exactly twenty-nine days from now, Sophie would hold the title to the building in her own hands. And Ella would never again have to worry about losing the only home she'd ever known.

Sophie couldn't let Ella down. She couldn't fail her only niece. She couldn't become another rotted branch on the careless Callahan family tree.

"Yes, all of the funds have been transferred from the account." Beth put on a pair of trendy violet-framed glasses.

Ella would've loved the smooth lightweight glasses. But the oval shape only sharpened the woman's gaze, as if that alone would force Sophie to focus.

Sophie was focused. On her empty bank account.

"There's a balance due for the wire-transfer fee." Beth closed the folder and pulled out her keyboard. "Usually that's deducted from the funds, but for some reason that didn't happen yesterday. Do you intend to clear that now?"

Sophie jerked back against the chair. "A fee?"

Her father had drained their joint savings account and left Sophie to pay the fee. Her back seemed to be pinned against the leather chair like the large Post-it note tacked to Beth's bulletin board with "I love you mommy" written in blue marker and stamped with a greasy fingerprint. Sophie had never written notes like that to her parents. Notes like that refused to stick to vodka and gin bottles. As for fingerprints—well, generations of Callahan fingerprints were well documented at police stations across the nation.

Perhaps Sophie should've written notes like that to her father. Perhaps if she'd been a better daughter, George Callahan might've been a better father. A better father would not have drained the savings account without telling anyone. A better daughter would've been more diligent in anticipating such a disaster.

Beth stopped typing and looked across the desk at Sophie. "Would you like me to deduct the fee from your checking account?"

Sophie nodded, her head going up and down like one of those bobblehead dogs stuck to a vinyl dashboard. Because ready agreement was expected from people in stunned stupors. Shock scratched at her throat, stealing her voice and sucking every molecule of fresh air in the cubicle.

Beth's smile was more of a flat grin, a quick twitch of acknowledgment that neither upset her glasses nor loosened her hair-sprayed updo.

Sophie's account could not be empty. Not after all the sleepless nights, tears and hard work. That money had ensured Ella a home. That money had ensured that Ella would be safe.

Sophie slipped her fingers under her legs to keep herself still. To keep herself from wringing her hands or running her palms over her jeans in some falsely soothing gesture. She peeled her shoulders off the chair, leaned forward, then lied through a grin that revealed all of her teeth. "My father is always looking for the best return on our money."

Beth offered another quick twitch of a grin. The twitch of a person who recognized a lie.

Sophie continued, "It was certainly thoughtful of him to move the money to a higher-yield bond."

The only bond Sophie's father knew was a jail bond. Had he taken the money to avoid prison? He'd never mentioned jail when he'd called for his weekly catch-up with Ella two nights ago. He'd mentioned a plan to Sophie.

But her father always had a plan. Always some new scheme in the works. That was nothing new. He'd told Sophie not to worry. But she always worried. And he'd told Sophie not to panic. Too late for that.

If only Sophie hadn't been distracted by an eighty-pound poodle petrified by bathwater, she might've asked more questions about her father's latest scheme. Then she might've been able to squelch the fear curdling up through her now. Sophie squeezed her leg. "Who doesn't want more money these days, right?"

Beth kept up her rapid typing. The hard strike

of each finger against the key seemed to punctuate every lie Sophie uttered. "We offer some of the best rates in the city." Beth pushed a receipt across the desk. "It's unfortunate your father didn't meet with me. I could've helped him."

It was unfortunate her father hadn't spoken to anyone, mainly Sophie. It was unfortunate that Sophie had believed her money had been secure. It was unfortunate her father excelled at finding loopholes and using them to his advantage. He'd just never used Sophie as his advantage before.

Until now.

Beth removed her glasses and considered Sophie. "I certainly hope your father didn't lock up the funds for a certain period of time given your balloon payment is due in less than four weeks."

Sophie stretched her dry lips. "There's one thing my father knows and that's money."

Her father knew how to invest in business ventures that stretched the legal limits, use small loans to place bets at racetracks and make timely deposits into slot machines in Reno.

But Sophie would not lose their home or her business. She'd been homeless at Ella's age. No child should experience that depth of fear, especially her niece, who faced every day with courage and a smile. Without Ella's smile, Sophie just might forget to smile herself. And if that happened, Sophie feared she might lose more than their home. She just might lose herself.

Sophie pushed out of the chair. She had to get outside. She needed to find more air. She needed to find something to stop the buzzing in her head. She needed to find her father. "I'll have the money for the loan payment by the end of the month."

"I'll be here when you're ready to make that payment." Beth smiled and swiveled her chair toward her computer. "Enjoy the rest of your day, Ms. Callahan."

Outside, Sophie leaned against the stone wall of Pacific Bank and Trust. Damp, cold air stuck to her cheeks like blistering hand slaps. Stoplights flashed in the thick fog, dull yellow flares of criticism and condemnation and failure. Even the pigeons nesting up inside the Pacific Bank and Trust sign never cooed, as if already aware she couldn't afford to waste even one crumb.

Sophie searched the silver mist that had spilled into the city after yesterday's winter storm, seeking the silent romance of the fog she usually loved. But only a dull grayness blanketed the streets. In front of her, a bus hissed to a stop. Its electric lines sparked and its brakes wheezed an acrid, bitter scent as its occupants spewed onto the sidewalk and scattered like bees from a harassed hive.

Cell phones chimed, coffee splattered the cement, paper bags with morning breakfast muffins crumbled as late workers rushed to their high-rise cubicles and corner offices. Inside the fog, the city pulsed, reminding Sophie that she was an adult and no longer ten years old, shivering and hungry in a one-room apartment with only her sister, who was just a year older than she was. Two little girls confused and scared and all because of George and Cindy Callahan.

How dare her father try to thrust her back into her past. She'd overcome her childhood with persistence and will and guts. He'd not put her back there.

She pushed away from the wall and strode along the sidewalk, stretching her legs into a run. Each smack of her running shoe on the concrete dislodged her panic and organized her thoughts, enough to quiet the frantic little girl that screamed inside her.

Her father had to be in some kind of trouble to take that much money. He knew what the funds were for. If he'd only told Sophie, she'd have helped him. He was her father. That's what good daughters did, even when their fathers weren't always good.

At the fourth block, she pulled out her cell phone and left her father a lengthy voice mail, pleading with him to call her. By the sixth block, she'd slowed to a fast walk and sent him four texts: two pleas, one appeal and one demand.

Eleven blocks later, standing outside the Pampered Pooch, Sophie wiped her forehead with the sleeve of her sweatshirt and checked her phone. No response.

Silence was nothing new from George Callahan. Her father had always drifted in and out of Sophie's life. The length of his stays had increased the last few years and he always surfaced eventually. Yet this time, Sophie couldn't wait. She had to find him and her money and soon.

For now though she had a business to run and a niece to get to school.

The bells chimed on the door. Sophie stepped inside, leaving that frightened little girl from years past outside on the sidewalk. Inside these walls, Sophie Callahan was a confident small-business owner and capable caretaker. There was simply no room for anything else, like doubt or nerves.

Sophie flipped the sign in the window to Open and greeted April, one of her three employees, the one who managed to be both her most reliable and most scattered employee in the same week. Sophie never quite knew which April would show up on any given workday. But even April not at her best was better than no one at all. "Did you get some sleep last night?"

April waddled over to settle on the stool behind the counter. A bandanna corralled her unruly burst of wild burnt-copper curls, and a tie-dyed sweatshirt almost contained her protruding belly. "Barely. The babies kicked all night and my maternity clothes barely fit anymore."

"You're seven-and-a-half months pregnant with twins—I imagine that's typical." Sophie used the rolling cart to prop open the swinging door to the back room.

"So is bed rest," April muttered.

"Bed rest?" Sophie gripped, in a bear hug, the fifty-pound bag of dog food she was hefting, needing to squash the kernels of panic popping through her core. "As in 'you have to stay in bed and can only get out to use the bathroom' bed rest?"

"Yes, that kind exactly." April rolled a pawprint pencil between her fingers, but wasn't able to hide the misery in her voice.

Sophie adjusted the bag in her arms and walked down the center aisle, feeling uneasy. Selfishly, she needed April in the store, not in bed. Reliable April was good with customers and calming for the pets, and lately she'd been helping Sophie organize the Paws and Bark Bash.

The gala would raise funds for service dog organizations and rescue groups that helped with homeless animals in the Bay Area. Now Sophie had her father to locate. Who'd run the store while Sophie chased down George?

She dropped the heavy bag on the bent shelf. She'd known April would go on maternity leave; she'd just assumed she'd have more time to prepare. Things were supposed to be different in four weeks when Sophie had paid her debts in full. Instead, all Sophie had was an empty bank account, a missing father and surging panic that'd consume her if she wasn't careful.

Sophie glanced over the top shelf at April. Tears filled April's eyes and slipped down her full cheeks. Sophie rushed to the younger woman, swiping the box of tissues from the far end of the counter. "You have to do what's best for your babies. It's going to be fine."

Everything had to be fine. Sophie had no other choice.

"I can't stay in bed all day." April pressed a tissue to her eyes. "It's best for my babies if I stay here during the day. With you and Troy and Erin doing the legwork, I could sit on this stool. Bed or stool, what does it matter?"

"Being in bed won't be that bad." Sophie handed April another tissue. "Besides, you have to follow the doctor's orders for the babies' safety."

"I can't do this." More tears dampened April's cheeks.

"We'll get through it." Sophie rubbed April's shoulders. "Everything will work out." Maybe if Sophie repeated it often enough and shouted it loud enough, she'd start to believe her own words.

Troy, full-time college student, part-time pet-shop worker, called out from the back room before he leaned around the cart in the doorway. "Soph, can you help with the morning arrivals?"

Sophie drew a deep breath. Her cell phone hadn't vibrated in her back pocket. Her father hadn't responded. She'd lost her entire savings and an employee in the same morning. That little panicked girl from her past tapped on the front window, wanting to be let in. Sophie turned her back on the store entrance. "I'll help you get the dogs settled, then call Erin to see if she can come in earlier."

The bell chimed on the front door behind Sophie, signaling the arrival of their first morning customer. Sophie ignored whoever it was. "April, do not move from this stool. If that customer needs assistance, I'll be right back." At April's nod, Sophie rushed through the back to the two outdoor play yards.

Doggy day care was almost full. Her rescued Lab-mix and two senior cats had finally been adopted into their forever homes yesterday. Sophie ran some calculations, hoping that would be enough to cover Erin's and Troy's overtime. One day she wouldn't have to budget by the hour. At least that had been the plan. In a notebook upstairs in her third-floor apartment, she'd designed an area for more kennels to offer long-term boarding services and allow her to take in more animal rescues. She'd mentally renovated the empty second-floor apartment for a vet's office. She'd drawn the layout for her modern storefront. She'd visualized the growth of her business, visualized making the Pampered Pooch a full-service one-stop that catered to a pet's every need, both house pets and service animals. Unfortunately, she'd never visualized the disappearance of all her money that'd ensure her future vision.

And, worse, she'd never visualized not living and working here, in this space. Their home. That rapping on the glass increased, the terrified tempo tripping through her. No, she wasn't that forgotten little girl. She'd find her money and save everything.

Stepping around a crate of dog treats in the storage room, she texted an SOS to Ruthie Cain, her best friend since freshman year in high school. They'd bonded while waiting to be picked joint last for the volleyball team in PE. She strode through the cramped kennel area and pulled up short to avoid slamming into the male back filling the doorway. The man's broad shoulders looked as if he could hold the weight of the world without stumbling.

But physical appearance wasn't an indication of the size of one's heart. She'd witnessed more strength of character in a thirty-pound toddler than in most grown men. That same toddler now stood just over four feet—a compact package of bravery, kindness and a pure heart who reminded Sophie every day that good still existed.

Her cell phone vibrated and she opened a new text from Ruthie. Help was less than ten minutes away.

"Excuse me." Sophie stuffed her phone into her back pocket and squeezed around the man in the archway, but she didn't manage to avoid contact. She popped out into the storefront and caught her running shoe on the wheel of the rolling cart. What was happening? She confronted the stranger, the rolling cart the only barrier between them. "This area has to remain clear." And it wasn't just for fire-code reasons.

"I'm attempting to clear the area now." The man grinned at Sophie.

There was nothing symmetrical in the small

smile that lifted only one side of his mouth, backed up into a sculpted cheekbone and sparked into his more green than brown eyes. She'd never quite understood that centuries-old fluttery feeling women described until now. She'd never liked being too warm or too queasy or too aware of those complicated emotional spots deep inside her. She blamed the single dimple denting his left cheek and wished he'd step behind the storage-room door. Instead, he studied Sophie as if she might be his next task on his own private to-do list. And made her wonder if she ranked first. Sophie told herself to focus and cleared her throat. "You need to move."

"If you step aside, the cart and I can clear the doorway."

Even his smooth voice appealed to her. But good-looking men were like designer shoes in the department store. She'd notice, acknowledge and keep moving. Designer shoes busted her budget; good-looking men busted more than her bank account, like her heart.

April slid a dented, damp cardboard box across the counter where she perched. "He offered to shelve the dog food in exchange for these little guys."

Sophie held the man's gaze and willed April not to open the box. Prayed April wouldn't open the box. Sophie didn't want to know what little helpless guys shivered inside. She couldn't accept any more rescues. "Our kennels are full."

"But there're five wet and dirty babies in here." April spread a lavender Pampered Pooch towel across the counter. "Five teeny, tiny kittens that can't be more than four weeks old."

Sophie gripped the metal handle on the rolling cart. She didn't want to know. Didn't want to look. It was a school day. She was losing her employee. And she had to find her father. Wasn't that enough for a Friday?

Mewling and scratching sounds drifted from inside the cardboard and stuttered against her heart. She didn't have time to call Dr. Bradshaw to examine the kittens or search for the heat lamp in the basement or reorganize an already too-crowded kennel. She had to save her home, not add more dependents to it. "We don't have room for your kittens."

"They aren't my kittens." He pointed over her shoulder. "I found them outside on your doorstep when I arrived."

"I'm sure your vet will take them in." Sophie tore off a corner of the waterlogged box flap and crushed it in her fist. That was the closest she'd get without risking her resolve. Neglectful pet owners, even the good-looking ones, made her tired and angry. "And while you're there, pay to have your adult cat spayed to prevent this from happening again."

"I'm not a cat person. I prefer dogs." He shoved his fingers through his chestnut hair, creating spikes on top of his head. "Those baby kittens would be invisible next to the size of dog I prefer."

"You're doing the right thing," she said. He was more appealing with his disheveled hair and earnest tone and tense dark eyebrows over his hazel eyes. He didn't like to be doubted. Sophie didn't like mistreated animals. Even more, she didn't like that this stranger made her want to check her teeth for spinach from last night's salad, pinch her cheeks for color and take off her baseball cap to fix her hair. *Notice, acknowledge and move on.* She'd noticed his charm. She'd acknowledged his good looks. Now she needed to move on. "I'm not accusing you of neglect or being a bad pet owner."

"Suggesting is almost the same." He rubbed his cheek, erasing his dimple. "In fact, suggestion is often confused with accusation."

Tension sharpened his voice and narrowed his eyes. Being accused of lying did not sit well with him. Sophie didn't care about preserving his pride. She was the voice for the abandoned and mistreated and neglected. "And we're thankful you're willing to surrender this litter."

Her placating tone hit another mark. He thrust his arm out and pointed at the corner behind the counter. "If your security camera was installed and not lying on the floor like a forgotten doorstop, you'd have the footage to show that I picked up the box outside your door." He leaned across the rolling cart toward her. "You'd also have the footage of the actual cat owner and you could harass that individual, instead."

Sophie leaned toward him, dropping her voice to a low menace. "I haven't even begun to harass you." That might be laying it on a bit thick, but she wanted him as unsettled as he made her.

"I don't suppose you'd consider it harassment." His voice softened, the edge receding from his words. "You're the self-appointed guardian of helpless animals."

Sophie stretched into every inch of her five-foot-five-inch frame. "Seven years ago, I opened the doors to this pet store and doggy day care to give working pet owners affordable and safe options for their apartment pets. I offer training and socialization classes. I foster and meticulously match every pet to each family. I've never denied a return or surrender. If there's a rescue organization in northern California, I've partnered with them. There's no 'self-appointed' about any of it. This is my business. My life."

"And my life is not animal neglect." He

crossed his arms over his chest and tipped his head, his gaze fastened on Sophie.

"There's an all-white one in here." April interrupted their stand-off.

Sophie held her breath. Don't let it have blue eyes. Please, no blue eyes. Sophie needed the cart moved. Needed this man and his kittens gone. She couldn't afford another rescue. She held the man's gaze, refusing to even peek in April's direction.

A squeak, and then April's words, softer than a sigh. "Both eyes are blue."

"Are blue eyes bad?" Concern filtered through her cat rescuer's voice.

"Over seventy-five percent of pure white cats born with blue eyes are deaf." She rambled off feline statistics as if it mattered. The kitten's second fragile mewl splintered through Sophie, mocking her resolve to ignore it. Sophie took the white kitten from April and wrapped it in the lavender towel.

Sophie hadn't really stood a chance. She couldn't have denied shelter to this abandoned litter, deaf kitten or not. Apparently, she hadn't yet reached her maximum capacity for helping those in need.

"Someone just abandoned a litter of kittens, and one or more might be deaf?" Outrage and confusion collided, deepening her cat rescuer's voice like a slow roll of thunder before the lightning strike. He glanced between the kitten in Sophie's arms and the one climbing over April. Finally, he looked at April, as if he didn't believe Sophie. When April nodded, he cursed under his breath.

Whether it was his outrage on the kittens' behalf, or that she'd insulted him and he'd refused to back down, Sophie believed him. He'd found the box outside. He wasn't the cat's owner.

"It happens more than we'd like." April kissed her gray kitten on its head and returned it to its siblings. "Sophie rescues anything in need. She'll fatten these little guys up and care for them like she cares for everything—the right way. Her DNA won't let her turn anyone away. Ever."

"Speaking of taking care, April, you need to get your feet up." Sophie placed the white kitten in the box with the others. None of them looked similar. It was as if each had been picked from assorted purebred litters, then tumbled together like mismatched socks. But they curled up as one, paws and tails entwined for warmth, security and survival, like a family. And now they'd be part of her family. "We can't ignore your doctor's orders. It sets a bad precedent."

"Back on the stool now." April frowned. "Resting."

"And you're swelling." Sophie pointed at April's ankles, which were swollen above her slip-on canvas shoes.

The man cleared his throat and pointed to the cart. "I'll just shelve all this and get that dog food I came in for."

Sophie dropped her hand on the cart and stopped the man from rolling it away.

"I ordered most of the dog food we carry and can tell you the best kind for your particular dog's needs," April offered in her excellent customer-service voice.

Of course, April had chosen today to contend for employee of the month, when unfortunately, these moments had become more and more rare. Still, Sophie frowned at the hope April injected into her voice. "You'll help by going home to bed."

"But we have customers, and you have meetings later this morning and only Troy here until this afternoon. And now kittens to clean up and create space for." April never budged from the stool. "Besides, I'm better here."

Sophie wrapped an arm around April's shoulders, nudging her off the stool. "I'll bring the laptop over this afternoon, and we can go over the table arrangements for the gala. While you wait, you can catch up on some daytime talk shows."

"I don't like those shows. They're always about bad relationships or weight loss." April yanked her sweatshirt down.

"Then watch reruns or read that mom-to-be book I gave you." Sophie grabbed April's purse from under the counter. "Just get into bed. The store will be fine today."

"What about tomorrow?" April refused to take her purse.

"One day at a time." Or, Sophie corrected, one crisis at a time. The cart rolled forward—or one customer at a time. She tossed April's purse on the counter and spun, gripping the cart handle and stopping the cart from moving another inch. "I won't let you shelve this dog food."

"You can't exactly stop me." He tipped his head toward April. The woman scooted her pregnant belly back behind the counter like the good employee she wanted to be.

Sophie frowned.

"She can't do any heavy lifting," her helpful customer continued, his voice all patient logic and reason. "And you obviously have a busy morning."

She'd already had too much *busy* in her morning. She wanted her normal routine. The one where everyone listened to her and followed her rules. "If you fracture your back on my property, you can sue for damages," she said. "I can't have a lawsuit." She most definitely couldn't have a lawsuit, not with everything else.

"I'm well trained in heavy lifting." He pushed on the cart.

Sophie shoved back, stalling the cart in the doorway and her customer, with his warm smile and easy banter, in the storage room. But she'd never trusted charm and understood all too well the power of false advertising. She'd purchased those trendy boots that had guaranteed flexibility and pillow-like cushioning and all-day comfort and only ended up with raw, open blisters on both heels after one day. Shoes and men were not mistakes she intended to repeat.

The sleigh-style bells chimed on the front door. April stashed her purse, settled on the stool and slid the kitten box closer.

Sophie never loosened her grip as she twisted around and exhaled. Everything was about to return to normal. She gave a quick prayer of thanks for the arrival of her practical, steady and composed best friend.

Ruthie stepped inside, threw her hands wide and grinned at Sophie. "Okay. Duke and Lady are out back running with their doggy friends. I've rescheduled my morning conference to this afternoon. I'm all yours until one o'clock."

The bells chimed again. Matt, Ruthie's fiancé since their Thanksgiving engagement, strode in.

"Sophie, please tell me that Ruthie won't have to work the cash register."

"April is still here to train me." Ruthie waved at April before jamming her elbow into Matt's side. "Besides, I can run that little credit-card machine without crashing it."

"Sophie, maybe I should stay here." Matt dropped his arm around Ruthie's waist and tugged her into his side.

There was nothing possessive or overpowering about Matt's embrace. It was as if he simply needed Ruthie closer to him in order to breathe. A sigh shifted through Sophie. Love suited her friends.

Matt grinned at Sophie. "We can send Ruthie to my job site. She'd be safer using power tools."

"I lecture to halls with over four hundred college freshmen." Ruthie pushed on Matt's chest, but he never loosened his hold. "I can handle this."

Sophie discovered her first smile of the morning. Her grip on the cart eased. She'd needed her friends. The ones that understood why doggy day care clients dropped their dogs off in the back, but entered the store from the front. The ones that followed the protocol and never wavered. Never altered Sophie's rules. Never commandeered rolling carts. If it had simply been important to Sophie, they'd have done it to appease her. But Sophie's priority was Ella's safety and her friends recognized that, too.

She spun around and faced her kitten rescuer. "You can get your dog food now. I've got this."

"Sophie, let Matt deal with that loaded cart," Ruthie said.

"Out of the way." Matt's strong hands landed on Sophie's shoulders and stilled. "Brad?"

Sophie's customer leaned across the cart and reached for Matt's hand. "I didn't want to interrupt. This must be Dr. Ruthie Cain, the fiancée you can't stop bragging about?"

Ruthie's voice echoed the happiness in her wide smile. "Still getting used to that."

"Ladies, this is Brad Harrington," Matt said. "I've been a consultant for Brad going back several years now."

Matt wore stained jeans, a plaid button-down shirt and steel-toed boots for his part-time job renovating historic buildings in the city. He also spoke more than half-a-dozen languages fluently and primarily worked as a translator contracted to the United States government for secret missions that Sophie believed saved the world, but Matt never confirmed nor denied. He was quite simply a brilliant mind wrapped in a handsome package. Sophie shifted her attention to Brad in his jeans, pullover and dimpled smile.

He *was* Matt's friend. But she didn't trust

him and definitely didn't want to know anything more about him. She was better off cata-
loguing Brad as that random kitten finder. "Do
you work with Matt on his renovations or on his
translation jobs?"

"Matt has the gift with languages. I'm in security." Brad edged around the cart, stepped behind
the counter and picked up the security camera
from the floor. "I make these work correctly."

Matt frowned at her. "Sophie, I could've introduced you to Brad a while ago. I thought you
got that taken care of."

"The manual to install it made it sound easier
than it is." Sophie took the camera from Brad
and set it on the counter. "I'll get to it."

"I bet you haven't fixed that front lower window yet, either." Ruthie eyed the kitten box.

"Some things came up." Like the trip to Chicago for a second opinion on Ella's eye surgery.
There weren't any extra funds for window repair. And now she was out of funds, thanks to
her father. "It's fine. The glass is taped and I
added a piece of plywood on the inside."

"Anyone can kick that in," Brad said.

"That's what I told her when she did it," April
added. The extra tablespoon of gracious, oblig-
ing customer service saturated any condescending dips in her tone.

"Anyone can bust through the glass door

if they really wanted to steal catnip." Sophie scowled at Brad and willed him to be stiff and cold and abrasive like those expensive red heels she'd seen in the window display on Union Street. An alarm was quite low on her list of things to deal with. If she didn't have a store, she wouldn't need an alarm. She wanted to pull out her phone and see if her dad had replied. Or, better yet, keep calling him until he answered.

"That's why you need that installed." Brad gripped the cart handle and pulled, rolling past her. His tone patient, his voice calm, his words all too reasonable.

Sophie crammed her hands into the wide front pocket of her sweatshirt and tipped her chin up, defiance tumbling through her words. "Show me someone who will install it for free and I'll get it done today."

"I'll do it." Brad smiled at her, distracting her with his dimple.

Sophie paused. Hadn't he heard her? "I can't pay you."

"We'll work out a trade."

"Other than dog food, I don't have much to bargain with," Sophie told him.

"The only Harrington in need of dog food is Brad's mother." Matt guided the front of the cart down the dog-food aisle, then glanced at Brad. "Unless you broke your own vow and adopted a pet, following in your mother's footsteps, after all."

Sophie watched Brad's shoulders stiffen as if he'd been poked with a thick needle. He hadn't liked Matt's comment. Brad pressed his lips together as if to keep his response from flying free. And Sophie wanted to know what he refused to say. Sophie wanted to know about his family. Sophie wanted to know about this man.

But that wasn't right. She wasn't interested *in* Brad. She'd given up on relationships and all that ten years ago when she'd climbed into the ambulance with her unconscious sister and her three-pound niece born with a drug addiction eight weeks too early. Love stories belonged to people like Ruthie and Matt. Sophie might dream about her own fairy tale in the darkest, quietest, loneliest hour of the night, but dawn always returned her to reality.

Ruthie nudged Sophie. "Brad's mother is the newly elected mayor of Pacific Hills. If you traveled down the coast at all last fall, you would've seen her campaign posters with the two greyhounds in shop windows and on the residents' lawns throughout the entire town."

"Your mother is Mayor Harrington?" Sophie had vowed never to follow in her own mother's shallow footsteps. But Brad's mother was mayor of the coastal town south of the city. Surely being like Mrs. Harrington wasn't a bad thing.

"She is," Brad admitted. "And I'm definitely not following in her footsteps."

His voice was tight and drew her in even more. "You don't want to be mayor?"

"I'll leave the politics to my brother." Brad lifted a bag off the cart and passed it to Matt. "And stick with what I know."

Sophie needed to stick with what she knew, too. And that wasn't Brad Harrington. Both Brad and Matt towered over the squat shelves that she swore groaned and pleaded for retirement every time she restocked. But the place was stuck in its current unpampered state, much like Sophie was stuck in baseball caps and budget lockdown. This was her life.

She pulled her baseball cap lower on her forehead. "You must have other clients or business to attend to. Something more important than installing a security system in a pet store for free."

"I'm crashing at our friend's place until my boat is ready," Brad said. "Zack can use the food for the dog he rescued on his last trip to the mountains."

"You're still setting sail, then?" Matt asked.

"Just waiting for the guys at Delta Craft to let me know the restoration is complete." Brad tossed the last bag to Matt. "Hopefully before the end of the month, I'll sail out of the bay."

"What about your job?" Sophie asked. "What about your family?"

"My partner is handling things in my absence," Brad said.

Sophie noted he never volunteered anything about his family. And again she wanted to know more. But he was leaving. What else mattered?

"Brad is the H in J & H Associates." Matt straightened the food bags on the weary shelf. "Always helps when you own the company."

Sophie nodded. She was a business owner herself, but leaving had never been a consideration. *Never.* Not even for a long weekend. She had to be here to maintain the business and provide for her niece. An indefinite hold had been put on vacations. Last fall, she'd taken a day trip with Ella to Chicago for a second opinion on Ella's eye surgery. Less than a twenty-four-hour turnaround, with most of their time spent in airports and waiting rooms. Definitely not Sophie's idea of a vacation.

"So, do we have a deal?" Brad wiped his hands on his jeans and smiled. "Security system for dog food."

"What kind of dog did your friend rescue?" Sophie was curious. "A Chihuahua hardly eats enough to pay for the cost of the security system."

"A forty-five-pound mutt with one blue eye and one green eye," Brad said. "I can be done installing this unit within the day."

A day. She could handle one day with Brad Harrington. Brad's presence was fleeting, like that wistful glance at the designer shoes in the department store window   noticed and forgot ten. "You have a deal."

"That gives you about eight more hours to harass me," Brad said.

The grin in his voice and the laughter in his gaze pulled her own smile to the surface.

"I'll be back after I pick up a few things." Brad looked at Matt. "Do you have a tape measure in your truck?"

"I'm parked out front." Matt hugged Ruthie and moved to the front door.

Sophie watched Brad head toward the broken window. "I'll replace that," she said.

Brad faced her and shook his head. "This one is on me. Can't put in a new security system when there's a broken window."

There was a stubborn set to his mouth, but something in his manner, how his head tilted just slightly, made her think he welcomed her argument. He wanted her to spar. Sophie stuffed her hands in her back pockets and held his stare, once again aware of that fluttery feeling in her core and her too-warm skin. His one-sided grin twitched into place as if he was aware of her feelings.

"Auntie!" Ella's panicked shout steamrollered over all those soft, romantic notions inside Sophie.

Nice smiles, belly flutters—but Brad Harrington didn't belong in Sophie's world. Her reality was a ten-year-old girl, eye doctors and abandoned things.

Sophie swung around as Ella stepped into the doorway, a neon-pink brush stuck in her knotted hair, her fingers gripped around her white cane. "Auntie, I told Charlotte I'd have braids today. She has braids today. And I promised we'd match for the field trip. We have to match. It's pairs day. You have to match your partner on pairs day."

Sophie hurried over to her niece and started working the hairbrush loose. "Well, it's a good thing Ruthie is here then, because there's no one better at braids than her."

Ella pushed her eyeglasses up her nose. "I thought I heard her. And Matt, too?"

"Good morning, Ella-Bell," Matt called from the entrance. "Need a lift to school today?"

"I don't want to wrinkle my dress," Ella said. "Auntie ironed it last night."

"Then we'll plan another date." Matt walked outside, letting the door swing shut behind him.

Ella smoothed her hands over her dress and whispered to Sophie. "I haven't wrinkled it yet, have I?"

"You look perfect." Sophie leaned in and kissed Ella's porcelain cheek.

"But am I wrinkled?" Ella stretched out the last word, unable to contain her concern.

"Not one wrinkle." Ruthie adjusted the bow at Ella's waist. "Now do you want one braid or two?"

Ella's shoulders lowered and the corner of her bottom lip disappeared between her teeth. "Charlotte says she has less hair than me. She says her hair is flat and mine is puffy."

"That's your curls, Ella." Sophie freed the brush and untangled the worst snarl. "Charlotte's mother texted me last night. She can't do French braids, so Charlotte will have two ponytail braids."

"Ruthie, can you do a French braid?" Hope pushed out Ella's words in a rush.

Ruthie squeezed Ella's shoulders. "How about two French braids? That will still look like two ponytails."

"You can do that?" Ella asked.

"Anything for you," Ruthie said.

"Careful, Ruthie, or Ella will call you over

every morning to style her hair before school."
Sophie handed Ruthie the hairbrush.

Ella shook her head. "Only on special occasions. I don't want to inconvenience her."

The sincerity in Ella's tone and seriousness in the firm set of her mouth ripped through Sophie's heart. Ella had feared being an inconvenience ever since she'd overheard a conversation between Sophie and her older sister, who was also Ella's mother. The little girl hadn't needed supersensitive hearing skills during that particular morning. Sophie had dragged Tessa into the shower, fully clothed, after her sister's two-day-long binge of drinking and drugs. Even through the hair pulling, kicking and continued resistance, Tessa had never ceased ranting about the inconvenience of family. The inconvenience of parenting. The inconvenience of children.

Sophie rubbed behind her ear. Her hair had grown back, yet the memory still lingered in vivid color. But the imprint on a young, innocent child was the deepest wound, and that unseen scar remained. No matter how often Sophie tried to prove to Ella she wasn't an inconvenience or encourage her to leave out that word from her vocabulary, she hadn't succeeded. But she'd never stop trying.

Sophie hugged Ella. "Okay. Ruthie, while you

braid, April can give you tips on how to use the cash register."

Ruthie groaned. "But you told me I wouldn't need to run that ancient thing."

"It'll be fine." Sophie pushed confidence into her voice. Her friend was a brilliant PhD, but far from tech savvy. "The cash register is vintage, that's all."

"And temperamental and finicky," April added.

Sophie plowed on. "We might not have any customers this morning. So this is just in case."

"It's Friday. The bell chimes at least eighteen times on Friday mornings," Ella said, and nodded, authority lacing her matter-of-fact tone. "I counted when I was home sick a few weeks ago."

"That was a rare day," Sophie lied.

"Auntie, you told me it was slower than usual that day." Ella frowned.

Sophie kissed her niece's cheek to distract her. "You stand still and get braided. I'm putting a load of laundry into the washing machine and checking on Troy. Then we'll walk to school. April, you have twenty minutes to talk Ruthie through things and then you're off, too."

"Are the babies coming?" Excitement lifted Ella's voice into a breathless pitch.

"Not today." Relief poured into Sophie's words

as she rushed through the back door. Delivering twins couldn't be on today's to-do list.

"I'll be here later this morning if Ruthie has any trouble," Brad called from the front of the store.

Sophie shook the smile off her face. That she liked the idea of Brad being here poked at her conscience; she'd buried these kinds of feelings so deeply inside her, so long ago, she'd assumed they'd be lost forever.

Sophie returned to the group and touched Ella's shoulder. "Brad rescued a litter of kittens this morning and he's agreed to put in the security system today."

"How many kittens?" Ella clasped her hands together. "Can we keep them?"

"Only until we find them their forever homes," Sophie answered.

"This could be their forever home," Ella said. "With us."

Sophie rubbed her forehead. First, she had to ensure Ella had a forever home. "You know the deal. We can't keep them forever, only for now."

"Can I hold one?" Ella asked.

"After Ruthie finishes your hair and only for a minute. You don't want to miss the bus for your field trip."

"Ask for the white one," Brad said. "She's a puffball and soft like a cloud."

Ella laughed. "She sounds perfect."

Sophie watched Brad walk outside. Something about him made her want to pull up a chair and ask questions. But Sophie didn't have time for idle conversations over coffee and cake. She'd never had time for the frivolous. Thankfully, she had less than twenty-four hours to spend with Brad because there were some things Sophie could never have. Brad Harrington was one of them.

CHAPTER TWO

BRAD NOTICED SOPHIE push the empty cart into the back room. For such a petite package, the woman remained a study in motion. She hadn't stopped moving since she'd wedged herself between him and the cart and demanded he stop shelving her dog food.

He wouldn't be surprised if she'd already found families for those kittens he'd brought inside.

She was efficient, competent and obviously guilty—like her father. There had to be a dark side to balance all that good, and he'd always been fascinated with exposing that shady inner core. And Sophie Callahan was too fascinating.

Matt leaned against his truck and tossed the tape measure at Brad. "Got a case you're investigating?"

"No." Brad caught the tape measure and avoided his friend's stare. He wasn't working a case. He was doing a favor. A favor for the widow whose late husband should be seated behind the Pacific Hills mayor's desk, instead of his mother. "Would it matter?"

"If it involved Sophie Callahan, then yes, it'd matter." Matt came over to stand beside Brad. "It'd matter a lot."

Despite his experience, and what it had taken to build his company into a high-end forensic accounting and surveillance specialist firm, Brad hadn't anticipated his friend's reaction. Brad tapped the toe of his boot against the corner of the plywood-covered window. If he rammed his foot into the adjoining window, he'd shatter the glass. Nothing unexpected about that. Whereas everything was unexpected about Sophie.

His grandmother had dragged him to the symphony when he was thirteen. He'd been struggling to fit into his height, cursing his pimples and praying Sarah Quincy wouldn't spot his braces. He'd lodged a series of complaints longer than any kid's Christmas wish list from the back seat of his grandfather's pickup, and still they'd arrived early to the performance. He'd slouched in his chair, dug his chin into his chest, convinced the evening would be torture.

But the music—the drive of the woodwinds, beat of the percussion and harmony of the strings—collided inside him and shoved out everything until only the sound remained. He'd never confessed to his grandparents, and even now his family didn't know his contributions put him in the VIP seats of the San Francisco Philharmonic's Stradivarian Circle, where he escaped to as often as possible.

Sophie Callahan was the first person to pull at him in places he thought only the music could reach. But, unlike the symphony, he wasn't interested in becoming a patron of Sophie Callahan's.

"Look, I carried in a box of kittens to her store this morning." Brad pointed at the counter. Ruthie held a gray kitten while Ella hugged the white runt. Brad's mother would approve of Sophie's dedication to animals. That wasn't Sophie's first rescue litter and she acted as if she knew it wouldn't be her last. Still, she remained committed.

Brad's commitment to his own one-man cause seemed slightly more selfish in the face of Sophie's passion for animal rescue. But he was doing what was best for him and his family: leaving. "Some jerk just dumped the box outside her place," he explained.

"Hold on." Matt yanked open the door and called to Ruthie, who laughed at his admonition to not get too attached to the kittens and lifted one of the kitty's paws in a tiny wave.

Matt let the door close. "Ruthie's sister has not one but two Great Danes that split their time between our house and Sophie's day care. They'll accidentally step on a kitten without ever noticing."

Exasperation was thick in Matt's tone, but he never masked the tenderness in his gaze when Ruthie was in his sights. Brad's friend would bring that kitten home in an instant if Ruthie asked, and he'd protect it with everything he had. Love suited his friend. But Brad doubted he could ever love like that. He carried too much Harrington DNA. His family put on the show of being loyal, but at their core it was every Harrington for himself.

Brad measured the window and glanced over his shoulder at his friend. "I've been told big dogs can be extremely gentle."

Matt watched Ruthie through the glass and grinned. "Don't pass that information along to the doctor."

"I'm sure Sophie already told Ruthie." Brad typed the measurements into the notepad app on his phone, straightened and handed the tape measure to Matt.

Matt never reached for it and instead stared at Brad. "I meant what I said. It would matter if Sophie were involved."

"Understood." Brad tossed the tape measure from one hand to the other. He'd already lied to his friend about not being on a case. Fishing for information couldn't be a worse offense than that. "Anything else I should know?"

"Sophie and Ruthie have been best friends since high school." There was a warning in Matt's tone and caution in his silence.

Brad waited.

Matt added, "Sophie Callahan is what I like to call good people."

He'd witnessed the darkness that festered inside good people enough times in his career as an investigator that he wondered if true goodness was more myth than reality. Only time would reveal if Sophie's goodness came from her soul—something he'd yet to witness—or simply camouflaged a more corrupt nature. Something that had become his norm. "And I'm not good people?"

"You're the bubble buster." Matt laughed and punched Brad's shoulder, breaking the tension and putting them back on familiar ground. "The harbinger of truth."

"Truth sets people free." Brad punched back. He was certainly free now that he'd learned the truth about his parents. Free from the manipulation. Free to pursue his own life on his own terms. He'd gained way more than he'd lost. And if he exposed Sophie's father, George Callahan, for the low-life thief that he was, then he'd set Sophie free as well, if she was innocent.

"And I don't always expose the full truth."
He knew when to hold back, like now, with
his friend. Brad rubbed at his neck. Surely that
wasn't guilt knotting his muscles. Guilt wasn't
standard procedure. "The Nikkos kids will learn
the truth about their arms-dealing father when
he goes to trial. And that wife of the fraudulent
banker hadn't wanted to accept the facts. But
the truth always comes out eventually, whether
a person is prepared or not."

"Your brand of truth alters lives. And you
know I agree with you, or I wouldn't have joined
you on those cases or any of the others." Matt
opened the lid on his toolbox. "But there's an
aftermath."

Brad tossed the tape measure inside and
closed the lid. If only that pinch of guilt was as
easy to discard.

Matt studied him. "But she isn't your case."

"No." Sophie Callahan was part of the aftermath. He'd skipped breakfast that morning and
assumed the gnawing in his stomach was from
hunger, not unease about Sophie. He'd never
stayed long enough to witness the ramifications
or the consequences. He'd always presented his
findings, ensured justice was done and moved
on.

Except for his last FBI investigation that had
resulted in a counterattack explosion, an inno-

cent woman's death and his resignation. Yet, according to Dr. Florence, he'd resolved his feelings of regret and blame in his yearlong biweekly therapy sessions. Though, now, he wasn't so sure, and despite leaving the Bureau, there was still always a next case. Still never time to review his emotions or stick around for the aftermath.

Matt squeezed his shoulder. "Besides, in a few weeks you'll be leaving the corporate embezzlers, cyber criminals and money launderers behind and seeking your own truth with the sharks, stars and open waters."

"Maybe when I return, I'll be good people, too." Brad feared if he stayed in the city, he'd become more like his mother. Matt would never consider Harringtons good people if he knew the full truth about Brad's family.

"You should at least have a good tan." Matt laughed before climbing into his truck.

Brad watched Sophie return to the storefront and help Ella into a fuzzy jacket that made her look like a baby polar bear: warm and bundled up and adorable. Sophie slipped into a similar fleece jacket that she zipped up to her chin. Brad decided Sophie looked entirely too huggable and tempting. For that alone, he needed to expose her secrets.

He shoved his hands into his jacket pockets

and strode down the sidewalk. Within twenty-four hours, he'd have Sophie's security system installed; before the end of the long weekend, he'd locate her wayward father and deliver the truth to his client. As for Sophie, she was either innocent or guilty. Right now, he'd bet on the latter. No woman had ever gotten under his skin, or rather sneaked under, until today. Either she practiced witchcraft or had perfected a legitimate cover that only made him all the more suspicious. No one would ever imagine the adorable pet-shop owner who rescued strays to be a master con artist. No one except him.

A forgotten section of the *Times* tumbled out of the mist as if the fog had printed its own dire headlines. He stomped on the newspaper, stopping its escape, and bent down, crumpling it in his fist. Somewhere he'd lost his ability to believe in good. To see hope. To imagine something better. He smashed the newspaper into an overflowing trash can, wanting to punch through his own cynicism. But he feared no matter how far he dug, he might never discover that missing part of himself. It was like searching for a rare penny in the city dump. An impossible task.

For now, he just needed to finish this case quickly. Then he'd do what he always did— move on. Or in this case, set sail.

CHAPTER THREE

"WE NEED TO HURRY." Ella pulled her hood over her braids and gripped Sophie's elbow. "I don't want to miss the bus."

"It's five blocks and the fog delayed the bus's departure." Sophie dipped her chin inside her jacket. The unusual chill never cut into Ella's enthusiasm. But the drizzle edged under Sophie's collar, and a shiver ran through her. "I remember when it took you over one thousand steps to walk to school."

"There's no time for counting today, Auntie." Ella squeezed Sophie's arm, the pressure matching the urgency in her tone. "We have to talk about keeping Stormy Cloud."

"Stormy Cloud," Sophie repeated.

"The tiny kitten that April told me is most likely deaf," Ella said. "She's soft like a summer cloud, but her purr makes her sound like a storm cloud. No one likes storm clouds, Auntie."

"I do," Sophie said. The same way she liked the city fog and its changing weather moods, except today, when she needed sun—bright, bold and encouraging.

"That's why we need to keep her," Ella said. "She'll just be an inconvenience to another family."

There was that word again. The chill settled deep into her bones as if it intended to become permanent. Sophie tugged Ella closer.

Ella plowed on. "Is Brad an animal rescuer?"

"No, he stumbled upon those kittens accidentally."

"That's too bad." Ella frowned. "I wanted him to rescue another litter so he'd have to come back to the store."

"You liked him?" Sophie asked. Ella's answer mattered. She didn't want it to matter. Brad Harrington had a temporary place in their lives. Still, the mention of Brad brought a welcome warmth inside her.

Ella nodded. "His voice is good like an extra glass of hot chocolate, but sticky, like the laughter is trapped in his throat and he just needs someone to free it."

"What's my voice like?" Sophie asked.

"You sound like a mom."

Before Sophie could ask if that was good or bad, Ella moved on, her conversation covering more ground in the five blocks to the school bus than most people covered in an eight-hour shift. "Papa George promised to take me to a concert."

Sophie winced. Papa George needed to call his daughter back. Papa George needed to return Sophie's money. Papa George needed to stop making promises he couldn't keep.

Giggles and the stomping of boots disrupted Sophie's irritation. Ella's friends crowded around, peppering her with questions about her gorgeous braids. Four schools in four years and finally they'd discovered a place where Ella could flourish. Sophie had never considered that the public school less than a mile from their home would be the best fit for her legally blind niece. But the proof embraced Ella on the cement sidewalk in a diverse circle of acceptance and friendship and trust. Moving Ella to yet another school was not an option.

Sophie hugged Ella. "Have fun today."

Ella gripped Charlotte's elbow and the group of girls headed toward the buses, a flurry of excited chatter. Sophie waved to Ella's teacher and Ella's aide before she rushed down the sidewalk, heading toward her morning appointment. She had to find her money and save their home. And soon.

Her father had to be in serious trouble. She'd always believed she was free from his shady tactics. That she was somehow different to him, and darn it if she didn't need to feel special, even for a moment, to someone. One time in her life.

No, she didn't need to feel special anymore. She'd craved that when she was a child. But she'd outgrown the feeling the same way she had outgrown her craving for cereals with marshmallows and stars and good-luck charms.

Sophie stepped inside the law offices of Evans, Hampton, and King, leaving the pigeons on the sidewalk to peck away at her impractical childhood wishes.

Kay Olson waved at Sophie from behind the reception desk and slid off her headset. Kay tweaked her gray hair back into place. She'd been Sophie's first customer for her dog-walking business a decade earlier. Kay's hair had been gray even before cancer took Sophie's grandmother and Kay's childhood best friend, and before her daughter, April, became pregnant with twins.

Kay's silver pixie cut was like battle armor, a spiked shield she wore to deflect the mess life seemed content to keep throwing at her. Her shield allowed her to believe in something better. Kay wasn't expecting a pot of gold at the end of her rainbow—she was more of a realist than that. Sophie wanted some of that same inner-battle armor, though, to forge through her latest roadblock.

"Before you ask, I sent April home to bed." Sophie unzipped her coat. "If you have the sponsorship check for the gala, I can take it and let you get back to work."

"Let's talk in here." Kay pointed across the hall. "You can sample the pastries from Whisk and Whip Pastry Shop. Everyone agreed last week the Whisk is the city's best."

Sophie followed Kay into a small conference room that might have been bright if not for the fog crowding against the wall of windows. "I promised April I'd head over with the laptop and we'd work on the gala table seating so she still feels included."

"April didn't want to listen to the doctor." Kay thrust her fingers through her hair, tightening the spikes. "She never wants to listen to any opinion that differs from her own, including her mother's."

"She'll do what's right for her babies." Sophie walked to the windows that looked out over a park, but the gray mist had swallowed the swing set and slides. Mothers had a duty to do what was right for their children. Yet Sophie's own mother had failed, and her sister struggled to put Ella first. Motherhood for the Callahan women was like standing inside the fog and never seeing the children's little hands reaching for them. Sophie feared if she became a mother, she'd get lost in the fog, too. And that would be unforgivable.

"Well, the father needs to be told. That's what's right." Kay smacked her palm against the table and released a sigh tinged with frustration. "But we don't need to have this conversation again."

"I've tried to ask April about the identity of the father, but she refuses to talk about what happened." Sophie searched the fog for the metal curve of the swing set. She'd wanted to help April, seeing so much of her sister in the lost woman. Even more, she'd wanted to help Kay, to give back to the woman who'd given Sophie direction and purpose so many years ago. "I'm not sure I've been much of a good influence on her."

"Nonsense," Kay said. "April wants to keep working at your place. This is the longest she has stuck with anything. She claims she needs the Pampered Pooch and the four-legged customers to keep her calm."

"She's wonderful with the animals, especially the injured and newborns." Sophie turned her back on the park and leaned against the window ledge. "She'll be a great mother."

Kay remained quiet and eyed the silver pastry platter in the center of the table. She began transferring the pastries back into a medium sized bakery box. "She isn't you."

"I'm not that special. I do what needs to be done. April will, too." Sophie remembered feeling desperate and unsure, but she'd found her way, with the help of Kay and Ruthie. "You raised her right."

"I raised her." Kay set a croissant in the center of a napkin. "Did my best. Questioned everything. Second-guessed every decision."

"Now you can second-guess your decision to be called Gigi or Nana or Grandma."

Kay smiled. "My grandbabies are coming."

"They are," Sophie said. "There's no second-guessing that."

April Olson was having twins, ready or not. The pregnancy might have been unexpected, but everything since that test stick turned pink had been expected, even April's reticence to reveal the father's name. No one stole away in the middle of the night against the advice of family and friends only to return a year later and reveal all of their secrets. Sophie and Kay had eventually discovered that April had been in LA pursuing her music career. The prescription stuffed inside April's jacket pocket for rest and hydration for severely bruised vocal cords was from a physician with an East Hollywood address. This was the only clue as to April's whereabouts during her eleven-month disappearance. Other than that, April had offered few details.

Kay leaned back in her chair and looked at Sophie. "What will you do without April?"

Sophie let April keep her secrets and April never pried into Sophie's secrets. There was a trust between the women. Now Sophie didn't have April. She couldn't hire and train another person fast enough to take her place. Not to mention, a full-time employee would expect health benefits. Employee health care was supposed to be part of Sophie's plans after she'd paid off the loan. And after the gala happened, which was supposed to help raise awareness for the rescues and fosters at the Pampered Pooch that desperately needed homes. Sophie smiled, but the tension throbbing in her head was hard to ignore. "Make it work."

"You've got the gala to organize." Kay pulled the end off the croissant. "And Ella to care for."

"I'll shift things around. I knew this was coming. It's my fault for not planning better. Sooner." But she *had* planned. Except she'd never planned on her father betraying her and ruining everything. "I didn't come here to whine. We can do that over Sunday dinner."

"I didn't bring you in here to stall, either. It's not like me." Kay crumbled the pastry into tiny flaky crumbs.

Kay had never been a stress eater; rather, she destroyed food when she was worried. Sophie eyed the mangled croissant. "Okay. Now I'm nervous."

"I don't have the sponsorship check."

"That's fine." And it *was* fine. Perfect, actually. Kay hadn't announced something that Sophie couldn't handle, like she had cancer or was moving out of state. Sophie would need to call her vendors and adjust the payment schedule, but she'd sort it out. She dropped into the high-backed leather chair across from Kay. "I can get it Monday."

Kay leaned forward and squeezed Sophie's arm. "I won't have a check."

"Won't. That's different." Sophie set her elbows on the table, refusing to wilt into the chair. She was starting to hate expensive soft leather chairs. First the bank. And now here. "What happened?"

"I'm not entirely certain." Kay crushed another bit of croissant into the napkin.

Sophie struggled to remain positive, but her hope deflated quicker than the crumbs beneath Kay's fist.

"Pete Hampton called this morning to rescind the sponsorship," Kay said. "But he wants you to keep the firm on the sponsorship list for next year, so it isn't a total loss."

"I have to get through this year before I can even consider next year." And getting through this year was in jeopardy without one of her largest sponsors. "I appreciate that he's the senior partner and busy, but can I talk to him directly?"

"Pete's on the road, heading to Phoenix, then Dallas, and won't return until the end of next week."

That'd be too late. Sophie needed to pay the caterer and the audio-visual guy on Tuesday after the holiday weekend. Kay avoided looking at Sophie, and her shoulders dipped forward as if she'd lost her only dog in a blizzard. Sophie asked, "There's no way to change his mind, is there?"

"That man is a mule—brilliant, but a mule all the same." Kay tossed the napkin into the trash. "I can bring it up with him when he checks in this afternoon."

Sophie shook her head. She didn't want Kay to jeopardize her own position within the company. Kay needed the health insurance that covered her pregnant daughter.

"Pete mentioned that the insurance company and the wellness center have also withdrawn their sponsorship. Is that true?"

Sophie pressed into the hard cherrywood table to keep from swaying backward. She felt pummeled like Kay's croissant: ruined and unrecognizable. The loss of two more sponsors threatened the gala's success. She had a vision for this gala. "They are my next two stops."

"It'll be fine. I'm sure Pete was mistaken." But Kay's voice lacked conviction.

"I don't understand. When we'd met not long ago, they were excited and willing to help with the event. Everyone believed they'd help the animals first and foremost, and also boost their brands or businesses in the process. It's a win for everyone." For the Pampered Pooch, Sophie was hoping the event advertising would lead to more sales and subsequently allow her to venture into service-dog training.

"Pete claimed he'd made another commitment that he couldn't break. And he mentioned something about the first-quarter budget."

"But he could break his word to me." Sophie cleared her throat. "Sorry, this isn't your fault. I wanted this to work." She'd wanted the Paws and Bark Bash to become the premier nonprofit event in the city. She'd wanted to make a difference beyond her small store. She'd wanted to do something that mattered. Ensuring forever homes for rescues and service dogs mattered.

"And it will." Kay pushed her chair away from the table. "You just need to find new sponsors. More committed sponsors. We'll think of businesses to approach."

"I approached most of the city a year ago

when I started planning the gala," Sophie said. "It was hard to get those sponsors to commit ten months ago. Now we're less than a month before the event."

And she was broke, aside from Ella's eye-surgery fund and the little she had in the Pooch business account. Final payments were all due within the next few weeks. She pushed out of the chair, trying to leave her distress in the leather imprint. She still had two more sponsors to visit this morning. And her father could call back or realize his mistake or return her money. She refused to give up—at least, not yet.

"I can help," Kay said.

"You're here more than sixty hours a week and you have April to think about." Sophie pressed the chair to the table's edge, trying not to panic.

"I want to help," Kay insisted as they left the conference room.

"I appreciate it." Sophie walked to the door. "I'll figure it out."

"I'll text you when I get home." Kay placed her headset back on.

Sophie nodded and hurried outside. She needed to check the contracts she'd signed and reread the section on cancelations and penalties. She couldn't handle forfeiting the 50 percent deposit she'd given the caterer and the venue. More than the lost money was the damage to her reputation and the Pampered Pooch. She'd forged relationships, given her word to service-dog breeders and foster organizations. She'd vowed to find homes for every rescue she encountered and minimize their costs with affordable vet services and discounted dog supplies.

An hour later, Sophie stood in front of the insurance corporation and stared at her distorted reflection in the silver-plated serving tray. She wanted to bash the platter against the cement wall of the building, but the dish was worth at least a hundred dollars at the silent auction. That money alone could feed a kitten like Stormy Cloud for several months.

Three sponsors lost in one day. A savings account emptied overnight. And her full-time employee on bed rest. The day was turning out to be something for the record books. She squeezed the embellished silver handles, wanting to absorb the steel into her spine, and stepped into the fog that refused to give way to the sun.

Her first encounter with the city had been on a foggy night, when she'd stepped off the passenger bus holding her sister's hand. Her grandmother had emerged from beneath a dull streetlamp to wrap both girls in her embrace. There'd been comfort in that night such that Sophie had always welcomed the fog. Greeted the fog like a lost friend.

Except today. Today, no one was coming forward from the mist to embrace her and lie to her about everything being all right, like her grandmother had done all those years ago.

CHAPTER FOUR

BRAD TOSSED THE wrapper from his breakfast burrito into the trash and checked the time. He'd planned on returning to the Pampered Pooch after a quick breakfast, but Evelyn Davenport had texted while he was in line at the Gourmet Burrito that she wanted to meet with him as soon as possible. He'd taken his burrito to go and messaged her that he was heading back to his temporary living quarters at his friend Zack's loft. She hadn't arrived yet, so he took a spot on the couch and left a voice mail at Delta Craft asking for an update on the *Freedom Seeker*'s restoration.

Two photos filled the screen of his laptop on the steel-and-chrome coffee table. One picture was of a well-groomed, debonair man in his early fifties. The other was a woman in her late twenties with a baseball cap, ponytail, purple sweatshirt featuring a familiar paw-print logo, and running shoes. Sophie and George Callahan might dress differently, but they shared a similar undeniable charm. Sophie was the girl next door every boy wanted to ask to prom, and George was the one the accounting floor went to happy hour with every Thursday night at Mac's Tavern—a guy's guy and a woman's best confidant.

People were masters at pretense: pretending to listen to their children, pretending to be committed to charity work, pretending to be good, honest citizens.

But there had been nothing fake about Sophie's interaction with Ella, from the tenderness in the kiss she'd pressed to the girl's forehead to the patience and understanding in her calm voice.

Brad's mother had treated her boys like adults from the time they could crawl. The Harrington boys did not need toys—Nancy Harrington's boys needed calendars to keep them on task, wristwatches to keep them to a schedule and foreign language tutors to keep them civilized. She'd happily listened to their Latin recitation and would never have pandered to such a nonsensical thing as pairs day.

But Sophie had given pairs day the utmost importance because it mattered to Ella. And that had touched Brad on a level he wasn't entirely comfortable acknowledging. Sophie's compassion hit somewhere close to that tender spot he still harbored from the morning his mother had summoned him to her sterile office to enlighten him about the truth of Santa.

She'd considered it a favor to her five-year-old son, who considered it a betrayal, a childhood robbery that stole the magic from the season. He'd bet Sophie gave Ella a Christmas full of magic, wonder and fantasy. Good thing he'd long since filed Christmas into one more retail marketing scam, or he might've entertained the idea of spending the holiday with Sophie and Ella, just for the experience. Not that it mattered, since he intended to be lounging on some empty beach on some forgotten island this December twenty-fifth.

A new email message from his assistant Lydia flashed on his screen. A very large sum of money had been withdrawn yesterday from the Callahans' joint account. That wasn't the update he'd expected on George Callahan. Fortunately, the teller at Pacific Bank and Trust was a former client of Brad's firm, and even more fortunate was the teller's penchant to divulge too much information.

He clicked over to Sophie's picture. Surely she'd given George the funds so that he could pay back the money he'd stolen from Evelyn Davenport. Now Evelyn was on her way over to surely tell him the matter was closed. Brad scrubbed a hand along his jaw, pleased to be done with the case. He could install Sophie's security system and move on, like he wanted. Like he planned.

It wasn't as if he wanted to see more of Sophie Callahan. She'd made him lie. To his good friend and then to her. Zack had never rescued a dog, although he'd talked about it on his last trip when he'd come across the stray near a dirt airstrip. Now Brad could stop with all his pretending.

A buzzer pulled Brad away from his indigestion. Opening the front door, he greeted Evelyn.

She thrust several large shopping bags at him and wiped her knee-high plaid rain boots on the welcome mat. "This loft is smaller than I expected, but it's much more lived in and comfortable than that last boxy, sad condo you referred to as home."

Brad walked into the kitchen. "It's like that because it belongs to my friend and not me."

"I should have known." She set a stack of three plastic containers on the table.

Brad peeked into the shopping bags and grinned at the cookies inside. "Let me guess. George Callahan returned your money with copious apologies and all is forgiven. Case closed."

"Bradley Trent Harrington, you cut off the bulbs of all my tulips and roses in my award-winning garden when you were four years old." Evelyn untied the thick scarf that matched her rain boots and frowned at him. "You of all people know I do not forgive easily."

"Nor do you forget." Brad opened the top container. "I just want to stress that I'd turned four the week before the garden incident."

"You didn't leave one flower intact." She ripped a paper towel off the roll and tossed it at Brad.

"I'd discovered the power of scissors." Brad lifted a still-warm banana muffin from the container. His mother had never baked anything, not even the ready-to-bake cookies that required only several knife cuts to complete. And now he blamed his mother for his insatiable weakness for home-baked goods.

"If only you'd stopped with the flowers."

"It isn't my fault Shakespeare liked to sleep away his afternoons in the garden."

"He never left the house after his haircut." She tightened the lid on the banana muffins.

"Shakespeare lived longer as an indoor cat. I did him a favor." Brad laughed and lifted the muffin toward her. "If these aren't celebratory baked goods, what are they?"

"Products of a guilty conscience." Evelyn unzipped her raincoat and draped the down jacket over a chair. "They're guilt goods."

"You made a mistake. Those happen." Brad finally sampled the muffin.

"I'm not guilty because I chose to date George. I was lonely and vulnerable and stupid. I'm working through all that." Evelyn pulled out the tall chair at the kitchen bar and sat, her shoulders dipping forward as if she was an inflatable pool with a leak. She was definitely not acting like a woman whose retirement account had been restored in full.

Brad stopped peeling the wrapping off his second muffin and studied Evelyn. "George hasn't contacted you, then?"

"Not even a text," she said. "Should he have?"

If he'd intended to pay back her money. If he'd intended to make things right. If he'd intended not to be prosecuted. Apparently George Callahan had other intentions. Brad shook his head. "There are too many desserts here not to be celebrating."

"It's quite the opposite," she said. "I admit I've tried to bake away my guilt. It seems I might've ruined George's daughter's event."

"I doubt that." Sophie hadn't looked defeated this morning. She'd been determined to help the kittens and turn Ella's day into the best one of the week.

"I've caused her stress." Evelyn straightened the stack of Tupperware, aligning the containers. "If she's innocent and not involved with her father's schemes, I need you to fix it. If she's like her father, then let it go."

He set the muffin on the paper towel. The first muffin fought for space beside the burrito. Unease oozed through his suddenly full stomach. "What exactly did you do?"

"Mary Kate Hampton was waxing on about her grandkids at yesterday's breakfast. No one else had a chance to talk. We don't invite her often because she can occupy the entire conversation. We invited her this time because she's dear friends with the owner of the new wellness center. The service is impeccable in their café and the manager comps our appetizers and smoothies, which is always helpful as this group prefers to eat out unless your mother is hosting. When Mary Kate finally paused to sip her Bellini, I mentioned that George had left me."

Brad leaned back in his chair. Evelyn's daily vocabulary did not include words that would stir up scandal. The Davenports were the only really honest political family Brad had ever encountered. Evelyn would never confess such a gossipy detail now and mar the Davenport reputation. "You told Mary Kate and the others about the money?"

"I told them George went off with a woman in her thirties," she said. "I left out the part about

George emptying my savings account on his way out the door."

Brad broke his muffin in half. "How does Sophie fit into this?"

"George and I attended the theater league ball last autumn. George always spoke about his daughter with such pride, and he mentioned to Mary Kate and her husband that his daughter was putting on an event that would rival the theater ball and he was certain she'd accept more sponsors. After several martinis, Peter promised to speak to his partners about sponsoring Sophie's gala." Evelyn rose and opened cabinet doors until she found a plastic sports cup and filled it with water. Zack's modern style didn't yet extend to his kitchenware. "That was the last I'd heard of it until this morning when Mary Kate phoned to tell me she had Peter rescind the firm's sponsorship. I've ruined Sophie's event because I was tired of listening to Mary Kate prattle about her exceptionally well behaved, musically inclined, 'ready to take the fashion world by storm and steal Disney acting parts' grandkids. All of her grandchildren are under the age of four."

Brad nodded, although he didn't understand. The law firm could've pulled its sponsorship for any number of reasons. "I didn't think you'd met George's daughter?"

"I haven't," she said. "She's protective of her niece and her situation."

"Situation?" Brad repeated.

"The little girl is blind. Can you imagine? George's daughter watches her while the child's mother discovers herself. She needs to discover her parenting skills, if you ask me. A mother belongs with her child."

Brad disagreed. He'd seen the love and affection between Sophie and Ella in the little girl's clutching of Sophie's hand to make her point. In Sophie's gentleness as she'd freed the hairbrush. In the softness in Sophie's gaze and the relaxing of Ella's stiff shoulders with the knowledge that her aunt would make her world right again. He couldn't recall going to his mother as a kid to fix his problems. Perhaps because he'd been too busy just trying to capture her attention. "The little girl might be better off with the current arrangement."

"You won't be better off without your mother." Evelyn tipped her water cup at Brad. "No matter what you've convinced yourself."

"We aren't talking about my mother." He pushed the half-eaten muffin aside. "We're discussing the Callahans."

"That's settled."

"What did I miss?"

"You'll make it right if George's daughter isn't a lowlife like her father."

"You want me to fund her gala?" he asked.

"I want you to ensure that gala doesn't fail because of me. I won't act as low as George. It's possible he gave my money to his daughter for her event." She dumped her water in the sink. "Bradley Harrington, stop frowning at me. I know that didn't happen, but still, I like that thought."

"Even if he did give the money to Sophie, which he didn't, George still stole from you."

"Yes, but at least the money would've gone to rescue needy animals and not to rescue George's own pocketbook."

"Perhaps the gala should fail. Perhaps you did Sophie a favor." Brad pressed his fingertips to his forehead. He kept getting stuck on images of dogs in bow ties, drinking from crystal water bowls. Whoever heard of a dog ball anyway? No doubt it was another Callahan con job. Nobody could be this altruistic without exploding.

"No. Sophie has a real purpose for her event, beyond her own needs. With patience and guidance, it could become a premier fund-raiser. But with a few blows, like a lack of sponsors, it'll be a mere afterthought. A *might have been*, like my relationship with George. No one deserves to feel like that."

"You want me to have George Callahan arrested and help his daughter?" Brad asked.

"Exactly." Evelyn wrapped her scarf around her neck before bussing his cheek and squeezing his shoulders like she'd been doing since he was four. Here there was the affection and trust and encouragement that Sophie and Ella shared. Evelyn continued, "I've provided you with ample snacks to fortify you. There's nothing complicated about this."

Brad felt irritation pushing away the comfort he usually found in Evelyn's hugs. This wasn't how his cases usually went. Not the protocol. Ever. There was an order. Steps to be taken. He'd labeled this a favor, not a case. Maybe he hadn't been lying after all. Favors were unpredictable and often unwieldy and usually snowballed into something bigger, something more involved.

But he wasn't getting any more involved with Sophie Callahan. Installing her security system was enough help. She was on her own with her dog ball.

CHAPTER FIVE

SOPHIE YANKED HER hair into a tight braid to keep from throwing her cell phone against the wall. Unfortunately, her older sister wouldn't feel the impact. Tessa was thousands of miles away in India and only visible on Sophie's phone screen thanks to modern technology and phone apps.

Sophie stared at her sister's thin, tan face filling the screen. Tessa looked rested, relaxed, pretty even. Her lips were stained red like their mother's, her eyes were sky blue like their mother's and her auburn hair was full of effortless curls like their mother's. And just like their mother, Tessa was a wanderer.

"My Yogi master suggested I stay for another six weeks to make sure I've fully committed to my new path." Tessa traced her finger over one naturally arched eyebrow.

"You told me the same thing eight weeks ago." Sophie tugged on her hair.

"No, I needed the last eight weeks to embrace my new path." Tessa leaned into the camera.

Her blue eyes were wide and clear and no longer haunted. "I need the next six weeks to commit."

"What am I supposed to tell Ella?" Sophie asked. "I told her two months ago that you'd be coming home. It's time to come home, Tessa."

"I left so I could become a better mother." Tessa leaned away, but Sophie caught the white of her teeth biting into her bottom lip. Her sister always did that when she was scared. She'd chewed her lip raw on their fateful bus ride to the city.

Tessa's voice lowered, her words tumbling out in an urgent rush. "Mom's voice is still too loud inside me. And you promised me that you wouldn't let me become like Mom."

Sophie had made that promise when Tessa had come home high and clutching a pregnancy test. But Sophie had long since stopped believing in empty words and put her faith in actions. Too often people claimed to be pet lovers, then threw away newborn kittens. Too often parents promised to return to their children, then continued moving on, sending an occasional postcard or making a quick phone call. Too often her sister said she'd put her family first and then disappeared.

But Tessa had booked her healing trip to India on her own. She'd made a plan for a new life.

She'd asked for Sophie's support. Now Sophie had to trust her sister would do the right thing.

"I need these last six weeks to become my best," Tessa said. "You understand, right?"

"Of course." Sophie wanted her sister to be home. To be healed. To be a parent. For once in Ella's life, Sophie wanted Ella to have a real mother. Not a stand-in aunt, who covered for her absentee mother with constant assurances of how much Tessa still loved Ella, even after all these years. But her sister feared coming home. She couldn't blame her. "No more after this, Tessa. You need to be here. There are decisions to be made about Ella's next surgery. Her parent needs to sign those medical forms."

"You have all the paperwork I signed before I left, Soph," Tessa said. "You just have to submit it."

"We aren't talking about that paperwork." That paperwork made Sophie more than Ella's aunt. That paperwork relinquished Tessa of her parental rights. That paperwork she'd stashed in the bottom drawer of her dresser under keepsakes from Ella's first year: hair from her first haircut, her pacifier and a milestone book of Ella's first five years. Sophie hadn't opened that drawer since Tessa had boarded the plane to India.

"Fine, but we need to talk about it sometime,"

Tessa said. "For now, I'll put the charges for the next six weeks on the credit card."

Her sister wasn't coming home and she expected Sophie to fund the extension. Sophie didn't have the funds for the electric bill. She closed her eyes and saw only the image of her sister after she'd given birth on her supplier's cold basement floor. Both mother and baby had barely been breathing. Sophie had vowed that night she'd do anything to keep her only family safe. She dropped her hair and let the braid unravel. "You're supposed to be teaching classes to help cover your room and board."

"I do teach," Tessa said. "Just not regularly. I'll pay you back. We talked about this before I left."

They'd talked about many things, some irrelevant like the weather and some relevant like missing Ella's ninth birthday. Sophie watched her sister wrap a silk scarf over her head. Ella's tenth birthday was next month. Shouldn't her sister remember her own daughter's birthday? If her sister had grown as a person from her year of discovery in India, then Ella's birthday should've mattered.

Sophie shook her head and prayed six more weeks was the answer to Tessa's lack of parental inclination. "Put the charges on the credit card."

Tessa kissed the phone screen. "I love you, little sister."

"I love you, too." Sophie meant those words and believed her sister did, too.

Sophie just wasn't sure that love mattered. Love was empty without support and commitment and trust. That's what made love a bond that lasted and endured. Sophie knew that love existed. She'd seen it with Ruthie's parents who'd recently celebrated forty years of marriage, and now between Ruthie and Matt. It was rare and precious and magical. But only children believed in magic and fairy tales. And a childhood built on abandonment and dysfunction severed any belief in happily-ever-afters. Instead, Sophie strove for happy-for-nows.

"I have to run," Tessa said. "Class begins in five."

"Wait." Sophie grabbed her phone. "Don't you want to talk to Ella?"

"I will soon," Tessa said. "It's better if you tell her. You can hug her and make her smile after delivering the news. If I tell her, then we'll all be in tears. That won't be good for anyone. She already thinks I'm a huge disappointment."

Tessa ended the call before Sophie could respond. Sophie stuffed her phone into her back pocket, checked the locks on the front doors of the Pampered Pooch and switched off the lights. She glanced at the boarded-up window. Brad hadn't made it back to the store. It meant she'd get to see him again. She might've warmed to the idea if her sister hadn't doused her with a cold bucket of broken promises.

The outside fire escape, with its sturdy thick wood stairs and reliable handrail connected the backyard to the third-floor apartment she shared with Ella. Sophie ran up the stairs, bypassing the empty second floor that would one day hopefully house a vet's office. This staircase meant Ella and she never had to go outside on the front sidewalk to deal with the steel gate at their main apartment entrance and they could avoid the strangers at the bus stop four steps from their front door.

She wiped her shoes on the mat outside the back door and strode through the kitchen down the hallway. She'd planned to cook a marinara pasta dish with Ella, but her appetite had disappeared when Tessa had signed off. Just thinking about adding garlic to her too-sour stomach made her insides cramp even more.

She pressed her palm on her stomach before knocking on Ella's bedroom door. "Hey, sweetie."

Ella sat in the middle of a queen-size bed in a room painted pale lavender and decorated with fuzzy pillows, plump stuffed animals and a thick down comforter. It was the room Sophie and Tessa had never had as children. Ella had picked out everything to make her bedroom cozy. Sophie wished Tessa had been there. Sophie wished Tessa could see how accomplished her daughter had become. Sophie wished...

Ella pressed Pause on her CD player, drawing a smile from deep inside Sophie. These days she couldn't order audiobooks fast enough for her niece.

"Do we have extra cotton balls?" Ella asked.

"In my bathroom." The colored markers Sophie had found at the craft store last week covered Ella's bed. Years ago, Sophie had taught Ella her colors through scent. Discovering scented markers had ignited Ella's other passion besides books: art. "How many do you need?"

Ella pressed her palm against the upper corner of a poster board. "Enough to glue here for my clouds." Then she frowned. "Or should the rainbow be above the clouds?"

"The rainbow can be anyplace you want it. So can the clouds." Sophie touched the intricate braids that Ruthie had formed into her niece's hair. She wanted so much for Ella to see how much she looked like a princess. "It's your picture. Your art to create."

"Do you think Mother will like it?" Ella asked.

Sophie's heart stalled as if clogged by those extra cotton balls. "She'll love it."

"After we add the clouds and I finish the

rainbow, you'll help me write 'welcome home,' right?" Ella ran her hands over the rainbow arc she'd formed with thin, flexible wax strips.

The joy in Ella's tone stole Sophie's heart, and her throat swelled, feeling stuffed by another bunch of cotton balls. "Whenever you're ready."

"She'll be home in nineteen days," Ella said. "So I need to be ready soon."

"About that." Sophie sat on the bed. "I talked to your mother today."

Ella's hands stilled on her picture. "Is she excited to come home?"

A guardedness tightened Ella's voice as if to protect the joy. Sophie swallowed her scream of anger. Her niece didn't deserve this amount of pain. "She's excited to see you." Sophie hugged Ella, wanting the contact to be more comfort than her empty words, but knew it'd never be enough. "But she needs to stay a little while longer."

"Then she isn't excited to see me." Ella dismantled her rainbow and her joy.

"Oh, sweetie, she wants to see you," Sophie said. "She wants to be home, but she needs to finish her therapy."

"She could do her therapy here." Ella twisted the wax strips in her fingers.

Sophie resented that small kernel of hope in Ella's voice. Sophie had had that same hope bubble when she was Ella's age. Her grandmother would pop it with the harsh truth. Over the years, Sophie's hope bubbles had shrunk in size until they were small enough for Sophie to hide in places her grandmother couldn't poke.

Ella rushed on. "They have yoga here. I heard Taylor's mom talking to another mom about their afternoon yoga class over on Market."

She hated that she'd stomp on Ella's hope now. She'd never wanted that for this precious girl. "It isn't the same."

How Sophie wanted it to be the same. To be that simple.

"It's better." Ella smashed the purple modeling clay in her fist. "Her family is here. I'm here. You're here. There's yoga here."

And there was nothing else Sophie could say. She couldn't promise Ella that Tessa would be home soon. Tessa always found a reason to delay. She'd tell Ella that her mother loved her as usual, but Sophie was too mad at her sister to spend the time to convince Ella it was true. Mothers weren't supposed to break their daughters' hearts. Her chest ached and her stomach tightened into knots no Yogi master could release. She'd tried to soften the hurt every time, but the pain was always there. "I'll go get those cotton balls."

"There's no rush." Ella pushed her drawing

across the bed and picked up her headphones. "I'm going to finish my book."

Ella rolled over onto her side, away from Sophie. Sophie ached. Ella ached, too. Yet no tears dampened either of their faces. But Sophie always dried Ella's tears and teased away the disappointment. The tissues she'd shoved into her pocket before talking to Ella remained untouched. When had they stopped caring? Ella could see the truth better than most people with twenty-twenty vision. She could see better than her own mother. Sophie's ache spread like a poison vine, strangling every bone, every vein, consuming her.

Sophie tapped Ella's shoulder. "I'm going to change over the laundry, then we'll figure out dinner."

Ella nodded and covered her ears with her headphones.

Sophie carried Ella's hamper down into the basement. She wasn't sure if she smelled the lavender-scented detergent first before she splashed into the water. Or if the water ran into her shoes up to her ankles before the lavender coated every breath, failed to calm her and instead encouraged rage.

She did know that the ancient overflowing washing machine with soap bubbles everywhere and a waterfall streaming up and over the lid became the topper to her rotten day.

She sloshed through the water and kicked the appliance. "Clean underwear. That's all I wanted." She kicked the machine again. "That can't be too much to ask."

It was too much to ask for her father to tell Sophie about needing money. It was too much to ask for the gala sponsors to show professional courtesy and give Sophie more time before backing out. It was too much to ask for her sister to come home when she'd promised.

But clean underwear was not too much to ask.

Except, apparently, it was.

Water squished inside her shoes. The sound made something switch inside Sophie, as if she'd sprung a leak, too. Or more than a leak. A burst pipe. A broken water main. A knocked-over fire hydrant.

Ruthie had given Sophie a wooden baseball bat for protection when the Pooch had first opened. Sophie had bought one for every floor of the building as her tightened security plan met a limited budget. She grabbed the bat from the hook on the wall and descended on the washer.

Sophie had definitely had enough.

How much was one person expected to handle? She lifted the bat over her head like a club.

"Clean underwear. That's all I requested." She

smacked the bat against the washing-machine lid. The impact vibrated up her arms, jolted through her shoulders, then splintered down each vertebra. But something aligned inside her or maybe some things finally aligned like the rage, despair, disgust and fear she felt. She smashed the lid again.

That pressure valve inside her twisted open another notch. Tears tangled with her eyelashes and splattered against her cheeks. Her attack on the washer continued.

A hit for her family's betrayal. A crack for her pain. A series of smashes for Ella's anguish.

Sophie hardly recognized herself, but she didn't care. The corner of the washer crumpled beneath the bat's assault.

"Why?" She slammed the bat against the top. Thwack. Thwack. Thwack. Added one more swing, and shouted, "Why?"

Each breath was more ragged and unsteady than the last. She set her stance, readied the bat. One last hit. Sanity threatened, but she had one final shot inside her.

"You piece of crap." She swung the base-ball bat. The front paneling caved in. A control knob flipped through the air, plopped into the water and sank. Sophie's anger slowed to a drip as if that valve had been twisted shut. Or maybe she'd used up her emotion and was like an empty well. Either way, clarity and reason finally spilled through her: she had to deal with the water. Now.

She tossed the bat aside and dropped to her hands and knees to search for the drain that was somewhere in the middle of the room. She'd replaced the plastic drain cover after it broke several months ago. Soapy water splashed her face. One more hit of cold reality.

How was she going to fix this? She had to fix this so she could have clean underwear on when she found her father. She needed clean underwear on when she walked into Beth Perkins's corner cubicle at Pacific Bank and Trust and paid off her loan in full in less than four weeks.

She would not be defeated by an ancient washing machine or her father.

She crawled through the suds, skimming her hands over the cement floor, keeping her search for the drain in the forefront of her mind and the panic at bay.

Sophie had been in the fourth grade when her parents had abandoned her sister and Sophie to their one-room apartment. Sophie had returned from school and found a handwritten note taped to the refrigerator where schoolwork and kids' drawings should have hung: "If you girls are wise and careful, you can make the groceries last two weeks until we return."

Sophie had managed the two weeks without panicking. She'd panicked on day twenty-one when all of the food was gone and her parents still weren't home. She'd panicked on the twenty-fourth day when Ms. Dormer, her fourth-grade teacher, had knocked on the apartment door after following the girls home from school. She'd been nervous when Ms. Dormer drove her to the pawn shop to sell her mother's gold necklace to buy the bus tickets from Tahoe City to San Francisco. And she'd worried during the first hour of the bus ride that the authorities would separate her and her sister before they'd arrived at their grandmother's house. She'd finally contained every molecule of anxiety when her grandmother had stepped out of that fog surrounding the bus station and wrapped one thin arm around Sophie's small but stubborn shoulders.

Sophie hadn't truly panicked since then.

She refused to panic now. A broken washer had nothing on her past.

She'd overcome this, too. She had to for another, more important child.

CHAPTER SIX

BRAD JAMMED HIS finger against the buzzer to Sophie's upstairs apartment. Everything remained dark inside the Pampered Pooch. The store had been closed for almost an hour. That wasn't his concern. It was the violent thudding that seemed to be coming from Sophie's basement. Sophie might be a con artist, but he didn't want her hurt until after he'd discovered the truth. Even then, the thought of Sophie suffering made his skin feel a little too tight. He really had to get the woman out of his system.

Another bang vibrated the night air. It wasn't the crack of gunshots or glass shattering. Still, he wanted inside.

This was the only access to her upstairs apartment other than the wooden fire escape at the back of the building that exited to the doggy play yard. There was an entrance to the alley leading to the yard with a back door to the Pampered Pooch and a door to the basement. This he'd learned from a quick text to Matt.

He rang the buzzer again and hit the call button for Sophie's cell number, also supplied in a text from Matt. Her voice mail picked up. Silence ricocheted between the buildings and that doubled Brad's urgency to get inside.

Just then a young voice echoed through the intercom. "Yes?"

Brad pressed the button. "Ella, this is Brad. We met this morning in the pet store."

Static coated Ella's voice. "Did you find more kittens?"

"Not this time." Brad inhaled, forcing himself to slow his words. "Ella, where's your aunt?"

"Hold on, Brad. Ruthie is calling and I have to answer or she'll worry."

Brad closed his eyes and rested his head next to the intercom, which Ella hadn't clicked off. She exchanged a rapid series of nonsensical words that he quickly deduced was a sort of code. He admired their concern for Ella's safety.

Ella paused, then said, "Brad rescued Stormy Cloud. He'll rescue Aunt Sophie, too."

He grinned at the certainty in Ella's voice.

Ella quickly followed with, "You and Matt stay there. I can let Brad in, right?"

The lock clicked and Brad yanked opened the steel gate. The main door swung open. Now he'd rescue Sophie. "Thanks, Ella."

Ella clutched the wooden stair post in one

hand and a cell phone in the other. "Did you make that banging stop, Brad?"

He wished. "You heard that, too?"

Ella nodded. "It wouldn't stop. And Auntie never came back from the basement."

"I need to get to the basement."

Ella spun, keeping her hand on the banister. "I know the back stairs the best."

Brad followed Ella up the double staircase to the third-floor apartment and down the hall-way through the kitchen to the outside landing. "Ella, you should wait up here inside with the door locked."

Ella shook her head, her mouth firm and the end of her braids whipping against her sweat-shirt. "I need to check on my aunt."

Brad wanted to insist she go back, but Ella's pale cheeks indicated her fear, the quiver in her bottom lip indicated her concern. He touched her shoulder. "Tell you what. You wait right here, by the door, but outside so you can hear my shout. If it's all clear, I'll call for you."

"And if it's not?"

"You'll hear me."

She lifted her cell phone. "And I'll call 9-1-1 and lock the door behind me."

"Exactly." He squeezed her shoulder and raced down the stairs.

Brad held tight to the rusted metal banister

and pulled himself to a stop on the bottom step. Soapy water covered the entire basement floor. Sophie crawled through the suds, muttering to herself.

Brad's legs wobbled as a wave hit, almost knocking him off balance.

He nudged the bat, bobbing in the water, with the toe of his work boot. She hadn't been under attack. She'd been the attacker. And the bashed-up washing machine had been her victim. "Who won?"

Sophie glanced over her shoulder, but her hands continued swishing through the water. "I will, as soon as I find the drain."

"Have you turned off the water?" He waded through the pond.

She paused long enough to scowl at him. "What are you doing here?"

"I said I'd come back this afternoon. Here I am." Brad scooted the washer away from the wall and turned off the water valve. "Thought I'd be less of an intrusion if I installed the cameras after hours."

"How did you get inside? Ella knows better."

"There were texts with Matt. Code words with Ruthie and something about rescuing another litter of cats." Brad sloshed through the water and strode up the stairs. "Be right back."

He shouted all clear up to Ella. Her face

peeked over the edge of the railing. "Should I come down?"

"The washing machine flooded the basement. Your aunt tried to fix it with her baseball bat."

Ella covered her mouth with her hand, but not fast enough to hide her smile.

Sophie came to stand beside Brad. Water leaked from her shoes and pants, puddling around her. She called up to Ella. "We have to head to the Laundromat. We'll be right up."

Sophie dripped a path up the stairs and left her running shoes on the utility porch before entering the kitchen. Brad followed.

"You know what's close to the Laundromat?" Ella asked.

Ella stood near the white cabinets lining one wall of a compact but quaint kitchen. Teapots from classical Victorian times, like the ones his mother stored in her china cabinet, to the modern glass-infused types to his personal favorites—the comical zoo animals—squatted in a glass-fronted cabinet, on the windowsill and on top of the refrigerator. Something about Sophie's kitchen made Brad want to pull a red vinyl chair up to the round fifties-style diner table with curved chrome legs and pour himself a cup of hot tea. But he'd never liked tea before.

Sophie washed her hands at the sink. "I thought we'd planned to eat in tonight."

Ella shook her head. "You don't want to eat at our house, Brad."

"Ella Marie." Sophie picked up a giraffe teapot, removed the lid and tipped the pot over. Coins dumped out onto the counter.

Ella shrugged. "It's true. We're learning to cook."

Sophie sorted through the change, setting the quarters aside. "I can cook."

"Noodles and cheese from a box," Ella said.

"Hey, no one can stir the noodles in boiling water quite like me."

"We're learning to cook *together*," Ella said. "Real cooking, with recipes and measuring cups and oil. But we aren't any good yet. You know what's really good?"

"Ella, we eat there every week." Sophie sorted through the change.

"Because it's good. They have the best burgers and I don't even need to try to read a menu there." Ella pushed her glasses up her nose and rushed on. "You just tell them what you want and they make it. Brad will like it."

Sophie's fingers curled around a quarter. Brad watched Sophie close her eyes and inhale, not in the impatient, "irritated by her obnoxious kid so she's trying to calm herself down" way. Rather, Sophie looked like she'd made a wish on the quarter and only needed that magic fountain to toss it into in order for her world to be all right again. Then one small, stiff shake of her head and she flicked the quarter on the pile as if she'd remembered magic didn't exist. She resumed her search for more coins.

"But do they have milk shakes?" Brad asked.

"Of course," Ella said. "So we're going to City Suds, then Roadside Burgers with Brad."

"I'm sure Brad has better things to do than wait for our clothes to dry." Sophie tossed the smaller coins back inside the teapot and avoided looking at Brad.

"If that's all I need to do to try the best burger in the city, then I'm in." Brad rubbed his stomach. "We can talk about your new security system."

"It's one camera in the store." Sophie looked at him, her gaze steady, but something in the way she clutched the giraffe against her ribs and the way she shifted from one foot to the other made him think she was nervous. Unsettled by more than her very wet socks.

Nice to know the feeling was mutual. He smiled at her. "You might want to change your clothes and find dry shoes. Walking to City Suds might get a little uncomfortable."

"We aren't walking all the way there." Nothing nervous about the authority in her tone. The finality in her words.

Brad studied her, letting his confusion dip into his voice. "Why not?"

"I can walk there," Ella said, her chin firm and her mouth set.

"The last time..." Sophie glanced between Brad and Ella.

"That was the last time," Ella interrupted. "This is this time."

"What's different?" Sophie set the teapot on the shelf and reached for Ella's hand.

"Brad is with us," Ella said. "And Lady can come along. We just need to call Ruthie."

"Lady is not a guide dog. You know that, right?" Sophie asked.

An edge of frustration settled into Sophie's tone, but her touch remained gentle and her hold on Ella protective.

"She's the closest thing I have until I'm older." Ella leaned in toward her aunt. "And we talked. She wants to be my guide." Ella gripped Sophie's hand between both of hers. "Can't we please try? That was last year before school started. It's ancient history."

Sophie hesitated and Brad saw the indecision in her gaze. Whatever had happened was clearly not ancient history for Ella's aunt. Whatever had happened had left an impression and Brad doubted it was a positive one.

"We'll all get in a cab if it's too crowded on the street." Sophie looked to Brad.

He nodded. He wanted Sophie to know she had his support. He *needed* Sophie to know she had his support. Not that it should matter, but somehow it did. Very much.

"Yes, but only if it's too crowded." Ella bounced up on her toes and tossed her arms around her aunt. Her smile lifted in joy.

Brad couldn't recall hugging anyone in his family with such pure freedom. Spontaneity. And ease. He'd been taught self-discipline as a child. There was nothing wrong with reserve and control. Still, as he watched Ella and Sophie, he struggled to repress the appeal of Sophie wrapping him up in a similar embrace.

Sophie leaned back and tucked a loose curl behind Ella's ear. "Without arguing, Ella?"

Ella tipped her head, her lips pulling together before she countered, "You won't drink my shake?"

"I'll only have a sample," Sophie said.

"Or five or six." Ella lowered her voice and looked toward Brad. "She usually finishes the ice cream in the metal cup."

"Fine. I won't drink your shake." Sophie pulled Ella closer.

Ella squeezed her aunt back. "Then I won't argue about taking a cab."

CHAPTER SEVEN

SOPHIE HELD OPEN the door to City Suds for Ella and Brad. He'd carried their laundry basket like a linebacker, ready to ram people out of Sophie and Ella's path for the past ten blocks. She was grateful for the assistance so she could concentrate on guiding Ella. If he'd been with them last fall, she might not have been shoved around in an unexpected crowd spilling out of the neighborhood pub. She might not have tripped into the street and she might not have been separated from Ella. Sophie blamed her inattention and still struggled to forgive herself for the fear she'd caused Ella.

Thankfully, there had only been a small crowd of college students at the corner of Bayview and Gate Street outside the pub. The evening was still early for the twentysomething group and their awareness had yet to be clouded by too many tequila shots. And once they'd seen Brad barreling toward them, they'd scattered like leaves in a windstorm.

Sophie grinned, turned on the dryer and

walked over to sit beside Brad. Ella lounged on Brad's other side, her back against the wall and her legs stretched out across two seats toward Brad, earbuds in and her audiobook on Play. "Thanks for carrying our laundry all that way. We really can manage from here." Sophie ran her palms over her jeans, not sure whether she wanted Brad to leave or stay.

"According to Ella, the best burger in the city is waiting for me after this." Brad laughed. "I can't leave now."

Sophie relaxed into the chair, unable to deny that the thin plastic chair beside Brad was the most comfortable one she'd sat in all day. But surely her sudden contentment had nothing to do with the man next to her.

Brad leaned toward her, his shoulder touching hers. "So about your washer?"

His low voice teased her, and the brush of his shoulder awakened a new awareness. He smelled fresh and clean like he'd walked through a midnight rainstorm, reminding her of a hidden mountain lake, one of those places she'd always wanted to escape to. He made her want to escape with him. She didn't want to discuss the washer now. She wanted to edge closer and pretend this was about more than a trip for hamburgers. But that was all wrong.

Escaping with Brad wasn't an option. And this was only about a hamburger.

She shifted in the chair and edged away from Brad. She'd lost it in the basement. Not her finest moment, but she was allowed a private outburst, wasn't she? She'd never expected to have a witness. "Its rinse cycle has been more soak than rinse recently. I should've replaced it a while ago."

"Not your first basement flood?" He leaned toward her again.

Only her first basement appliance beating. "I fixed it with a new gasket and an internet how-to video last time."

"And this time?"

His rough voice was part laughter and part understanding and too many parts temptation. "The bat seemed the most appropriate tool."

Sophie jumped up and pretended to check the timer on the dryer. Something about Brad pulled her to him when she needed to pull herself away. He wasn't part of her world. And the feelings he stirred inside her had no place in her life.

Her phone buzzed in her back pocket, breaking into her fascination with Brad. She glanced at the screen and accepted the call.

"Soda-Pop."

Only one person called her that. "Dad." Sophie stepped outside and leaned against the City Suds window. This was her world. "Where are you?"

"No need to worry about that now." Her father's smooth laughter swirled through the phone. "I've got a plan. A real good one, Soda-Pop."

Her father had taken Sophie Diane and turned it into Soda-Pop while Sophie learned to crawl. At least she hadn't been nicknamed Teapot. Tessa had been labeled with that one. Sophie squeezed her eyes shut. "Where are you?"

"It's going to be fine, like I've always told you."

Sophie ground her teeth together, willing herself to keep control.

"I haven't failed you." His voice was sincere, his words urgent, but he'd always talked in a rush. As if he feared slowing down might make Sophie doubt him or question him or refuse him.

Her father rambled on. "Remember when you wanted a bicycle for your birthday and I got you that skateboard to get you to school faster than any bike. Or when you needed a car and I brought you a motorcycle so you could always find parking. Or that time…"

"Dad, stop." She didn't have time to debate the appropriateness of his gifts. He'd only ever been trying to help her in his own misguided way. "Where are you? Where's the money?"

"There's no time to discuss all that now."

"We have to discuss this. *Now*." A shout crept into her throat. "You know what that money means."

"You know I love you girls. This is for us. You know you can trust me. I'll get your money back with an extra bonus." His voice went from earnest to firm. "Now, listen."

"Dad," Sophie said, her voice one notch below a full screech. "You need to *listen* to me. Is that a train behind you?"

"Don't worry about that." Her father plowed over her. "If anyone comes to the store asking about me, you tell them you don't know where I am."

"I don't know where you are." Sophie plugged her other ear with her finger. "That sounds like bells and horns?"

"You let them know I'll be in touch soon," he said.

"Who is them?"

"Nobody important. I'll make everything right, that's a promise. That's what good plans are for. Always have a good plan, Soda-Pop. Don't ever forget that."

"Dad…" Sophie tapped the cell phone against her forehead. He'd already hung up. Sophie stuffed her phone in her pocket and turned toward the door, her focus falling on Brad, dwarfing the flimsy plastic chair with his tall frame. Had Brad shown up at the shop looking for her father? He was in the security business. But what did that really mean?

Surely he'd have told her if he was after her father. Matt would definitely have told her. She yanked open the door. The wall of heat from the spinning dryers surrounded her and kindled her doubt about Brad. She knew nothing about investigators and how they worked. What could she offer him as a starting point? She couldn't even guess her father's location from the background noise during their phone call.

"Everything okay?" Brad asked.

"It's fine." Sophie cringed, feeling she sounded as false as her father. She sat beside Brad and stared at the blur of whirling clothes. Talking to her father always made her feel as if she'd been set on a rapid-spin cycle. She wished it was as easy to wring the truth from her father as it was to squeeze water from the towels. "So you own a security firm. You can install security systems. What else does your firm do?" Sophie blamed her father for her lack of tact. Clearly she hadn't found her balance yet. "Do you provide bodyguards?"

"That's my partner's area," he said. "I manage the investigations."

Could her father be an investigation? Was that

why he was stocking her dog food, installing her alarm and carrying her laundry? "What do you investigate?"

"Corporate and insurance fraud mostly."

Corporate America wasn't her father's playground. "You must have many overseas corporate clients since you use Matt to translate a lot."

"It isn't all fraud." He grinned. "Sometimes it gets a little more complicated."

"I suppose those are the cases you prefer and the ones you can't talk about," she said. "So if my kitten abandoner was a money-laundering arms dealer, then you'd step in and bring him to justice?"

"Maybe," he said. "But it's usually a little less Hollywood and a lot more mundane than that."

But much bigger than her careless father. Her father had taught her not to trust as a child, and she prided herself on being more open and less closed off as an adult. Until one phone call from her father had made her suspicious of everyone, including herself. One phone call had made her doubt that decency existed.

Brad had rescued a litter of abandoned kittens, offered to fix her security camera for dog food and was a mayor's son. The son of Mayor Nancy Harrington who had campaigned with her greyhounds. Sophie should have thought of that sooner. Something close to hope swirled through her and she shifted in her chair to face Brad. Maybe Brad was an answer to her problems, not another problem. But if he was using her for information on her father, then she wouldn't feel the least guilty about her next move. After all, George Callahan had lectured his young daughters that turnabout was fair play, never mind any moral objection. "Can I ask you a favor?"

"Sure."

His warm smile eased through her like melted marshmallows into homemade hot chocolate. But she'd burned her tongue so many times she'd lost her craving for even a sip of the deliciously rich drink. "Would you introduce me to your mother?"

CHAPTER EIGHT

No. No. No. That wasn't the right favor. Brad wasn't agreeing to that. Her father had drained her account. She should want the money back. She should want to find her father. Unless she already knew where he was laying low.

"I've spooked you." Sophie waved her hands at him and then at herself. "I wasn't asking to meet your family as if this was…you and I… as if this was something. Because it's nothing. We just met. You're temporary. That sounded mean. It could be something. Maybe, not that it is." Sophie covered her face, inhaled and held her breath.

Brad stared at her cheeks reddening between her spread fingers and forgot about George Callahan. Sophie was flustered, stammering and quite simply too adorable.

"You could help here," she muttered behind her hands.

He'd never seen that deep shade of red before, not even in Evelyn's prized garden. Evelyn's roses had never been such an inviting crimson shade. Maybe if Evelyn's roses had been as appealing as Sophie's cheeks, he wouldn't have cut off the heads all those years ago. "I am."

She glared at him.

He grinned back. "I'm politely waiting while you collect yourself."

She dropped her hands and pointed at him. "You know this isn't anything. We met less than twenty-four hours ago. I'm not interested in becoming a Harrington." She jerked back. That warm red washed from her cheeks, and her dark brown eyes widened.

"What are you interested in?" Brad reached out and grabbed her hand instead of brushing his fingers across her cheeks to coax that warmth to return.

She studied their joined hands, then looked up at him. "Surviving."

His mother was interested in her own survival, as well. "You believe my mother will help?"

"Your mother is known to be a strong animal advocate and notable dog lover. I lost several key sponsors today for a dog ball I'm planning. The Paws and Bark Bash will raise funds to benefit therapy and service-dog organizations as well as rescue outfits around the Bay Area."

"And?" he asked. This had to be about more than donating to some dog organizations. Fundraisers required extensive preparation and work.

If his mother attached her name to an event, she expected something in return. What did Sophie expect to gain from her bash? More marks for her father to scam?

She linked her fingers with his, tightening their connection. "A successful gala will help the Pampered Pooch move from a mom-and-pop pet store to a legitimate business."

"What's wrong with remaining a mom-and-pop store?" Brad squeezed her fingers. There was something natural and safe about their joined hands. Something he liked a little more than he should. "You have a solid customer base, and you can cater to their needs consistently and reliably."

"It's not enough." She dropped her other hand on top of their joined ones. "You don't understand. You have a successful business with a partner, employees, profit."

He'd stepped into a family business. Partnered with his cousin with his mother's blessing. Hired more relatives with his mother's encouragement. Then built the entire business on his mother's political agenda and the profit that came from his mother's clients. Family loyalty had called him home, and family loyalty had allowed him to be manipulated again. A one-man shop that he'd built from the ground on his own terms, his own way, would matter. He envied Sophie her independence. "And with all that comes more responsibility, more problems, more heartburn."

"It can't be all that uncomfortable. You're sailing away for a sabbatical without a return date."

He had no choice. "Well, like you, I'm interested in surviving."

Sophie studied him, and he studied her back, each searching for some truth in the silence. Her lips parted, her head tipped toward her shoulder. Brad waited. Waited for her to probe. Waited for her to ask. Waited for her to come to him.

But Sophie simply released his hand and walked over to the dryer.

Brad leaned back in the plastic chair, a little surprised she hadn't pried. She'd wanted to ask more. He'd seen the interest swirl through her deep molasses gaze. The bigger surprise was that he'd have answered. He never spilled any of his secrets to virtual strangers. Never had the slightest inclination. Until he'd held Sophie Callahan's hand. Every minute, this favor for Evelyn Davenport became more and more complicated. He hated complications.

"There's less than five minutes left on the dryer." Sophie picked up the laundry basket. "I'm sure you have better things to do than hang out at City Suds."

Ella dropped her headphones around her neck.

"Brad can't leave until he's tried the best milk shake in town."

Brad looked at Sophie. "I can't leave without sampling a milk shake."

Sophie wanted to argue. Brad could see it in the way her mouth thinned and her eyes narrowed. And suddenly he wanted to stay. He wanted to rattle her even more until he could control his own response to the woman. Until he could prove her guilty. Yet he feared the truth about Sophie might not be enough to sever his interest in her.

"I'll get the laundry, then." Sophie shoved the basket against the dryer and tossed the clothes inside, not bothering to stop and fold any garment.

Brad leaned toward Ella. "I'm thinking a chocolate shake and cheeseburger."

Ella shook her head. "Boring."

"That's classic comfort food," Brad argued. "Simple and tasty."

"There's more flavor if you add bacon to your milk shake and to your burger."

Sophie returned. "Ready?"

"Ella wants me to put bacon in my milk shake." Brad gripped the laundry basket and pulled, but Sophie's grip remained firm. Heaven help him, but he enjoyed being around this woman.

"It's so good." Ella laughed and stood. "Can we teach Brad to guide?"

Sophie released the laundry. "He's on basket duty."

"After dinner, then." Ella picked up her cane and gripped Sophie's elbow.

Brad held the door open and watched the pair exit, their movements synchronized. There was a trust between Sophie and Ella that Brad suspected would be there even if Ella wasn't blind. Yet there was more in their whispered words and in their soft laughter that showed their love for each other. There was a bond that Brad recognized. He had something similar with his older brother, but he suspected the love between Sophie and Ella was unconditional and always would be. He wondered just how far Sophie would go to protect their relationship. Brad fell into step on the other side of Sophie.

"Never mind about the introduction to your mother," Sophie said.

"I'll pick you up Sunday at ten and take you to meet her."

"I shouldn't have asked."

"But I agreed." He adjusted the basket in his arm and widened his stance, brushing against a guy encroaching on their space. "Sunday at ten. Now about my favor."

Sophie frowned. She didn't look at him, and

her focus remained on her surroundings. "I wasn't aware I'd agreed to a favor."

"This one is easy," he said. "You'll let me install the security system I want in your shop, not the lame one I picked up off your floor."

"That system was rated five stars."

"Maybe for a week five years ago," he said. "Technology has come a long way since IP cameras and DOS computers."

"It isn't that old," she argued.

"The next time you pick up your bat, you can use it on that camera," Brad said.

Ella giggled.

"That was a one-time thing." Sophie's chin clicked two degrees higher as if to punctuate her statement. "My bat days are behind me."

"That's unfortunate," Brad said. "You'd kill it at a piñata party."

A smile lifted the corner of her mouth, disrupting the tension in her stiff chin. Brad's laughter mixed with hers. What was wrong with him?

He must've inhaled too much lint or bleach fumes in the Laundromat. He didn't skip across city intersections with his own laundry, let alone a stranger's. But with Ella and Sophie he was tempted. He used teasing as a deflection. But with Ella and Sophie, he wanted to laugh for the simple joy. He didn't find contentment in holding a woman's hand. Until today.

He squeezed the plastic handles on the basket. The laundry was the only thing keeping him from reaching for Sophie's hand. That'd be a mistake. If he held her hand again, he might fall under her spell. But he was finished with women maneuvering him for their advantage. So he'd concentrate on his own agenda and keep his hands to himself. Then nothing could go wrong.

CHAPTER NINE

A LONG GLASS WALL with two sets of French doors overlooked an infinity koi pond. A pair of detailed cement staircases framed the pond and led into an English-style garden. The entire view made Mayor Harrington's home office feel more like a lavish sunroom than a staid place for civic duty.

Inside the room, hand-carved white paneling, white antique furniture and white marble floors urged a person's eyes to nature's ever-changing color palette just beyond the glass. And if a visitor tired of nature, a volume of Shakespeare's *A Midsummer Night's Dream* sat waiting to be enjoyed on the expensive chaise longue beside the ornate gas fireplace. And if Shakespeare wasn't to a person's taste, then there was certainly something to be discovered among the well-stocked shelves of the floor-to-ceiling bookcases.

Sophie would've preferred to use the chaise longue as intended: to faint on. She uncrossed her legs and straightened in the Queen Victoria–

style armchair with white linen fabric that she'd expected to have been covered by thin plastic to protect it from wine stains or pet-shop owners covered in cat hair.

Brad hadn't mentioned they'd be interrupting his mother's monthly bruncheon with over a dozen of her society friends. Brad hadn't mentioned his mother and her gang had a theme for each gathering and that today's was an elaborate Mardi Gras event complete with feather headpieces and Venetian half masks inlaid with rhinestones and green velvet ribbons.

Sophie smoothed her palms over her jeans, then straightened her top. At least she'd left her baseball cap on the door hook at the Pooch. Still, there was no denying her running shoes had seen more miles than an Olympic cross-country star. She was the scrubbing-floors Cinderella to Mayor Harrington's queen mother.

And there wasn't a fairy godmother ready to materialize in the solarium and rescue Sophie.

Only Mayor Harrington, who appeared now with her royal purple suede four-inch heels, and matching poise. The mayor offered another apology to her guests and closed the connecting door, blocking out the women's chatter blending with Brad's deep laugh and the clinking of silver forks against fine china.

Sophie'd lied when it came to turnabout. An

eye for an eye had never been her style. Her stomach dropped.

She was here, though, and needed to drown her nerves in the bottom of that koi pond. Sophie inhaled, dragging in as much of the vanilla scent from the candles on the mantel without choking. She could've stuck the pillar candle under her nose, but wasn't sure that'd be enough to ease her anxiety.

Mayor Harrington sat behind her desk and removed her pointy-toed slingbacks. She pulled a pair of chestnut-colored sheepskin boots from under her desk and grinned at Sophie. "I suggested a polar bear–plunge theme today precisely so that I could wear these boots. However, given the calendar, we had to celebrate Mardi Gras. The heels are necessary for the added height, but these boots are my private reward."

The mayor's boots were as worn as Sophie's running shoes. Sophie eased her feet out from under the chair.

"My son hasn't brought anyone home in quite some time." Mayor Harrington stretched her legs out, flexed her feet and studied Sophie. "This, I must admit, is a bit of a surprise."

"It isn't… We aren't together like that." Sophie touched her head, searching for her familiar baseball cap. The mayor's cool gaze was sharp and clear-cut. "It's a bit more underhanded, in fact. I asked Brad for an introduction. I caught him at a weak moment and used it to my advantage."

"I see." Mrs. Harrington's laughter was short and compressed, but there was something genuine in the sound. "I assume if you requested an audience via my son, then you're here for business. I'm not exactly the sort of celebrity one wants to spend the day with unless I can push an agenda. What's your agenda, Sophie Callahan?"

Sophie's agenda involved preserving the only stability she'd managed to give Ella. Sophie wanted to keep the home she'd built for them. But she wasn't here to play the sympathy card with Mayor Harrington.

Even in her worn shearling boots, the mayor of Pacific Hills exuded confidence, like the timeless elegance of the hand-carved armrests beneath Sophie's elbows. Sophie didn't doubt Mayor Harrington had an agenda. Always. And she lived it without apology or excuses.

Sophie's agenda included Mayor Harrington. She believed the mayor could take up sponsorship of the dog ball. Sophie could stretch a dollar since she'd had to in the fourth grade when her parents had left. She'd do that now. She just needed the endorsements. The mayor loved animals, owned dogs and supported animal causes. The woman was a natural sponsor for this event.

Now was the time to convince the mayor to share her vision. "I'm organizing an event to benefit service animals. Your love of animals is well documented and the journeys of your greyhounds are photographed and blogged about." Sophie looked out the windows, past the gardens, at the expansive trimmed lawns that would make a lovely dog park complete with fenced runs, rest and water-play areas. A five-star doggy day care.

Sophie strove for three-star accommodation and five-star care.

She turned to the mayor and snapped her backbone in place. It was time to own her agenda. "As a fellow animal supporter I'd like to offer you a sponsorship position at the Paws and Bark Bash."

"The bash is your creation?" the mayor asked.

April had crafted the name when she'd helped Sophie design the graphics for the event. The concept had evolved from an impromptu evening of wine and what-ifs with Kay. "Yes, it's my event."

Other than the quick, successive foot flex, the mayor was still and contained, every movement regulated, along with her voice, which neither peaked with interest nor lowered with disgust. "When is your event?"

"The second Saturday in March," Sophie answered. The mayor was calmness to Sophie's need to move. Sophie wiggled her toes inside her shoes, wanting to pace the marble tiles or better yet run across the lawn. Her fingers twitched and her palms dampened from the unease.

"That's less than a month away, but you shouldn't collide too much with the Saint Patrick's Day festivities." Mrs. Harrington studied a desk calendar. "Where is it being held?"

"The Pavilion at the Reserve," Sophie said.

"The Reserve can be lovely this time of year," she said. "The Plaza Ballroom or Piazza Pavilion?"

"Plaza Ballroom," Sophie said.

"You might consider the Pavilion and request use of the lawns, providing you'll promise to keep all dogs leashed and under proper supervision. I've witnessed a spooked terrier scale the six-foot fence and plunge into traffic because of a careless handler."

Sophie nodded as the urge to pace receded. Certainly Mayor Harrington would've returned to her guests by now if she wasn't interested. Surely she'd not offer suggestions. Encouraged, Sophie plunged ahead, padding the numbers. "The guest count is currently close to seven hundred fifty."

"Commendable attendance for your first

event." The mayor made no move to leave. "I presume there is a silent auction."

"Yes, local businesses have donated over two hundred items, including Napa weekend getaways and handcrafted jewelry." At least she planned to have more than two hundred items and a live auction, but she needed more than stainless steel hors d'oeuvre trays.

"You should ask local artists to hand-paint fire hydrants for your live auction, if you wanted to add a unique flair."

Sophie just wanted flair. It didn't have to be unique. None of her current customers were local artists. And she didn't even know where to begin to collect old fire hydrants. Time to return to her agenda and forget the distractions. "I've allotted for a full three-course dinner. There will be a runway show to highlight the dogs up for adoption."

"You might consider a buffet with carving stations and smart, easy food choices to avoid the fuss of a formal dinner," the mayor said. "Your guests could mingle with the animals and each other."

Buffet carving stations added to her catering budget, an already very limited one. "We have a cash bar. However, I fully intend to offer drink tickets with the purchase of event tickets next year."

"You've given thought to this event beyond your first year?"

Sophie soaked in Mayor Harrington's approval. "Absolutely. I intend for this to become one of the city's premier fund-raisers."

"Then you're prepared to put in the work to scale such an event to the size you foresee?"

"I wouldn't be here, using your son for an introduction, if I wasn't prepared to put everything into it."

"You've picked a worthy cause," Mrs. Harrington said. "I've discovered people often have a softer spot for animals than their own family. You shouldn't lack for sponsors."

She didn't lack for sponsors. Or she hadn't lacked for sponsors until three days ago. "I have a pet store as a résumé, Mrs. Harrington. Not hedge funds or political connections or family lineage. But I have a passion and belief in my cause."

"That isn't always enough, is it?"

Sophie shook her head. "But this gala will happen. It'll grow and those same businesses that refused this year will come forward, and I'll add them to my growing wait list."

"Unfortunately, my dear, you'll have to add me to that wait list."

Sophie's breath wheezed out as if she were a deflated balloon. Of course she'd encouraged one of those childhood hope bubbles to blossom in the last fifteen minutes. Hadn't she learned her lesson as a child? Mayor Harrington wasn't like Sophie's grandmother, but her words pierced all the same.

Mayor Harrington pulled two thin leashes from a drawer in her desk before opening the adjoining door to the dining hall. "Bradley, we'll talk while I let the dogs run before I return to my guests. Evelyn, once you finish your plate, will you see to Bradley's guest?"

Mayor Harrington turned and smiled at Sophie. "Ms. Callahan, it has been my pleasure."

Brad hovered inside the doorway and glanced between his mother and Sophie. "We've taken you away from your guests long enough. And service has started."

"You'll walk with me, Bradley. The dogs will run, then I'll join the ladies." Mayor Harrington, still in her boots, opened the door wider and handed the dog leashes to Brad. "You've known most of my guests since you were in diapers, so we're both aware they're not waiting for me to return before eating. Move aside, so that I may introduce Evelyn to your friend."

Brad passed the dog leashes from one hand to the other and searched Sophie's face. She lifted her chin and pulled her dry lips into a short smile. Finally he moved out of the doorway and walked outside to retrieve the dogs.

"Sophie Callahan, this is my dear friend, Evelyn Davenport. She'll entertain you while I speak to my son." The mayor smiled, but her gaze assessed Sophie as if she was waiting for something.

Sophie wasn't about to beg for more time with the mayor or plead with her to reconsider or whine to the woman's friend. She refused to show her desperation. She jerked her gaze away from Mrs. Harrington and looked at Evelyn Davenport in her peacock headpiece. "Pleasure to meet you, Mrs. Davenport, but you don't have to entertain me."

"It's nothing." Evelyn touched the rhinestone choker at her neck. "And I've just the thing for this occasion. I'll be right back."

Mayor Harrington opened the French doors when Brad appeared on the balcony with two greyhound dogs and a toy ball launcher. "We won't be long."

Sophie stared at the orange ball clasped in the throwing stick Brad held. If only chasing her survival was as easy as fetching a neon ball.

CHAPTER TEN

BRAD SQUEEZED THE leather dog leashes in his fist. He'd miscalculated badly. He'd expected Mayor Harrington, the shrewd politician, to identify the imposters from the legitimate, discredit the pretenders and expose the frauds. The one woman who'd have been immune to Sophie's adorable face and persuasive story. The mayor should have needed less than five minutes to escort Sophie and her sham of a bash out of her office.

But that hadn't happened. The mayor was in full Mrs. Harrington mode, hosting the monthly bruncheon for her closest friends, whom Drew and Brad had long ago affectionately coined the Myna Birds for their incessant chatter. That she'd slipped into her favorite boots in Sophie's company proved she'd hung up her mayor hat for the afternoon.

Evelyn hadn't mentioned the bruncheon when he'd talked to her yesterday and the topic never came up when he called his father last night to check in. So Brad had dropped into the gathering like fresh birdseed, drawing everyone's attention. Fortunately, he'd adapted quickly by stowing Sophie in his mother's office. He'd intended to sneak out of the house, but his mother had swooped in—a mom thrilled to welcome her son and his friend to her home. The Birds would know he hadn't been home in almost a month. They also knew he hadn't brought a woman home since his senior prom and that was simply because his date was the youngest daughter of a Myna Bird.

He pulled off the Velcro strap on the fleece coat and tightened it around Poe's stomach. How had he misstepped so badly? He wasn't usually so careless.

Thankfully Poe and Gunner needed to run or he'd be trapped in his mother's office. He didn't know how Sophie could stand it. Why she wasn't rubbing her arms from the cold chill embedded in the marble floor. Or why she hadn't thrown the French doors wide open and thrust her head outside, like a dog on a road trip, for a reprieve from the lung-clogging vanilla scent. At least he hadn't seen her perched on one of those pretentious white chairs. That furniture had never fit him, even as a child.

The only time he'd ever had his mother's full attention was when she'd summoned him to her sanctuary. Somehow even those moments in her office had never been enough and he'd always left feeling emptier than when he'd entered.

His mother joined him on the small crest beyond the gardens. "It's interesting you'd bring Sophie Callahan here to ask for my help when you know full well I could never support her. Evelyn is a dear friend."

"I never gave you Sophie's last name." He unhooked the dogs' leashes and used a hand command to get them to sit.

"That young woman looks like her father, George Callahan. They share the same deep brown eyes and bone structure in their cheeks." She took the launcher from Brad, signaled to Poe and threw the ball. "Aside from the physical similarities, there's only one new gala being organized in the Bay Area. George boasted about his daughter at the theater league ball we all attended together. How do you think she garnered such lucrative sponsors?"

"Those same sponsors also pulled out, but you already know that, too." Brad pulled another ball from his pocket and launched that one for Gunner.

"I can't sponsor an event my dear friends don't support." His mother picked up the ball Poe had dropped beside her boots and handed it to Brad. "What would they think of me?"

"Anonymous donations are made all the time."

Unless his mother suspected Sophie of some sort of deception.

She shook her head. "Much too obvious. Sophie had a private audience with me and within days her gala is back on course. That's rather convenient. Besides, we must all carry the burden of our own guilt. It cannot be shared or lessened by someone else."

"I have no guilt."

"You're investigating Sophie's father for something more than sleeping with younger women."

He opened his mouth to argue.

"Save your breath." She waved him silent with a sharp flick of her hand. "You and Evie can share her secret. I have enough confidences to keep. I don't need the burden of another. Yet the fact remains that you're looking for her father and you haven't told Sophie the truth."

"I haven't lied to Sophie." She just hadn't asked.

"Omission is the same," his mother said. "I should know. I've turned it into an art form the past decade. But I'm curious as to why you brought Sophie here."

Brad watched the dogs sprint back, eager to return to his mother. He was suddenly eager to run away. What would his mother think if he explained that he doubted a woman who'd unselfishly stepped up to raise her niece and planned a dog ball to benefit service animals, of all things? She was likely to take the ball launcher and rap him on his head.

His silence failed to deter his mother. "You expected something from me. But from the frown embedded in your cheeks, I haven't delivered."

This would've been much simpler if only she'd called Sophie a fraud. Then he wouldn't be standing here debating whether he was more irritated with his mother or himself. "Why did you introduce Evelyn and Sophie?"

"I suppose for the same reasons you brought Sophie to me," she said. "We both wanted a reaction."

Seemed neither of them had gotten the response they'd expected. Except he wasn't sure what reaction his mother wanted. "So you've been prying into Evelyn's personal life after all."

"One can never have enough information. When that information proves to have value, it's even more important to own." Her smile spread, but she restrained it from being too wide like a beauty queen accepting her crown, or too natural like a child on Christmas morning. But there in the familiar grin, Brad saw the politician he knew all too well: the calculating, ruthless, focused woman who'd raised him. He'd seen that look too many times when he'd been discovering the truth on one of his cases.

"What game are you playing now?" His grip tightened around the plastic handle of the ball launcher. "Evelyn's your lifelong friend."

"How do you expect me to protect her without all of the information?" she asked.

"You can't investigate everyone for secrets and information you might find useful later on."

"I can't, but you will. That's your job."

"Not anymore." He'd already paid the final invoice on the *Freedom Seeker*'s restoration—in effect, a cease-and-desist order for his mother.

"You'll do something for me."

"I stopped doing favors some time ago." When he'd realized that he hadn't atoned for anything while working as his mother's lackey. He'd only become more jaded than when he'd left the agency four years ago after his witness had been killed. But he wasn't here to rehash the past. "Besides, you denied Sophie your sponsorship."

"You can't know that." His mother leaned over and kissed Gunner on the top of his head.

"Disappointment was written all over Sophie's face. She wasn't clutching a check and hugging you in gratitude." Of course his mother never hugged people, but still, he'd expect Sophie to embrace her anyway in her enthusiasm. Sophie's gaze, however, had lost its joy, and that had burrowed through to his core, leaving him as hollow as Sophie's forced grin.

"You should be pleased." She handed him Gunner's ball. "You're investigating her father—and Sophie, by extension. You wouldn't want the mayor of Pacific Hills connected to a fundraising scam."

Brad threw the ball, watching Gunner tear across the lawn. He felt as if, instead, he'd run for the ball and suffered whiplash, just inches from securing the prize. He'd reached the end of his leash. "Then you think it's a scam?"

"I think I want tickets to Ms. Callahan's bash."

Surprise knocked him back. He scratched at his neck. "You refuse to sponsor her gala, but you want tickets to attend and, on top of that, you believe it's a scam?"

"You're the one who seems to think it could be a scam."

He hated arguing semantics with his mother. She'd had too many years of practice and had perfected her skills in the political realm. "Why?"

"Animal causes are very dear to me."

"You don't have to attend to open your checkbook." Brad squeezed the ball Poe, obedient and dutiful, had dropped at his feet. Everything Brad used to be. "This isn't about the money, is it, Mother?"

"If Sophie released her severe ponytail and applied lipstick and eyeliner, I imagine she'd be quite attractive."

"She's beautiful because she's natural and understated." Brad launched the ball. It was easier to keep up with the dogs' simple agenda of playing fetch, rather than his mother's.

"You never had a preference for her type before," his mother said.

"I never had a preference for scotch either, but tastes evolve."

"It's good her niece shares her bone structure and porcelain skin," his mother said. "A natural beauty."

"Sophie mentioned Ella?" Brad was confused. Five minutes with his mother and surely Sophie would've realized his mother lacked the DNA structure for empathy.

"The internet can be very helpful." If his mother believed tsking was something other than vulgar, she would've done just that, he was sure. Instead, she patted Poe's head, her tone condescending. "Bradley, dear, I don't need you for every detail."

"No, you only need me for the details that end careers, ruin marriages and implode personal lives." His mother's campaign trail was littered with collateral debris and masked by the adventures of her greyhounds. He needn't look any further than Evelyn and Richard for evidence.

Worse, he'd loaded the gun with proof of Richard's backroom promises to a construction lobbyist to guarantee votes in the primary. His mother had promised Brad that she'd fix everything. Instead, she'd pulled the trigger that had alerted the press; it resulted in key unions transferring their support from Richard to his mother, thereby granting Nancy Harrington the primary win with a clear path to the Mayor's seat. If only he'd kept silent.

"I vowed to deliver the truth to the people of Pacific Hills," she said. "I've done just that and haven't failed my supporters."

"You deliver your version of the truth, you mean."

"You grew your company and exemplary reputation on my truth," she said. "You made a lot of money and established yourself as a premier expert in your field. I fail to see the problem."

He felt as if Poe's orange ball had been lodged between his ribs. He'd enjoyed his work, been fulfilled by his cases. And sold himself on his own lies of justification like his mother. "I have a new truth now." Which was to find the man he used to be before he'd derailed into the corruption and become someone he didn't even really like.

"Yes, the boat you intend to sail away on." She walked farther on, away from the house. "The only truth you'll discover alone in the blue waters is that you and I aren't so very different after all."

"You're wrong, Mother. You wanted me to be like you, but I've finally grown up."

"Our family roots run too deep inside you to be severed that easily." She spun and smiled at him. The sun lit her from behind as if she was some prophet sent to deliver the good news. "You'll learn that one day."

"I won't be you, Mother."

"You already are. I thought you'd be tired by now from fighting that truth for so long." She tipped her head. Her laughter was light and quick, making it obvious he'd failed to mask his surprise. "Come now, Bradley, all those stunts in high school, those incidents in college and now this boat expedition—they've all been attempts to make a stand, to prove you were different, not like the other Harringtons. But you've only proved you are as driven and dedicated as me."

"Dedicated? Is that the campaign buzzword these days?"

"You've been dedicated to your task of not becoming like your mother, but I have to wonder what would happen if you'd simply accept that you're just like me."

"I'm never entering politics, Mother," he said. "You'll have to look to Andrew for your legacy."

"There's more to life than politics, Bradley."

A small burst of laughter escaped. "But there will only ever be life in politics."

"I never told you that."

"You didn't have to," he said. "Drew and I lived it every single day with every single breath. Heck, Drew still lives it."

"There's no shame in being a Harrington with a strong heritage of people who've served in political roles." She lifted her hand, signaling for the dogs to return to her side. The motion was almost unnecessary as she assumed everyone around her simply understood her commands and responded accordingly. She passed the dogs' leashes to him. "It's time I returned to my guests. Please see that Gunner and Poe get their lunch."

Brad led the dogs to their private kennel area, which was an oasis complete with fountain and plush beds that any person would be jealous of.

His mother was wrong. His heritage wasn't the problem. His shame came from the fact that when he looked at the world now, it wasn't with hope. When he looked around now, he suspected the long-time, exemplary finance officer of falsifying accounting reports to cover his fraudulent transactions. He doubted the sincerity of an injured employee, assuming she took off her neck brace to run errands across the bay where no one would recognize her. He questioned the appointment of a top political advisor to a popular legislator, wondering who he'd paid off to claim the position. Distrust tainted his insight and polluted his perception of the world. And he hated himself for that. Feared he might never stop looking for the bad in every corner and every shadow and every laugh.

Despite everything, his mother still believed in her cause. Still believed she'd made a positive impact. He almost envied her for that.

Then there was Sophie Callahan. The goodness practically oozed from inside her. But he held himself back. He could lose his heart to a woman like that. But if she proved to be another lie, that'd be a blow he'd never recover from.

Besides, too good to be true always exacted a price.

CHAPTER ELEVEN

SOPHIE GLANCED AROUND the mayor's pristine office. She'd wasted the entire morning when she should've been chasing down her dad, not chasing her dream of the gala. All of this had come about because she'd wanted to avoid talking with Brad about her phone call at City Suds. She could've just said the call was from a frustrating family member.

But there was something about Brad, protecting her hand inside his own, his eyes kind, his smile open, and she'd almost blurted out everything. Yet trusting someone not in her inner circle wasn't in her nature.

She should never have held his hand. Never entwined her fingers with his to draw him closer. She'd lost too much already and her heart wasn't up for bargaining.

But there was something about Brad…

She watched him and his mother through the window as they stood on a small incline. He interacted with the two large greyhounds, rewarding them with gentle pats on the head and quick rubs to their ears. But that same ease and comfort was absent between mother and son, and the distance between them was more than simply physical space. The mayor looked like she might touch Brad several times, but her hand always lowered to stroke one greyhound's neck or rub behind the other's ears. But Sophie never claimed to be an expert in family dynamics.

Laughter and muffled chatter escaped from the closed door that led to the dining room. Sophie considered crashing the luncheon and scoping out potential sponsors. She wouldn't ingratiate herself to the mayor, but Mrs. Harrington hadn't ingratiated herself to Sophie. Nonetheless, she grudgingly admired the mayor's meticulous care of her greyhounds with their plaid fleece coats.

The door clicked behind Sophie and she turned to see Evelyn Davenport approach. She'd removed her headpiece, and her layered white-gold hair swayed against her jawline. Mayor Harrington made Sophie sit up straighter. But Evelyn Davenport swept welcome and color into the monochrome office. Evelyn Davenport was the guidance counselor every high school student had expected and never gotten. Sophie wanted to hold the woman's hand and pour out her every frustration.

"I prefer Irish coffee over mimosas." Evelyn handed Sophie a glass mug with a diamond wedge-cut base, crystal handle and hourglass bowl.

"The whiskey warms from the inside out." Evelyn clinked her mug against Sophie's. "This is my special recipe."

"I'm sorry I've disrupted the morning and taken you away from your friends." Sophie sipped her drink. The cheery comfort in the coffee was at odds with the formal glass, much like Brad and his mother.

"We'd moved from gossip to categorizing our aches and pains. I don't mind the reprieve. They'll be debating the best surgeon for each body part about now. I'm not much for hospitals." Evelyn tipped her glass toward the windows. "Besides, Nancy is thrilled. Her son sought out her assistance."

Sophie frowned at mother and son. They didn't look thrilled.

"Nancy did offer her assistance, didn't she?" Evelyn asked.

"Broadway tickets for a silent auction at an event I'm hosting."

"Lovely seats. I spent an evening in the theater to see *Phantom*." Evelyn leaned her hip against the doorframe and considered Sophie. "But the tickets aren't what you'd hoped for."

"Not quite." Sophie shifted her focus to the older woman. Would Evelyn consider becoming a sponsor? Or perhaps change Mayor Harrington's mind. They'd been friends for years according to the mayor. Surely there was a statute on when you transitioned from friend status to family. Evelyn must be practically family to the Harringtons. "Do you have pets?"

"Not since my husband passed," Evelyn said. "Nancy and my late husband, Richard, had the passion for animals. Bradley's father and I indulged them."

"A pet can be a wonderful companion after the loss of a loved one."

"That's what Nancy and my other friends tell me."

"I can be of assistance." Sophie handed her a business card. She might be using the back door to get to the mayor, but she didn't care. And there was something about this woman that Sophie responded to. She wanted to help her. Maybe it was Evelyn's loneliness, not so revealing or open or obvious, but then neither was Sophie's, and perhaps that was why she could spot it. "When you're ready. I foster at my pet store and work closely with several rescue organizations. I can make you a perfect match."

"When I'm ready." Evelyn tucked the business card into the pocket of her slacks. "Do you have children, Ms. Callahan?"

"Sophie. And none of my own. I've been watching my niece until my sister returns."

"How long has your sister been gone?"

Since Ella's birth. "Too long I'm afraid."

"How old is your niece?"

"She turns ten next month."

"I imagine you've planned a big party."

"Ella hasn't quite decided what she wants. She's only told me that she'd like to do something special with her mother." Sophie swallowed more Irish coffee, hoping the hot drink might melt that icy disappointment still lodged inside her. Ella wanted her mother and got Sophie. Not the birthday present she'd choose to give her niece. "I imagine Mrs. Harrington would throw a spectacular party for her granddaughter."

Evelyn sipped her drink and shrugged. "If it fit into her agenda, I'm certain she would."

"I wasn't aware that granddaughters and daughters were items on an agenda." Sophie and her sister had never been on their parents' agenda. And Sophie strove every day to make sure Ella never felt like a task on her to-do list.

"Perhaps not to you or I." Evelyn watched Sophie over the rim of her glass. "I'm sure Ella's grandparents have plans to celebrate her birthday."

Ella's grandparents had plans, but they'd never included Ella. Even in her father's most recent call, he had mentioned a plan and his love for his girls, but not a plan *for* his girls. "Unfortunately, a granddaughter was never a priority of theirs."

"That's unfortunate."

It was more than unfortunate. It was disastrous. But Sophie never liked to air her dirty laundry. And already she revealed too much. She frowned into her mug and blamed her whiskey-laced coffee for softening her tongue, but nothing else. "How long have you known the Harringtons?"

"Since Bradley was four and took a pair of scissors to my garden." Evelyn battled between a smile and a frown.

But the fondness in how the older woman said Brad's name made Sophie like her even more. "That must've been a surprise."

"When he was in high school and started a job as a bagger at the grocery store, he sent me tulips on Mother's Day and red and white amaryllis bulbs on Christmas. He hasn't missed either holiday since."

Such a lovely sentiment. Sophie's heart sighed.

"Nancy is returning. That's my cue to get back to lunch." Evelyn tipped her glass toward the French doors and finished her coffee. "But I suppose this year I'll get a conch shell and a coconut from whatever island Brad has dropped anchor at."

Sophie seized the bit of anxiousness before it curled through her toes. Her heart had never flip-flopped over a man before. She wasn't about to start now. She didn't need plumeria leis, seashells and empty promises mailed to her from overseas. She wasn't a fool. When Brad finally set sail, her heart wouldn't be his stowaway.

CHAPTER TWELVE

BRAD DROVE ALONG his parents' winding driveway and glanced at Sophie. "Sorry my mother wasn't feeling more charitable."

"She offered two box seats for the silent auction." Sophie pushed on her sunglasses. "So it wasn't a total loss."

Brad rolled his eyes. His mother's box seats had been gifted to her before he'd been born. In the thirty years she'd been attending the theater, she'd never paid for one ticket. But he appreciated Sophie's upbeat tone as she tried to put a positive spin on the morning. His fingers tapped against the steering wheel as he clicked through possible reasons for his mother's interest in attending Sophie's event. She had an angle, he just couldn't see it yet. "Why don't you cancel and regroup? Hold your fund-raiser next year?"

"Because I've signed contracts and paid deposits."

"Those can be broken." Contracts were broken as easily as glass bottles, New Year's resolutions and wedding vows.

"For a penalty."

"But the penalty might be less than the money you still need to raise to fund the gala."

"I gave my word. Canceling is not an option."

Brad backed off. Maybe it was due to the sharp staccato of her words or the force in her tone, or perhaps because there was more she wasn't revealing and too much he already knew. Sophie was low on funds, whether she'd given her father the money or he'd taken it without her knowledge. Sophie was desperate. But the Sophie Callahan he was coming to know wasn't a quitter. And that was one more thing he liked about her. "You'll find someone better than my mother to support your cause."

"Your mother is strong and dedicated."

Brad frowned. Not that word again.

Sophie rushed on. "She brought your family through that scandal when your father lost the governor's race, and then she used her law degree, entered the political world and now sits behind the mayor's desk of Pacific Hills. That's sheer will and conviction."

His mother's PR team had spun a tale that the media adored and the public swallowed like elixir from some forgotten gods. Sophie had sipped from the same chalice. Breaking a spell so deeply held in a person's heart was like locating a computer hacker's physical location. Next to impossible.

The real truth was Mayor Harrington was more dedicated to her own cause than her own family; otherwise, she'd never have used her son to secure the mayor's seat. "All mothers are dedicated."

"Not all mothers."

The catch in her voice betrayed the indifference in her tone. Sadness made her whisper seem even weaker. He squeezed the steering wheel to keep from reaching for Sophie. His hands needed to stay put. Reaching for Sophie would be a lie. And no matter what his mother called him, he wasn't a liar.

Reaching for Sophie implied he cared. That he wanted to know more. That he was here for her.

But he was here to expose Sophie. To prove the apple hadn't really fallen far from the tree and she was in all ways George's prodigy. It would prove he was right to not lose his heart over a woman like her.

Now his heart called him a liar. Good thing he knew the folly of letting his emotions lead. He opened his mouth, ground his teeth together, then blurted, "So your father must've been the dedicated parent?"

He almost wrenched the steering wheel off

the dashboard. At least he hadn't asked about her mother.

"It seems our parents defined their roles differently."

He tried to loosen his grip. "What was the Callahan definition of parenting?"

"Absentee." Sophie hugged her purse on her lap. "I last saw my mother when the Bay Area Angels pitcher threw two no-hitter games in the same season."

"That was almost twenty years ago." Brad stopped at a red light and looked at Sophie, pulled by her matter-of-fact tone as if she were reciting nothing more interesting than her grocery list. "You're telling me you haven't seen your mother since you were ten?"

"I was nine. My sister, Tessa, was ten."

"I don't know what to say."

"I'd like to say it's fine, but that's not entirely true. However, it is what it is." She pulled on her seat belt, rubbing her chest beneath the strap as if that was the cause of her too-tight voice. "I don't have a mother, and you have one you want to get away from."

Brad slowed at another red light. He'd never known his mother not to be there, even as a child. She might've been occupied with work or fund-raising and not available for her sons, but she'd always been within reach. She'd always been home. He chose to leave now, secure in the knowledge that his mother would be here when he returned. But Sophie had never had that safety. Never had her mother, perhaps, when she'd needed her most. Sophie deserved better than that.

"You aren't going to deny it, then?"

He shook his head. "I'll miss my father."

He wouldn't have been more surprised if his car had lifted into the air like a jet when he stepped on the gas. Why'd he confess that? He would miss his father. That was true. But he didn't need to say it out loud to another person. To Sophie.

"What is your father like?"

Her question broke into his stupor. "He's a good man." He snapped his mouth shut before more truths escaped. Or, worse, some feelings he'd considered long buried. "How about your father?"

"He tries to be good."

"And has he been successful?" He'd clearly exited the freeway and driven into another dimension. One where his mouth and his brain had stopped communicating. He already knew George Callahan wasn't a success. Nor was the man good.

"Until recently," she said. "He'd been dating a woman for the past seven months and she'd been good for him. At least, I thought they were good together."

The wistful note in her voice stuck with him. That could be the only reason for the next absurdity to blurt out of his mouth. "What happened?"

"I suppose he wasn't good. I don't know the details, but I heard him tell someone on the phone that they'd decided to explore other options."

"You never met her?" Clearly his mouth had no interest in listening to his brain. He seemed unable to shut himself up. Although he hadn't given in to that incessant twitch to grab her hand and give her his support.

"I haven't met any of my father's girlfriends since Ella was two." At Brad's look, she sighed and zipped her purse as if preparing not to lose too many personal items. "It's complicated. My father likes women. He just doesn't like to keep women around long. And the revolving door of girlfriends can get confusing for Ella."

And for innocent daughters. Brad suspected her father's girlfriend train extended deep into her childhood and had left an impression on a bright-eyed young Sophie. "You thought the door might've stopped revolving with his most recent girlfriend?"

"I'd hoped so," she said. "Not just for him, but for Ella. He'd sounded content, almost settled."

She'd left herself out, but Brad knew she'd hoped for herself, too, that her father had finally changed. That George had discovered some sort of redemption. Because somewhere inside Sophie was a little girl who still wanted her father's love. He knew because he supposed somewhere inside him was a little boy who still wanted his mother's love. Wanted to know his mother loved him more than her career and political agenda.

He'd really derailed. Perhaps if he'd exited on Fifth Avenue he'd have avoided the self-analysis. He turned onto Market and paced a city bus beside him.

Maybe when he found George Callahan, the man would want to be the father Sophie deserved. Then again maybe his car would fly.

The vibration of his phone disrupted his impossible thoughts. Two more chimes indicated new text messages.

Sophie tapped her nail against his phone screen. "I thought you were on sabbatical."

"It won't officially begin until I hit open water and lose cell reception." Brad eased over into the far right lane behind the bus.

"I can't imagine being totally disconnected." She turned her own cell phone over in her grip. "I don't think I've ever had my cell phone off. Not sure I'd like being cut off from everything."

"I plan to get used to it really quickly." Brad

turned into an alley and parked. "Sorry. It's the office and it looks like they aren't going to quit until I answer."

He responded to several texts before calling his lead on a corporate fraud case. Ten minutes later, he dropped his phone in the drink holder and pulled out onto the road. "Sorry about that. It couldn't wait."

Sophie set her phone beside his. "I answered a few texts myself. But your call sounded more successful than the new items for the silent auction my friend Kay delivered this morning to the Pooch."

"This case is going better than we anticipated."

"You obviously enjoy your work." Sophie shifted in her seat and leaned against the car door. "You haven't been that animated since I met you. Yet, you just intend to leave it all behind."

He nodded. He loved preserving the reputations of the innocent and seeing justice served. He loved the black-and-white cases. But recently there'd been so much gray, lines crossed and boundaries pushed. Somewhere he'd lost his own moral compass and his personal why. He needed to discover that why before he returned.

"It's just such a large pendulum swing from all of this to nothing."

"I'll have a boat to take me anywhere in the world I want to go. Whenever I want to go. So I have something."

"Alone." Her distaste was obvious in the way she stretched out the word. She offered no reprieve. "You don't seem like a loner." Again her low opinion of solitary people echoed in her voice. He half expected her to correct herself and use the word *loser* rather than loner.

"What kind of person am I?" He wanted to know what she saw when she looked at him. He wanted to know if his inner cynic had finally pushed through to the surface and dimmed his gaze and cracked his smile.

"You're the kind that pulls over to answer texts. The kind that sends flowers to widows long after an apology's expiration date. And the kind that installs security systems for free for someone you just met."

He made a show of changing lanes, leaning forward to look in his mirrors as if he couldn't see perfectly fine. As if a small car squatted in his blind spot. Just to avoid glancing at Sophie. She was clearly the one who couldn't see. After all, she made him sound almost good. Almost decent. He rolled his shoulders against his leather seats, but the tension remained. "You didn't mention a sailor."

"I don't see that." No apology lingered in her flat tone.

"Thanks for the vote of confidence."

"Maybe you just need to find some balance in your life."

He intended to find that on his boat. "Maybe you need to find some balance with respect to your fund-raiser. Not shoot for the stars on the first one, but build it up each year."

"I don't have that kind of time."

He didn't have that kind of time, either. The more time he spent with Sophie, the less balanced he became. She seemed to make him lose his footing and forget his purpose. But they weren't friends trading confidences. She was a potential suspect and he had to stop forgetting that. He stopped outside the Pampered Pooch. "I'm going to check your security camera from a remote location and then I'll be back with the laptop."

She reached for the door handle and grinned. "A remote location as in your office."

The teasing lilt in her voice curled through him, squeezing around some of those somber places deep inside. He couldn't recall the last time he'd had a conversation that was more easy banter and kidding and less demanding with expectations and consequences. "Maybe."

She climbed out and then leaned into the truck. "It's okay to admit it out loud."

"Admit what?"

"You're going to miss your office." She shut the door and walked to the Pampered Pooch.

At this rate, he was going to miss more than his office. He waited until Sophie stepped inside before pulling away from the curb and his own stupidity.

CHAPTER THIRTEEN

SOPHIE YANKED OPEN the door to the Pampered Pooch. Normalcy reigned inside and once that door swung shut behind her, surely she'd return to her usual self. The self that didn't spill her history or tease good-looking men. Had she really been trying to steal Brad's laughter for herself? As if she'd wanted to be included in the amusement happening in his mother's exclusive dining room.

She didn't have time for light, playful moments. Weaving down the aisles on her way to the back, she straightened the canned cat food, tossed several cat toys back into their bins and returned her focus. She'd wasted the entire car ride talking to Brad instead of texting her dad or making a list of potential sponsors to approach. But she still had the afternoon free.

Across the aisle, she sorted dog beds, piling them neatly on the shelf while she piled items onto her to-do list, items that didn't include Brad. Things like litter boxes and a Plan B in case her father failed again. Worry bulged like the fluffy filling against the worn seam of a well-loved dog toy.

Checking the time on her phone, she tossed it on the counter and grabbed the litter-box scooper and small garbage can. Ella would return from her cake-tasting adventure with Ruthie and Matt in a little over an hour. That gave Sophie sixty minutes to help the two foster families coming for supplies, search for her father and sponsors, and pull herself together. Sixty minutes to stuff the worry, panic and desperation so deep inside her she'd struggle to find them again. And Ella wouldn't sense anything more than business as usual.

As for Plan B: an inventory of the antique furniture in the attic she could sell quickly. She'd conquer that once Ella retreated to her room for homework.

Brad infiltrated her thoughts at the last cat kennel. She'd almost managed ten minutes without a Brad interruption. She dropped the cat litter in the outside trash already full with the Pampered Pooch bags ruined by the basement flood. The basement should've been an ideal storage place for the paper bags. But nothing had been ideal lately. Except Brad's willingness to help her, despite the fact that he'd seen Sophie at her less than ideal. Dog food hardly seemed like a fair return. One of Grandmother

Callahan's favorite insights whispered through her: *the only real helping hand you'll ever find is the one attached to your arm.*

Sophie needed to figure out what she had that Brad wanted.

A bark and long whine cut in, yanking Sophie back to her to-do list. She ushered her foster dogs into the yard and watched the trio chase one another around, wishing she could share in their excitement. But desperation gnawed at her and dread pricked like a thousand flea bites. She might've only chased her tail the last few days, but she hadn't collapsed in exhaustion yet.

She still possessed one potential lead in the search for her father. A weak lead, but a lead, nonetheless. If she hadn't kept her distance from her father, she might not have lacked the information about where to look for him now. She couldn't go to the police. He hadn't actually stolen the money, since he'd been listed as joint owner on the savings account. He wasn't even an official missing person since she'd spoken to him the night before. If her last lead failed, she'd consider hiring a PI. Problem was she didn't know any, except for Brad. Asking Brad for recommendations might force her to confess even more secrets. She shoved hiring a PI down to Plan F.

She washed her hands and wiped her palms on her jeans before pulling a business card for the Makeover Studio out from under the cash register.

This was all she had. And she couldn't even recall what number Charlene Raye was on her father's list of girlfriends. She remembered her father had suggested Charlene Raye's services to Sophie for some special Christmas evening at the opera, as if Sophie had the funds to attend the opera. And Tessa had continued as Charlene's client, despite Sophie's objections, up until the week before her sister had boarded her flight to India. Not even a novice gambler would agree to this bet, the odds so slim that the hairstylist had even seen her father lately, let alone knew where he might've gone.

Sophie tapped the business card on the counter, her hope evaporating.

Yesterday's call to her father's landlord had depleted her optimism and inflated her debt. Not only was her father several months behind on his rent, his landlord—and Sophie suspected one of her father's former love interests—expected Sophie to cover the overdue costs, as if Sophie was to blame for her father's laundry list of delinquencies.

Now Sophie wondered what complaints Charlene Raye would air against her father. Although her father always preached about the importance of appearances, never approving of Sophie's baseball hats and rubber band hair ties, maybe she'd catch a break here. Clean shaven, hair trimmed away from his ears, and plans were the staples of George's existence.

Sophie punched in the number for the Makeover Studio on her cell phone, not surprised when the voice mail answered on the second ring. It was late Sunday afternoon. The bells chimed on the door, disrupting Sophie's simple message for Charlene Raye.

An unfamiliar gentleman stepped inside. Sophie ended her call. "We're not officially open."

The gentleman pointed down the dog-food aisle and smiled. "I only need a minute."

Sophie nodded. There was something offputting about the man. His neat khakis and pin-striped white-and-blue dress shirt with the sleeves rolled up to midforearm were standard-issue business casual for anyone working in the financial district. His dirty-blond hair with small traces of gray at the temples was tidy, his two-finger-wide goatee nicely trimmed. Even his nose had only the slightest bend, as if he'd tripped into a doorway rather than used weekly bar brawls as his exercise program. Without socks, his loafers couldn't hide more than a butter knife.

Still, Sophie glanced at the camera Brad had

installed. Each blink of the red light reassured her that Brad might be watching on the other end.

Her unwelcome customer dropped a fifty-pound bag of dog food on the counter. "You look like your father, Sophie Callahan."

The jolt of her instincts screaming *I told you so* made Sophie's heart beat double time. She focused on the man's scarred knuckles. His weren't the hands of a number-crunching accountant, no matter how manicured his fingernails. She tried to keep her racing adrenaline from leaking into her voice. "You're a friend of my father's?"

"Business associate." He ran his palm over the list of all-natural dog-food ingredients. "He recommended your store for the best prices on pet supplies."

Sophie didn't need her father recommending her shop to his business associates, or anyone for that matter. She watched the black titanium bracelet shift over the man's wrist. Too many sleepless nights, she'd channel-surfed through infomercials lauding the benefits of the magnetic bracelets for energy, balance and pain. She wondered if the bracelet balanced him out while he delivered the pain. "We try to stay competitive in the market. It's all about customer loyalty. Is this all, then?"

"Not quite." His fingers dug into the bag. "Since your father spoke so highly of you and all you've accomplished, I was hoping he might be here."

This was the last place her father would be. Sophie gripped the scanner as if she'd picked up one of her baseball bats instead. "I haven't seen him in over two weeks."

He covered the bar code. "I need to speak to him."

He needed to get in line behind Sophie if he wanted to speak to her father. But first the man needed to get out of her store. "You aren't the only one. I'm sorry, but I can't help you." Sophie tugged on the dog-food bag, but he pressed down, keeping it in place.

"Your father and I have an unresolved financial matter."

His voice remained pleasant, almost kind, but a warning lingered. The man's implied threat punched through her core and made her heart sprint around her chest. Her father was definitely in trouble and it was more than back rent he owed. But he'd promised to return her money. She had to believe he'd return her money, or her entire relationship with her father would've been an illusion. One more lie in an already distorted childhood. Sophie squeezed the scanner. "I have a business to run. You should pay or leave."

The bells chimed above the door, and her heart slowed like a dog trained to sit on command. One of her foster moms waved before she moved into the dog aisle. Not the person she wanted, but relief spilled through Sophie now that she had a witness.

"On second thought, I'll stick with the name brand from the box store across the bay. When you talk to your father, tell him to call Teddy Gordon." He pulled a marker from the pencil holder and scratched a phone number in thick black ink across the dog-food bag. "Until next time, Ms. Callahan."

No next time. Not with this man. Not if Sophie could help it. His plastic smile stretched up, sparking into his gaze as if he knew exactly what she was thinking.

But there was no way she could prevent another meeting. And they both knew it.

He tipped his head toward Sophie's new arrival before he walked out of the Pampered Pooch and hopefully out of Sophie's world. The bells chimed at his exit, but the shudder inside Sophie remained stuck on repeat.

"Let me get this out of the way." Sophie pulled the dog-food bag off the counter and shrugged at her foster mom. "Apparently this food upset his dog's stomach."

When in fact it was the man who had upset Sophie's stomach.

She moved into the back room and squeezed

the heavy bag, trying to force the tremor out of every bone in her fingers. The queasy tumble of worry and fear increased as if she'd been dumped in the bay at night, the rough current trapping her under the surface.

Since Ella had come home from her extended stay in the newborn intensive care unit, Sophie had been careful to keep her niece's world separate from her father's. Now his world had invaded the sanctuary Sophie had struggled so hard to build. She wanted to lock the doors and run upstairs to hide with Ella. But hiding had never been an option.

She needed to revise her strategy. The part that included a quick influx of cash must jump to the forefront. But she'd also need to be prepared in case good old Teddy returned. For now she'd concentrate and take things one step at a time.

The first step was to dump the dog-food bag. The second was to deal with her foster parent. She'd work out the next steps as she went.

Sophie turned in a slow circle, searching for a spot to leave the food. Finding empty space in the kennel area was like finding dollar bills on a money tree. Finally she shoved the oversize bag behind the food bins she used for her foster dogs, making sure that the phone number faced the wall. Pressing her palm into her roiling stomach, she tried to channel some of her sister's meditation tips. Nothing, not even the ten even, deep breaths or mind warps quieted the wave of nausea. Her regularly scheduled life waited.

BRAD CRADLED A candy dish against his chest and searched through the chocolate-peanut morsels for a blue one. He always ate one color at a time in reverse rainbow order, ending with red. Usually, by the time he reached the end of the rainbow, he'd found a solution to whatever dilemma he was contemplating. And the colorful candies brought the only point of interest to his otherwise monochrome office with chrome fixtures and deep walnut-stained shelves.

He reminded himself to leave a thank-you note for the refill on his assistant's desk. He popped a blue candy in his mouth and wondered what date for his maiden voyage Lydia had picked in the office betting pool. Clearly, Lydia suspected he'd be in this weekend, or she wouldn't have bothered replenishing the candy dish. He popped two more candies in his mouth and considered looking on Lydia's desk for the spreadsheet. But even he wasn't certain what date he'd bet on to leave.

Sophie's laptop sat nearby. Security cameras filmed her outdoor play area, the kennels and her storefront. Last he'd checked, she was finally sitting down behind the counter after darting between the yard and the kennels, covering more miles in that small store than a triathlete. Perched on the stool, her shoulders had hunched forward, but her gaze stayed fixed on a business card she held. Her body might be exhausted, but her mind was active.

He'd watched her for over a half hour before picking up the candy dish. If she'd been working a con, she wouldn't have wasted her alone time tending to dirty litter boxes, cuddling kittens or throwing tennis balls to the dogs. The high-resolution digital security cameras would've revealed even the tiniest transgression.

Ironic that Sophie was the one on film, every expression, every movement, every action recorded, and yet he felt fully exposed, as if those same cameras were peering into his soul and dismantling his secrets. But it wasn't the cameras.

He blamed his mother for his discontent and uncertainty about Sophie. Mayor Harrington should've recognized the con in Sophie's fundraiser; his mother should've exposed the pretender in Sophie Callahan. Instead, his mother had offered her personal box seats as a silent-auction donation and requested a table at the gala.

Why couldn't he just believe that Sophie might simply have a good cause and a desire to help? Why couldn't he look at Sophie without connecting her to George's dark deeds? He'd tracked her every move on the cameras, anticipating some sort of deception. But he'd only witnessed her meticulous attention to cleanliness, her endless devotion to the smallest detail of her store and her tender care with every animal. He suspected she'd put the same dedication into a relationship. But how long before she manipulated her partner's loyalty for her own gain and twisted the ugly out of their love? That was a con at its most simplistic. The cracked candy shells pricked at his stomach as if in revolt; the chocolate hardened into a clump of self-disgust.

He paced over to the large conference table and abandoned the candy dish to its usual place on a black woven place mat in the center of the tinted oval glass. Pulling his phone from his back pocket, he dialed Delta Craft. He'd never gain perspective if he stayed in the city.

Movement at his doorway caught Brad's attention. His brother leaned against the archway as if he'd been there for several minutes, observing Brad's unusual behavior. He should've heard his brother when Drew had stepped off the elevator. His brother matched Brad's height, but Drew was built like a linebacker and he'd never moved with stealth or lightness, even as a kid.

Brad's edges had softened, his instincts dulled.

The *Freedom Seeker* couldn't be lowered into the bay soon enough.

Drew marched across the office and grabbed the candy bowl. "Never known you to leave the blue ones in the dish."

"I'm learning to ration. I won't have an endless supply on the boat." Hopefully he also wouldn't have such a narrow outlook.

"Why wasn't I invited to family day at the old homestead? At the very least, you could've hung around until Dad and I returned from the golf course." Drew tossed candy into his mouth, one piece after the other like an automatic tennis-ball launcher stuck on rapid volley.

"You could've invited me to the range." Brad dropped into his office chair, ignoring the security camera feed on the open laptop.

Drew swallowed and his hand stilled in the dish. His gaze zeroed in on Brad as if Brad was the sole cause of his hung jury. "You haven't been to the golf range since high school."

His freshman year, his mother had signed up Brad for golf lessons, but he'd flirted with the lifeguards instead, refusing to morph into his mother's version of a proper Harrington. "Maybe I'm ready to pick up a nine iron."

Drew sat in a chair, his gaze still fixed on Brad. "Sophie Callahan must like golf."

Brad shifted forward, but the flinch of his

brother's eyebrows indicated he'd already anticipated Brad's response. Brad leaned back, stretching his voice into casual disinterest. "How do you know about Sophie?"

"You brought a woman home to meet Mom during her bruncheon." Drew elongated every syllable of bruncheon as if to better spotlight the evidence. Then he flung a candy into Brad's forehead.

There were over two dozen different ways Drew could've learned about Sophie and none of those ways included their own mother. Brad rubbed his forehead. "Never mind."

"What were you thinking, introducing Sophie to Mom?" Drew shoved the dish onto Brad's desk.

Brad squeezed his temples, wanting this questioning to end. "She needs help funding her dog ball." Or funding her father.

"Dog ball?" Drew repeated.

"It's a fund-raiser to benefit service and therapy dogs." There. Now he sounded convincing—no skepticism had leaked into his tone.

Drew set his elbows on his knees and inched forward. "Good cause."

"Mom offered her theater seats to the silent auction and demanded reservations at the event." She hadn't fully endorsed the bash with a sponsorship check. But then she hadn't denounced

Sophie as a fraud, either. That she'd apparently leave for Brad. That chocolate knot heaved sideways in his stomach, as if rebelling against the idea of proving Sophie a fraud.

"Mom wants to attend?" Drew scooped out another handful of candy and seemed to be considering Brad.

"Any idea why?"

"Doesn't matter to me." Drew shrugged. "How can I get tickets?"

"Not you, too," Brad said. "This isn't some sideshow for our family's entertainment. This event means a lot to Sophie." At least she'd seemed passionate about it, determined enough to ask for a meeting with his mother. Resolved enough not to cancel it. But he'd seen cons put on worthy acting performances before. And he'd discovered that people who built their reality around their own lies were often the most convincing. Was Sophie just a convincing liar? His heart deemed him the liar while his head commanded that he look at the facts.

"I'm not joking." Drew tossed another candy at Brad. "How can I get tickets?"

"There's supposed to be a link on the Pampered Pooch website." The link was definitely there. Brad had confirmed that several days ago. He'd also confirmed that gala registrations dropped into a database and the payments into a separate third-party PayPal account. He rubbed his stomach. He'd never questioned his methods or tactics on any case prior to this. He wasn't about to start now.

Drew nodded and typed on his phone.

His brother couldn't be serious. He wasn't letting his entire family get conned by Sophie's dream fund-raiser. "Aren't you supposed to be preparing for trial next week?"

"Continuance." Drew never looked up from his phone screen. "Nice website."

Brad ignored that comment. "Does Mom know you've got some free time?"

Drew tossed his phone on the desk. A broad smile stretched across his face. "Thanks to your impromptu visit this morning, there hasn't been a chance to discuss anything else like my impending trial or personal schedule."

"Glad I could help." There was nothing pleasant about his voice.

"I figure I have Sophie to thank." Drew's smile spread wider.

"So you want to repay her by attending her dog ball?" He wasn't able to rein in the disbelief.

"You could've saved yourself a visit with Mom if you'd called me first." Drew tipped his head and studied Brad, as if he expected Brad to know already what he was referring to.

Once again Brad was missing something. And

with Sophie Callahan involved, that seemed to be his MO lately. "Because you've suddenly developed an interest in helping the service-dog community?"

"Wow, you're either really distracted by one Sophie Callahan or your mind has already set sail on the *Seeker*." Drew rubbed his chin and watched Brad. His brother was a good cross-examiner, patient and thoughtful, yet insightful and forceful. Drew wasn't one of the top attorneys in the city by accident.

But Brad was good, too. One of the best in his field. And he schooled his expression, neither confirming nor denying his brother's allegation. He certainly hadn't set sail. That might've been the simpler option at this point. And distracted by Sophie... He'd never admit that, even to his brother.

Drew stretched out his long legs and leaned back in the chair as if he'd settled in for an evening marathon session of some legal TV drama. "How's the boat?"

"Still in dry dock," Brad said. His brother was giving him a chance to remember something and he was failing. Quite miserably.

"Must be Sophie Callahan causing your brain lapse, then." Drew laughed. "Two years ago you attended a wedding for the son of one of your biggest clients. I believe there was a certain brunette in the bridal party who occupied your attention most of the evening."

Now a certain blonde seemed to occupy all of Brad's attention, even his dreams. "I've been to over a dozen weddings for—"

"But this one featured a golden Lab," Drew said. "A therapy dog named Sadie. She walked the aisle with the bride."

Brad sat back. How could he have forgotten that? "They'd make perfect sponsors."

"Yes," Drew said. "I'll even make it happen in exchange for a favor."

His family had always operated on the quid pro quo system; that was the Harrington way. However, helping his brother had never been a hardship or a burden. But then again, they never asked each other—the support was always there, no questions asked.

Brad clenched the leather armrests. Maybe that was what set him on edge now. His brother wouldn't have asked before. "You're sounding a bit too much like Mom, and the instinct to refuse is suddenly very strong."

"You might be on the verge of your sabbatical, but you haven't lost your instincts yet." Drew chuckled. "Why are you here anyway? I thought they'd have locked up your office by now."

Brad must have looked offended or surprised. Drew flicked his arms wide. "It isn't as if you had anything to pack up. There isn't one personal item in this sterile square box you call an office."

Brad glanced around. He didn't have vintage furniture like his mother or fake happy family photos of his adorable pets littering the shelves. He didn't even have a plant on the window ledge or a miniature water fountain to soothe visitors. He worked here—he didn't live here.

Of course, his old apartment had looked much the same, or so Evie had always accused. Sterile and cold, she'd called it. But that didn't matter. Soon he'd have a boat and ocean sunsets to color his world.

"My assistant won't padlock the door until I leave the dock. Apparently the entire office has a betting pool on how long it'll be before I'm on my boating excursion." Brad turned the laptop toward his brother. "As for why I'm here. I jumped on a conference call with my team about a new fraud case while updating the software on Sophie's computer, so I could test her new security system."

"Who do I need to contact to get in on the office bet?" Drew asked. "Lydia in charge?"

"Don't encourage them," Brad said. "About that favor?"

"You need to fix the buffering. The feed is frozen." Drew tapped on the keyboard, then frowned at the screen. "Is Sophie open on Sundays?"

"Not officially. A few foster families planned to stop in for supplies." Brad heard more quick typing and watched his brother's eyes narrow on the monitor. "Why?"

"Either Sophie isn't happy with her customer, or he isn't from one of her foster families." Drew spun the computer toward Brad. "Hit Rewind."

Brad watched the video feed and pressed his fist into his thigh. He should've installed sound. He'd have violated all sorts of privacy issues, but at the moment he hardly cared.

A regular-looking guy in khakis and a dress shirt faced Sophie at the counter. Sophie strangled her cash register scanner, her mouth tense and firm. He backed up the footage to the customer's arrival and noted Sophie's quick glance at the camera. Was that relief on her face, or was it his imagination? Had she hoped he'd been watching?

He was watching now. Sophie flinched when her customer grabbed something to write with and scrawled across the dog-food bag. Then he noticed her fear. Quick glances at the camera, her teeth digging into her bottom lip. She wasn't pretending now. He'd left her alone and afraid with someone harassing her. All while he'd paced his office and doubted her.

Anger ambushed him, pointing a gnarly finger at him. "Definitely not a puppy lover." Brad slammed the laptop closed. "I need to go."

Drew shoved out of his chair with a speed that mocked his size. "I'll drive. I'm parked out front."

"That's a no-parking zone." Brad grabbed his jacket off the chair, reached for his gun and came up empty. He wasn't on official duty or a case. This was a favor.

Drew hurried down the hall. "I've got a special permit."

"There's no such thing." Brad followed his brother into the elevator and punched the button for the lobby. He'd rather punch the jerk who'd scared Sophie or—even better—her father.

"Maybe not for you." Drew pulled car keys from his pocket. "Or perhaps you just don't know the right people."

Brad strode through the lobby. "I know you. Heck, I'm related to you."

"I'm definitely not the right people." Drew pushed open the glass door and clicked the alarm on his mini SUV.

Brad slid into the passenger seat, swiped the yellow paper off the dashboard and stuffed it into his jacket pocket. "Now I know the right people."

"You can't keep that. It's registered to my car." Drew eased into traffic.

"And now you don't know the right people." Brad forced a laugh, trying to disrupt the tension coiling inside him. He didn't need his brother interfering in this, too. "Vehicle information can be easily altered upstairs inside my office."

"You're sailing away soon. You need dock space, not city parking."

Thankfully, the streets weren't overly busy. If they hit the stoplights right they could be across town in less than ten minutes. Inside Sophie's place in less than twelve minutes. "I'm here now, so I'll keep your pass."

"For another favor." Drew cruised through a yellow light and turned onto a side street to avoid getting stuck behind a city bus.

"I'm not sure I agreed to the first one." Brad glanced at the clock in the dashboard and stopped his fingers from tapping against his leg. Surely they'd just discovered the longest stoplight in the financial district. "Which was what, by the way?"

Drew's phone rang inside the car, and he clicked the answer button on his steering wheel.

Brad shoved his brother's shoulder when the light turned green and Drew hesitated, distracted by his paralegal on the phone. He nudged Drew again at the next red light, sending him down a one-way street. He should've driven. Directing Drew through the city wasn't distracting enough.

Questions about Sophie's customer preoccupied his brain. He doubted the man was Sophie's ex. Beyond his research that indicated Sophie hadn't dated in a while, there was Ella. Sophie was fiercely protective of Ella, and he didn't think she'd introduce random men to her niece.

He pointed for Drew to turn again, but his brother ignored his assistance.

Brad tried to ignore the thought that Sophie might be pining for a past old love. He aimed the air vent into his face and turned up the fan speed. He'd never been the best passenger, and the car seemed too warm all of sudden. And too confining. And too slow. He could've run to Sophie's place faster.

What did he care if Sophie burned a candle for an old flame still? It wasn't as if he wanted her to burn a new candle for him. He just wanted to believe she had room for a new love. Nothing wrong with that. He tapped the fan speed to superblast, hoping the cool air might dry out his lies.

If the guy wasn't an ex, who was he? Definitely not a customer interested in the latest dog toys or foam mattress pet beds. That left George Callahan. He had to be connected to George. Brad just needed to find out how—then he'd know what the guy wanted with Sophie.

Drew pulled into the loading zone at the corner near the Pampered Pooch. Brad pointed to a guy down the street leaning against cement stairs, talking into a cell phone and drawing a deep drag from one of those e-cigs with the pale red tip and vapor plumes. "That's our guy. Recognize his bare ankles from here."

"Dude needs a tan." Drew looked over the top of his sunglasses.

"Follow him. Get me a license-plate number and an address." Brad jumped out of the car.

"I'm an assistant district attorney, not a detective."

Brad leaned back inside the car. "You love this stuff."

"I should go and check on Sophie." Drew motioned toward the pet store. "You can chase the bad guys."

Brad frowned at his brother, unable to relax his voice enough to suppress the possessive bite in his tone. "I'm checking on Sophie."

"And I'm calling Lydia." Drew shoved his sunglasses on. "I want in on your office bet."

"What's that mean?"

"Can't chat now." Drew turned his steering wheel, shifting the wheels away from the curb. "I have a bad guy to catch."

"Convenient." Brad tossed the crumpled

parking pass on the passenger seat. "You might need this."

"Thanks," Drew said. "You're accruing quite a list of favors."

"You'll have to get in line." Brad shut the car door and rushed toward the pet store.

CHAPTER FOURTEEN

SOPHIE STEPPED AROUND the counter and hugged Beverly Baker. Since becoming a foster parent three years ago, Beverly liked to fill Sophie in on every milestone, big or small, of the dogs in her care. Sophie extended their conversation, inquiring further about each dog's improvement and care plan. Beverly had been content to update Sophie and Sophie had been content to listen for the past fifteen minutes.

Still, that tremor inside Sophie's bones refused to recede. Even Beverly's animated tale about the bug guy letting Rex, the Jack Russell terrier, out and returning the wrong dog to her backyard failed to disrupt Sophie's fixation with the front entrance. Each time Beverly paused to breathe, Sophie collected her dread and waited for Teddy Gordon to step back through the door.

The bells chimed. Sophie concentrated on not tensing as she stepped away from Beverly. Over the woman's shoulder, she watched Brad enter the shop.

His strong shoulders filled the small center

aisle. His height drew her focus, and his confident stride chewed up the distance from the door to the counter. Finally that tremor inside her faded to a ripple. If Teddy Gordon returned, he'd definitely hesitate once he noticed Brad. She'd hesitate, too, but perhaps not for the same reasons.

Brad offered to help Beverly with her packages, but she smiled and shook her head. One last goodbye to Sophie and the woman left, the bells issuing a small chime.

Sophie glanced from the laptop in Brad's firm grip up to her security camera, then back to Brad. His expression seemed to be set in neutral—relaxed, yet not open. But there was something in his steady gaze that searched her face. Concern or wariness, she wasn't sure.

How much had he seen on camera? How much would she need to confess? How much did she want to explain? Surely it was enough that he was here. Nothing needed to be said. Her lips made a wide smile and she hoped it broadcast delight and welcome. "You're back, so everything must be working."

A crease shifted between his eyebrows. He didn't believe her fake smile. "It's better than I expected. Busy afternoon?"

"A few foster families." Sophie edged around the counter. He wasn't asking specifics and she wasn't revealing details. "Nothing I couldn't handle."

Brad set the laptop on the counter. "Ready to watch the video feed?"

"Not really," she muttered, avoiding Brad's gaze.

"Worried about how you look on camera?"

She was more worried about how other people looked. More precisely, how detailed one man's khakis and threats looked on camera.

"Who wants cake?" Ella's excited shout saved Sophie from replying and silenced the chime of the bells above the front door. Ella called out from her perch on Matt's back. "We brought samples!"

Matt's huge smile matched Ella's and Sophie wasn't sure who'd conned who into the piggyback ride. She dashed around the counter, wanting to wrap her arms around Ella, happy to know that for now the child was safe.

Ruthie waved several Whisk and Whip Pastry Shop bags. "Matt and Ella loved the s'mores cake. I liked pink champagne. Ella and I really liked red velvet."

Matt knelt and let Ella slide down to the floor. Ella grimaced and added, "No one liked the coconut lime with blueberries."

Matt took the bags from Ruthie. "So now you get to sample, too. Even you, Brad. I could use another male vote." Matt started to unload the first bag. "Do we go with a classic white-chocolate raspberry, or the exotic grasshopper with mint and chocolate for the wedding cake?"

Matt waggled his eyebrows at one of the cake containers. Clearly, he and Ella had a favorite and had failed to win over Ruthie.

Ella nudged Matt with her elbow. "Brad should try the s'mores cake first before he ruins his taste buds with the champagne one."

"The pink champagne was terrific." Ruthie took one of the bags from Matt and thrust it at Sophie. Ruthie frowned at Matt, seemingly disgruntled that he'd even suggested that they stray from tradition. "Sophie will agree with me."

Matt and Ella shook their heads in unison as if Ruthie was an unfortunate lost cause. Sophie grabbed the cake samples and set the bag on top of the laptop, content to banter about cake. Content to pretend that choosing a flavor was the most pressing problem to be solved today. Content to pretend this was her normal. "Isn't there supposed to be a groom's cake?"

"Already taken care of." Matt wrapped his arm around Ella's shoulders and squeezed. "Ella and I picked Creamsicle. Now we need help with the big one."

"The one Matt gets to smash in Ruthie's face," Ella added.

"Not if I get to him first." The challenge was there in Ruthie's voice, but laughter danced through her gaze.

Happiness radiated out of her every pore, making Ruthie the quintessential bride. Terror would ooze from Sophie's every pore if she were the bride-to-be.

Brad leaned toward Ella. "Who do you pick in the wedding day cake battle, Ella?"

"You'd pick Matt because he's bigger and a boy." Ella pushed her glasses up. "But I'm going with Ruthie because girls are faster and a lot smarter."

"You might be right." Brad rubbed his hands together. "When does this sampling begin?"

Sophie warned Brad, "We're trying the pink champagne first."

"But I used to make s'mores with my dad when my brother and I were kids." Brad ran a hand along his jaw as if replaying a favorite memory. "I'm sure Matt shared the same fun times with his dad."

Sophie narrowed her gaze at his earnest tone. Distrust shifted through her when Brad slung his arm around Matt's shoulders like Matt was his wingman and they were headed out for a good time.

Brad held Sophie's stare, then finally shrugged.

"Fine. I made s'mores once with Evie in her fire pit in her backyard."

Sophie quirked one eyebrow. "And?"

"And I was in college, not grade school. Still, the s'mores were some of the best things I've ever tasted." Brad fist-bumped Matt and smiled at Sophie. "You should ask Evie about that night."

Sophie shook her head. "Pink champagne first."

"Then the s'mores." The hope in his tone made him sound like one of Ella's contemporaries.

"There's nothing traditional about a s'mores wedding cake." Sophie put her arm around Ruthie's shoulder in support.

"Do you want a traditional wedding?" Brad asked Sophie. Surprise filtered through his voice and pulled his eyebrows down together.

"It isn't my wedding day," Sophie countered. *Thankfully.* Ruthie had been the one envisioning her wedding day steeped in tradition and history ever since they'd been in high school. Sophie hadn't envisioned extending a relationship beyond the first date. And her wedding: she'd never envisioned that. Not when she was a kid and not even as an adult. She'd only ever pictured herself as a bridesmaid—a spectator, never a bride.

"But if it was?" Brad persisted. He tipped his head and studied her.

Sophie wondered if he was trying to picture her as a bride. Then she wondered how he would picture her like that. But she never wanted to be a bride, did she? Surely she would've thought about her wedding day before now. Before this moment, with Brad watching her as if she were a suspected runaway bride.

Ella leaned forward—obviously she didn't want to miss Sophie's response. Ruthie's gaze ping-ponged between Brad and Sophie, a look of speculation blooming across her face.

Sophie blamed Ruthie. Her best friend wanted everyone around her to fall in love because she was deliriously in love. But Sophie would need to trust love in order to give her heart to someone. And she'd learned years ago the danger and pain that came with matters of the heart. No, love was a mistake she'd never make.

"It's Ruthie's wedding, not mine." Sophie took another cake sample bag from Matt. "What I might want or not want doesn't really matter."

Brad watched her, opened his mouth perhaps to disagree, but quit before anything more than air escaped.

Ruthie linked her arm with Sophie's. "I thought we'd sample more cake after we all had dinner at Rustic Bistro."

The way Ruthie stressed the word *we* set Sophie on edge. Rustic Bistro wasn't the restaurant they'd agreed on that morning when she'd dropped off Ella at Ruthie's. Now Ella smiled and nodded. Her niece loved the bistro's soft candlelight and fireplace; they reminded her of a castle. Ruthie hadn't known Brad would be here, though her best friend's matchmaking attempts were anything but subtle.

Sophie couldn't spend an evening crammed into a booth, sitting thigh to thigh with Brad, discussing wedding plans. She might forget that she could never fall in love. Never lose her heart. She might start picturing her own wedding day. Panic swirled like a funnel cloud, preparing to touch down, forcing Sophie to blurt out, "We already have plans. Brad is teaching me how to use the security system tonight."

Matt nodded his approval. Ruthie's look turned even more speculative. Brad crossed his arms over his chest and glanced between Ruthie and Sophie as if more than content to let the women hash out his evening schedule.

"That means Brad will join us for Sunday-night surprise." Ella raised her arms over her head in a cheer. "I have to call Charlotte so I can finish my project before we start dinner."

Too late, Sophie realized her error. She'd be alone with Brad now. For Sunday-night surprise.

Certainly their Sunday homemade dinner would not be a disaster again. Certainly with Ruthie gone, she'd pull her thoughts away from weddings and hearts and love. Certainly she could prepare a simple meal. Nothing complicated about it.

"Maybe you guys should catch a bite with us, then work on the system." Matt jumped in, worry thick in his voice. "We could go to someplace more casual, like the diner on 8th."

"We shouldn't intrude, Matt." Ruthie released Sophie's arm and patted Matt's cheek. "It's clear they have their evening all organized."

Brad scanned the adults, then finally leaned close to Ella. "What's Sunday-night surprise and why does everyone look worried?"

Ella giggled. "It's a surprise."

Matt slapped Brad on the shoulder. "Text me later if you're still hungry or need some antacids."

"Stop scaring him, Matthew Wright." Sophie pushed Matt away from Brad, wishing she could push away every thought about Brad, weddings and love. "Food poisoning isn't on the menu."

"There's always a first time." Matt laughed and dragged Sophie into a hug.

When Sophie didn't return the embrace, Matt squeezed harder. She spoke into his shoulder. "You can't insult me, then make it up with a hug."

"I'm not letting go until you hug me back." Matt tightened his hold.

"Take it back," Sophie said.

Matt sighed. "Sophie wouldn't intentionally poison anyone with her cooking, but things happen."

Sophie shook her head and laughed, giving him a quick hug. "I'm not sure how my very sensible, completely sane best friend can love you."

Matt gripped Sophie's shoulders and looked her in the eyes. "If you figure it out, do me a favor and don't tell her."

"Only if you promise to stay for Sunday-night surprise." Sophie raised her eyebrow and held his stare. Her challenge thrown.

"You have to check with the boss." Matt lifted his hands in surrender and looked at Ruthie. "I'm not in charge of our social calendar."

Ruthie hugged Sophie. "We'll leave you three to hone your culinary skills. We're scouting out wedding venues in Napa next week, so maybe we can schedule Sunday-night surprise some time after that."

"Culinary skills take months, sometimes years to master, Ruthie." Matt retreated several steps.

"You might want to leave." Sophie shoved Matt in the chest, pushing him toward the door.

"I'm getting ready to sharpen my knives. A chef needs sharp instruments and things to practice on."

Matt laughed and ducked around Sophie to kiss Ella's cheek. "You have my number."

Ella nodded. "So does Brad."

"Want to make a side bet over who calls me first—you or Brad?" Matt whispered.

Ella touched Brad's arm, trailed her fingers along until she clasped his hand in hers. "We're a team. We got this."

Brad's strong hand engulfed Ella's as if he'd been holding the girl's hand since she'd learned to walk. Simple, easy and natural like a father with a daughter. He never flinched. Never pulled away. Just moved closer to Ella's side. A band twisted around Sophie's chest as if a professional linebacker had tackled her to the ground.

Brad grinned at Matt. "We'll take care of each other."

That band tensed again, as if she were at the bottom of a pile-on, flattening her lungs and stealing her breath. That squeeze might've been around her heart, but she vowed to ignore all things heart related. Still staring at their joined hands, Sophie speculated what it would be like to hold Brad's hand and trust with every cell inside her body that he'd protect her. That she'd protect him. That they'd take care of each other forever and always.

But that was the problem. She could hold Brad's hand, but she wasn't built to trust. And, without trust, she'd always doubt. She'd leave the hand-holding to a couple like Ruthie and Matt. Sophie moved the cake samples off the laptop and lifted up the computer. At least now her hands weren't so empty.

Ruthie grabbed one of the bakery bags and reached for Matt. "I guess it's just you and me, a bottle of wine, and another red-velvet sample."

"Sounds like a perfect evening." Matt held open the door for Ruthie and called out to them, "We left the other cake samples so you won't starve later."

Sophie pushed Matt outside with her hip, locked the door behind the happy couple, and turned to see Brad and Ella disappearing together into the back, the bakery bags in Brad's firm grip and Ella reciting the day-end tasks: water in all kennels, preferred food choices for each foster and favorite toy. Ella's voice lost some excitement when she reached number four on the list—litter boxes.

Sophie stopped in the doorway and watched the pair. Their heads touched as they both looked into Chester's open kennel.

Ella stroked the orange cat's large body and

pointed out his damaged tail and clipped ear, explaining that Dr. Bradshaw wasn't certain if the injuries had come from a car accident or animal attack. Brad reached inside and Chester stretched out beneath his touch.

Ella felt around the kennel, her hand sliding under the bed and returning with a stuffed mouse. "This is Chester's favorite toy. He needs it in his bed so he can sleep good every night."

Brad picked up the bag of cat treats Sophie had left on the table and added a large handful to Chester's bowl.

Ella covered her mouth and giggled. "Auntie says Chester is on a diet and he can't have more than one treat a day."

Brad set his head against Ella's. "I'm not telling her. Chester is eating the evidence. Are you going to tell her?"

Ella chewed on her bottom lip. "She might make us clean out the litter boxes if she finds out."

Sophie crossed her arms over her chest and considered the pair. "I already cleaned the litter boxes."

"That's good news." Ella remained where she was, never turning toward Sophie.

Brad dropped a few more treats into Chester's bowl before sealing the bag and placing it back on the table. He stuffed his hands into his pockets and faced Sophie, all innocent and un-apologetic.

Ella took her time closing the door on Chester's kennel before twisting toward Sophie. Another picture of innocence, but there was a definite sparkle in her smile. "Then it's time for Sunday-night surprise."

With everything else locked up, Sophie put her keys in her pocket, considered the adorable pair and let them off the hook for the extra treats, even though Ella knew better. She tried to convince herself it was because she didn't want to dim that sparkle in Ella's smile. But she'd noticed a challenge in Brad's gaze, as if he dared Sophie to ruin their fun. Well, she knew how to have fun, too. "You leading or am I?"

"It's Sunday. No deliveries, so no new boxes to block my way." Ella grinned. "I got this."

Sophie, on the other hand, wasn't sure she had this. She didn't have time for fun. She didn't have time to want to have fun. To think about fun, just like she didn't have time to think about relationships and love and wedding days. Brad made her consider all that and more.

Sophie switched off the lights and caught the red dot up in the corner. Her new security camera, turned on, watching and filming. Recording her secrets, her failures and her problems.

How much had Brad seen? Would he ask questions? Would he want to help her? She didn't want his help, did she?

CHAPTER FIFTEEN

BRAD STROLLED AROUND Sophie's compact kitchen, studying her array of teapots. The realization that he still wanted to sit down for that tea and cake surprised him. The teapots charmed him. He favored the squat giraffe teapot with the neck for a handle, although he'd gotten a better look at the pumpkin teapot and now he had a competition going for his top pick.

Sophie darted back and forth, gathering cookbooks from various cabinets and shelves. He wasn't sure she wanted him there, and yet she hadn't rescinded her offer, either. She'd seemed more appalled at the idea of dinner at Rustic Bistro with Ruthie and Matt than dinner with Brad at her place. Her movements weren't stiff from anger or hasty from irritation, but she'd developed some type of edge he couldn't quite place since she'd walked up the back stairs.

He'd seen the softness in her gaze when she'd caught Ella and him giving the hefty orange cat too many treats. Here, she hugged the stack of cookbooks against her chest as if she were guarding against an attack.

He wouldn't have left now for anything.

Sophie dumped the dozen cookbooks onto the table beside the chair Ella sat in.

Ella swung her legs back and forth, the toes of her fuzzy boots scraping against the linoleum floor. She reached over and tugged on Sophie's arm. "We have a boy here tonight. Boys don't like vegetables."

"Neither do nine-year-old girls." Sophie stood beside the table. "Brad, do you eat vegetables?"

"Only when my mother makes me." He leaned against the counter near the sink. Sophie never looked at him, but he saw the quick flash of her smile.

"I know that feeling." Ella nudged the toe of her boot into the floor.

"It's my choice." Sophie sorted the cookbooks, placing them around the table. "You had last week. It isn't my fault you chose chicken and Chinese."

"I wanted chicken-fried rice." Ella grimaced. "Not spicy Szechuan stir-fry."

"It wasn't that bad," Sophie said.

Ella gripped her stomach and rocked forward as if wounded, using the classic body language for *gross* known by every kid around the world.

"Okay, it was. It'll be better tonight." Sophie

glanced over at Brad. "Sunday-night surprise works like this. The chooser picks a protein from the piglet teapot. Then a cuisine style from the cow teapot." Sophie pulled a colored cardboard piece from each teapot. "We've got French cuisine and fish as our protein. We can work with this. Now comes the surprise part." Sophie sorted through the cookbooks and picked up *French Food Made Simple*.

The daring taste buds of the pair interested and surprised Brad. He appreciated their culinary spirit and how organized and efficient Sunday-night surprise was. When he was a kid, he'd wanted only burgers and French fries. Matt and Ruthie's worry seemed unnecessary and overblown. He asked, "You make any recipe from that cookbook?"

"Not exactly." Ella leaned her elbow on the table and rested her chin in her palm. "We make the recipe on the page number Aunty picks."

"What if we don't like that recipe?" Brad asked.

"You have your cell phone in easy reach, right?" Ella asked.

"Yes," Brad said.

Ella grinned against her fingers. "Perfect. You might want to put The Boot Pizza into your contact list."

"We've only called them twice." Sophie

gripped the cookbook like she was a harassed librarian ready to swat rowdy children with it.

"Last week was close," Ella said. "We've called almost every time it's been your turn, Auntie."

"I haven't had very good luck," Sophie admitted.

Defeat eased into her tone and she looked like she wanted to smack her own forehead against the cookbook. Or cry. Brad wanted to bring back Sophie's smile. Bring back Ella's bright laughter. He should leave, but he wanted the experience he'd been promised: the surprise, the adventure and the food. Their execution needed a little refining, but he'd deal with that next Sunday. Not that there'd be a next anything. But there was tonight. Tonight, he'd stick to their plan.

"Maybe Brad should pick." Ella straightened, hope lifting her shoulders. "He might have better luck."

"I'm already intruding on your tradition," Brad said, even though he wasn't sorry to be there and planned to enjoy the rest of the evening with them.

"It's hardly a tradition." Sophie bent the soft cookbook cover, her thumb running over the pages. "We just started at the beginning of the new year."

Ella giggled.

"And you've called The Boot Pizza how many times?" Brad asked.

Ella clutched her stomach and laughed harder.

Brad tried not to catch Ella's contagious giggles and noticed Sophie struggled to contain her smile, too. Pleasure whipped through him.

Sophie's laughter tinged her next words. "Well, we're having fun spreading our culinary roots."

"We just fly back to our Italian ones each Sunday," Ella said.

"Understood." Brad pulled out his cell and moved closer to Ella's chair. "I'll just add The Boot to my favorites now."

"We could just order now," Ella suggested.

"That's being defeatist." Sophie held out the cookbook and eyed it with a wariness that suggested every recipe was written in French and she'd skipped those classes in school. "We have to at least pick a recipe."

"And then we call," Ella said.

"Or we cook," Brad offered.

Ella paused and pushed her glasses up. "Can you cook?"

"I know my way around a kitchen and a spice rack." No thanks to his mother. Cooking hadn't been a required skill in the Harrington household. He'd learned in grad school, trying to impress a pastry chef who lived in his apartment building. He'd never won over his neighbor, yet he'd had fun in the kitchen and enjoyed attempting new recipes and creating different flavors. He cooked at home more nights than he ate out and often brought the leftovers to work for his staff.

"We don't have a spice rack." Doubt and disappointment coated the earlier hope in Ella's voice.

"But we do have a spice drawer." Sophie pointed at the cabinets.

She'd leveled up the positive beat in her tone, but in her eyes he still saw the skepticism over his culinary skills.

"We have a *cooking drawer*." Ella touched Brad's arm. "The spices share space with the measuring cups and spatulas and spoons."

"How did you cook a spicy stir-fry?" Brad asked.

"We were too lazy to go to the store." Sophie restacked the cookery books as if that was the end to Sunday-night surprise. "So we improvised."

Brad cringed. *Improvised* was the culinary equivalent to deconstructed, and never a good sign on those TV cooking shows he watched every night.

Sophie avoided him, edging around the table rather than crossing in front of him to return the cookbooks to the shelf. She wouldn't look at him. He'd already guessed from the last ten minutes that she probably wasn't the best cook on the West Coast or even the city block. Not that it mattered. She was trying to build something special for Ella. She was making memories for herself and her niece: good memories that lasted.

A warning flared inside him, telling him these memories belonged to Ella and Sophie, not him. But he barreled on past the exit-now sign flashing in his mind, very much determined to add to their memories. Yes, Sophie's stove was more vintage than practical. He'd bet the temperature in the oven hadn't been calibrated in over two decades. And if he guessed correctly, only two of the four burners worked. Yet he wanted to make dinner here with them. Against all good sense and logic and rationale, he wanted to experience prepping and cooking in this kitchen with this family.

"How about this?" Brad grabbed a cookbook from the top of Sophie's stack, enjoying the surprise in her gaze. "Sophie, you play around with the laptop and the cameras. Ella will introduce me to the spice drawer and help me do a Sunday-night surprise Brad Harrington style."

"That's a lot of work." Sophie reached to take the cookbook from Brad. "We can call The Boot, and Ella—"

"Will help me locate everything I need after we discuss our menu." Brad firmed his grip on the cookbook as Sophie pulled harder.

She refused to release the cookbook and he refused to give it up. And then he knew. Maybe it was the hesitancy in her gaze or the firm set to her mouth or her white-knuckled grip on the cookbook. But he knew this wasn't a tug-of-war over takeout or home-cooked. This was about control and giving that up inside her own home. He softened his voice and added, "You'll be within jumping distance if we get into any trouble, which we won't."

"I know I can't light the stove." Ella jumped from her chair and crossed to Sophie's side. "But I can do a lot of other things."

The determined confidence in Ella's voice impressed Brad and tugged at his heart. The tension drifted from Sophie's face. She tugged once, then released the cookbook. "The pots are under the sink. It's the only cabinet tall enough." She pushed Ella's chair into the table and adjusted the towel before it slipped off the rack and onto the floor. "We usually cook at the kitchen table. It's easier for Ella to reach."

"Or she could use the stool at the counter, near the sink. Closer to the water," Brad suggested.

Sophie rounded on him and gave him a silent are-you-nuts glare.

Ella interpreted the tense silence. "I won't fall. I do balance activities in gym at school."

"You aren't at school, you're near a hot stove," Sophie countered.

"Ella won't fall. I won't burn myself." Brad opened the laptop on the kitchen table and plugged it into the wall socket beneath the table so Ella wouldn't trip on the cord. "But if it makes you feel better, you can sit here at the table and watch your video footage of this afternoon while we cook. After we have dinner, then we can continue our conversation from earlier."

Sophie made a show of dragging out the chair and plopping down as if under duress. Her fingers punched at the keyboard, but he figured she'd rather be poking at him. He'd invaded her kitchen and reminded her that he hadn't forgotten about her unwanted customer. He was two for two at rattling her. And there was time left in the evening. Brad smiled before switching his focus to Ella. "Did you pick out those apples in the basket on the counter?"

Ella nodded. "I tested each one for soft spots."

"Then we have dessert."

Ella frowned. "Those are my healthy snack before dessert."

"Not if we bake them into a pie."

Ella beamed. "We can do that?"

"Definitely," he said. "But we need supper first."

Ella tapped her chin. "I like noodles with butter."

Brad opened the refrigerator and spotted the package of chicken breasts and a bag of shredded mozzarella cheese beside a premade pizza crust. He had a protein. "Where do you keep those noodles, Ella?"

Ella opened two cabinet doors. "My friend Charlotte has a closet with all their food in it. You can walk inside and everything."

"Pantries come in all sizes. As long as you have certain staples, you can make dinner."

"Do we have staples?" Ella whispered.

Brad picked up a can of tomato sauce. He preferred crushed tomatoes or, even better, a dozen fresh Roma tomatoes from the farmers' market. But he'd make it work. "How do you feel about chicken Parmesan?"

"Does it come with noodles?" Ella asked.

"Any kind you want."

Ella opened a box and picked up a dry noodle. "Bow ties are my second favorite." Closing the box, she reached for another one. "These are my favorite. I like the twisty shape."

"I like those, too." Brad grabbed another can of pasta sauce from the cupboard and closed the door. "Now it's time to show me that cooking drawer."

The joy in Ella's smile was enough to tell Brad that he'd made the right choice in staying. Now if he could only get Sophie to stop punching the keyboard and join in the fun, then the evening might be a resounding success.

CHAPTER SIXTEEN

SOPHIE PACED ACROSS the kitchen and shoved the cooking drawer closed, the five steps hardly enough to release her irritation. The drawer had to be kept closed or Ella might run into it. Not that Ella was leaving Brad's side anytime soon. They didn't appear to even know Sophie was still there. From the flattening of the chicken breasts with a small hammer, as Sophie had never owned a mallet, to the seasoning of the bread crumbs, Ella and Brad kept their heads together, moving in tandem like a well-choreographed team.

Ella stood on a stool in front of the counter, her attention fixed on Brad's instructions, nodding when he paused and repeating each step back to him. At his praise, her thin shoulders straightened and pride blossomed across her cheeks. Brad secured Ella in his embrace, standing behind her with his arms framing her on either side as they worked together to roll out a piecrust.

Sophie chewed on her lip. Buying a piecrust in the pan already assembled wasn't a bad option, and, even for store-bought, the crust tasted perfectly acceptable.

Ella's joy filled the kitchen, bouncing around the teapots on the swirl of her laughter. "I'm making a real pie."

Brad's gentle encouragement stamped a deep imprint on Sophie's heart. She needed to close down her senses, protect herself and Ella from his charm and strength. But with every breath, she inhaled the enticing aromas from the chicken Parmesan baking in the oven. Heaven help her, she'd never known her kitchen could smell quite this delicious. And the delight in Ella's expression and the kindness in Brad's hooked her, pulling her away from the laptop over and over again.

But this wasn't reality. And she needed to bring all of them out of this culinary fantasy before bad things happened, like a kitchen fire or lost hearts.

Sophie moved over to the pie-assembly station and picked up an apple peeling. He'd even shown Ella how to peel an apple in one loop. He'd seriously downplayed his skills in the kitchen. And Sophie had seriously downplayed his effect on her. But she'd find her focus; she had to. "I imagine you'll be having mangoes and pineapple from Baja soon. Unless you intend to travel north first, but that would mean colder weather."

The apple peel twisted around Sophie's fingers like a chain twisting around her emotions. Brad glanced at her, a curious glint in his gaze. Everyone needed this reminder, so she plowed on. "You are sailing south first, right?"

Brad picked up the pie dish and shrugged. "I haven't quite mapped out my exact course." Then he steered the conversation back to Ella and their impromptu cooking lesson. "Now we press the dough into the pie pan."

"Then the filling and then the top." Ella brushed her hands together. "Brad knows how to cook so many different foods, Auntie. He's gone to so many places."

Awe and admiration colored Ella's voice. But apple pie was classic American fare. Sophie didn't need to be well traveled to chop up apples and dump them in a premade piecrust. *Thank you very much*. Then she noticed Brad had assembled a barrier of cans around the cutting board as markers for Ella to know how far to roll the pie dough. But anyone could've thought of that to help Ella.

Brad waited while Ella felt around the pie dish for the size and then together they lifted the dough into the pan. But his ease with Ella... Not everyone managed that with her niece, and more often their discomfort and uncertainty revealed itself. Brad didn't treat Ella as if she was a fragile keepsake best left on the shelf, but just like any other kid. Yet the teamwork, the trust Ella seemed to have in Brad and his trust in the little girl, in turn, continued to both weaken and irritate Sophie.

Ella and Sophie were the team. They only trusted each other. That's how it'd always been. And how it had to be now for the good of everyone.

"If only we had vanilla ice cream." Ella helped dump the apple mixture on top of the crust.

"There really aren't many things better than warm apple pie and ice cream," Brad added.

Sophie crossed her arms over her chest. "I'm not going out to buy ice cream." She definitely wasn't leaving these two alone. She might return and find Brad moved into the guest bedroom and her bags packed.

Ella pouted until Brad suggested they all go out to get ice cream after dinner.

Sophie knocked her head back against the wall, jarring that chain around her emotions. He was too accommodating. Too considerate. Too everything. But she'd locked herself away. She was untouchable. Still, she should've ordered takeout or accepted Ruthie's invitation for dinner at Rustic Bistro. This was fast becoming more than a simple dinner.

Brad opened the oven, dipped a chunk of

bread into the pan and handed it to Sophie. She blew on the steaming sauce, then took a bite and lost her focus. Forgot about feeling displaced. Forgot about those locks and chains. And tumbled into the culinary wonderland Brad had created.

Two servings, a glass of wine and a quick trip to the corner market later, Sophie still hadn't quite recovered her focus or located new dead bolts for her emotions. She couldn't recall the last time Ella had requested seconds of any meal that wasn't takeout. She couldn't recall having so much fun cleaning up. And she couldn't recall what her kitchen was like without Brad in it. She shook her head, blaming the wine for her memory failure.

This was only a moment and, like all moments, it had to end.

Sophie watched Brad cover the pie with tinfoil. "You can leave it out. I've figured out how to justify a second piece."

He glanced over his shoulder at her. "How's that?"

"Kay left more silent-auction items in the downstairs entryway this afternoon. I've been storing everything in the attic to keep it out of Ella's way."

He rubbed his stomach. "If I help carry, can I have more pie, too?"

"Whoever carries the most stuff can have the biggest piece." Sophie headed down the hall, stopping in Ella's bedroom to tell her they'd be in the attic. Once again, she blamed the wine for the happy skip in her step.

Four trips and over three hundred and fifty steps later, Sophie adjusted her grip on a tin of assorted pet toys and blankets.

Brad followed her into the attic, carrying a box with a spa gift basket and a movie night goodie package. "Where do you want these?"

"Under the window." Sophie set her pet tin on top of another box and started rearranging things. Thanks to Kay, the items for the silent auction had doubled.

"You'll need a larger attic soon." Brad edged a stack of donations closer to the wall and left to retrieve the last box from the entryway.

She wasn't about to stop Kay from collecting more items. She wanted the gala to be a success. She stepped back to give Brad more room and bumped into reality. The smack of her elbow against her grandmother's armoire cracked through the illusion of the evening, the stinging pain angling her attention back to her plans.

Brad wasn't part of her plans. He wasn't part of her future. Her future was uncertain. And every minute she didn't concentrate on finding her father and getting her money, she failed to secure a future for herself and Ella.

She ran her hand across the antique armoire. "How much do you think someone would pay for this?"

Brad opened the armoire's etched doors and pulled out the drawer inside. "It's solid, real wood. Well crafted." Brad inspected the matching dresser and headboard. "Beautifully maintained."

And the last of her grandmother's possessions. All that remained of the woman was there in the attic. "It was my grandmother's. All handmade by my grandfather."

The only tangible connection Sophie had to the grandfather she'd never met. Even as kids, Tessa and Sophie couldn't fill the void their grandfather's passing had carved inside their grandmother. In the detailed lines and intricate patterns of the furniture Sophie had discovered the love and true happiness shared between her grandparents. When Sophie wrapped her fingers around the thick bedpost, she stopped resenting her grandmother for refusing to let Sophie believe in the impossible. When she traced the curved edges on the side table, she understood that a tragic loss had made her grandmother a realist and that she'd only wanted to prevent Sophie and her sister from suffering the same pain.

The pain of dreams broken, hope shattered and love lost. "The sharp edges on the coffee table and thick bedposts were too dangerous for Ella. I worried she'd trip as a toddler and hit her head. I didn't want to alter the furniture so I moved it up here."

"It's your history." Brad scrutinized the bedside table. "Why would you want to sell it?"

Sophie knelt in front of a matching pair of bookshelves and flipped through one of her grandmother's blank journals. Friends and family had gifted her grandmother floral-covered notebooks on every birthday and holiday. But her grandmother had stopped writing after her grandfather's death, as if there was nothing worthwhile to commit to paper, not even the upbringing of two lost granddaughters. "Feels like it's wasted up here in the attic. Useless."

Which was what Sophie refused to be. She wouldn't be useless. Her future wouldn't be blank. She now had a backup plan to find the funds to keep her and Ella in their home: sell Grandmother's furniture and any other valuables that might be discovered in the attic.

"If you're serious, I know someone who could give you better advice than me."

The vintage furniture in Mayor Harrington's office had been authentic. She imagined the entire house carried a similar look. No imitations or replicas for the Harringtons. Sophie smiled at Brad. "Your mother?"

He shook his head, his eyes wide, as if he'd never considered his mother an authority on furniture or anything else. "No, my admin's partner is an interior decorator and she designs furniture on the side. They'll know what to do—estate sale, internet listing, auction."

"Thanks. I'd like to talk to her." Sophie skimmed through another journal. More blank pages, but various newspaper clippings had been tucked inside. The highlighting on one caught Sophie's attention. She tugged it free and read a short blurb about the arrest of Henry Mason, whose real name was George Henry Callahan.

Sophie stared at the yellowed clipping and remembered the "who will Daddy be today" car game she'd played with her parents and sister as they'd driven to new towns, found new apartments. But she'd only been five or so at the time, and her memories were unreliable. She'd been an innocent child enjoying the name game. But this old highlighted article signaled much more. Was it possible her grandmother had kept track of George Callahan's aliases? Her grandmother hadn't been a child playing a game. She'd been a mother tracking her son's misdeeds.

Sophie stuck the clipping back in the journal

and set it on top of the bookshelf to look through after Brad left and Ella fell asleep.

Brad glanced over at her. "Your sister won't want this stuff, will she?"

Sophie struggled not to snort. She'd already ignored several calls and texts from Tessa that week, certain Tessa only wanted more money. Sophie wanted Tessa to make a claim and it wasn't on the antique furniture. Her sister needed to claim Ella and accept her responsibilities as the girl's mother. "It's not really her style."

Tessa's style was more likely to claim half of the profit from the sale. Sophie doubted her sister even remembered the furniture. Heck, Tessa couldn't seem to remember her own daughter's birthday. Certainly she'd forgotten an old bedroom set and living room furniture.

"What about Ella?" Brad asked. "Maybe she'll want the connection to her great-grandmother."

"My grandmother was difficult to bond with and Ella was young at the time." Besides, Ella was the reason Sophie had to sell the furniture. "She'll still have my grandmother's early journals and a few pieces of her jewelry. Ella is more connected to the things we've picked out together."

Brad closed the armoire doors and leaned his shoulder against the tall piece. "I'm not sure I've seen a stronger mother-daughter bond than you and Ella."

That word speared through her core and numbed every cell. She wasn't a mother. She couldn't be a mother. Surely Brad saw that. She'd failed to bond with her grandmother. Her own mother had abandoned her two young daughters. And her sister had begged Sophie to let her relinquish her parental responsibilities every day. Sophie's family tree was filled with rotten branches of unsatisfied wanderers.

Clearly the Callahans lacked the mother gene. No, she couldn't be a mother. Callahan mothers failed and she couldn't fail Ella. "I've been a good aunt," she qualified. "I've done what I had to do to give Ella the home she deserves."

Brad stepped close and grabbed her hand. "I didn't mean to upset you."

"You haven't."

But he must have heard the catch, that dry crack in her voice, and he tightened his grip.

Sophie clutched his hand in return, unable or perhaps just unwilling to break the contact yet. She had to convince him she wasn't a mother. He had to understand so she could dismiss the impossible thoughts he stirred up for her. She was on emotional lockdown. There couldn't be any more Sunday-night surprises Brad Harrington style. No more burgers and laundry. No more trips to the corner market like they were family.

Sophie wasn't homemade, home-cooked or homegrown. She was store-bought, artificially sweetened and a substitute. "Ella has a mother. My sister. I'm her aunt."

"But her mother isn't here," Brad said. "Hasn't been here. But you've been here, through every step, every tear, every moment—good or bad."

"Someone had to be." Sophie tightened her grip, as if the force would make him understand.

"No, you didn't have to be," Brad said.

Sophie jerked away, losing contact. He wanted her to admit to being someone she could never be. He wanted her to admit she loved Ella more than... No, it was enough that she loved Ella with everything she had. "I couldn't leave that innocent child alone."

"Why not? Her own mother left."

"That's not fair." Sophie crossed her arms low over her stomach. His words poked into her like a balloon in midflight pricked from multiple sides. "You don't know Tessa. You don't know what she's been through. How much she has suffered."

"And you haven't suffered?" Brad asked. "Or don't you matter?"

"What do you want from me?" Sophie curled into herself, trying to plug those holes, but she sputtered into a nosedive like that erratic balloon. Tried to block the betrayal in his words. Tried to remember who she was. Who she'd always have to be to survive.

"I don't want anything." Brad pointed to the stairs. "But there's a little girl nearby who thinks of you as her world. As her everything. As her…"

"Don't say it." Sophie lunged forward and pressed her palm over his mouth. "I'm better as Ella's aunt."

Brad reached up and pulled her hand off his mouth, anchoring her with their linked fingers, catching her before she'd crashed into the ground. He'd exposed her, split open those secret places inside her and now held her while she gathered herself together. Sophie searched his face, noted the emotions swirling through his gaze and the words backing up against his closed lips. Maybe he finally understood.

"I lied." His voice was low, as if dredged through the darkness. "I do want something from you."

Sophie watched him and waited. The attic closed in as if embracing them, but a shiver shifted through the air, rippling across her skin. "What?"

Brad tugged her against him. "This."

The attic sighed; the walls closed in on them

as his lips fell against hers. He never let her lock herself back down. Every obstacle she threw up, he destroyed. First with his words. Now with his touch. He teased, he pried and he learned. And he offered—temptation, tenderness and safety.

Sophie stopped fighting, stopped running and stopped hiding. There was so much she couldn't be. Couldn't have. But this moment, she'd take this.

Sophie pulled away before she took too much. Before she fell too far. Before she discovered too much of the heart she refused to recognize. "I better check on Ella. It's a school night." She spun and raced down the stairs, hoping to outrun her budding feelings for Brad.

Brad scrubbed his hands over his face and let his forehead thunk against the antique armoire. Nowhere in the great golden state was there a bigger fool.

He'd wanted to reach Sophie. Reach into her heart, past her fears, and when his words had failed, he'd kissed her. He'd wanted her to see herself as more than an aunt. He wanted her to see that she was everything to Ella. That she could very well become his everything, too. His world.

He wanted her to be a part of his world.

He rapped his head against the armoire again,

hoping to jar his sanity loose. He had to be insane. He couldn't find peace in the arms of a woman like Sophie. He doubted Sophie's innocence in her father's scam, didn't he?

He rubbed his palms up over his face and let out a deep breath. His world wasn't made for hearts and soft sentiments and Sophie with her adorable niece and inviting kitchen and endless rescues. He'd taint Sophie's world even more than her father, teaching her to twist his love into something darker.

He really needed to leave. He needed to jump on the *Freedom Seeker* and shove the engine to full throttle. He needed to speed right out of the bay, drown his heart in the current and let his emotions sink to the ocean floor. Then he could forget Sophie and how right she seemed to fit, whether holding his hand, stepping into his embrace or settling into his heart.

No, that wasn't right. And the longer he stayed here with Sophie the more he lost himself.

Time to leave and not look back. That meant no more impromptu dinners. No more stolen kisses. And no more favors for Sophie.

Besides, he'd fulfilled his commitment to her. He'd installed her security system and introduced her to his mother as she'd requested. And she'd obviously handled her unwanted customer. He had no business rushing into her store like her protector. He had no business inviting himself into her traditions as if he belonged. He had no business here other than what he'd promised.

And he'd promised Evie he'd bring George Callahan to justice. Time to fulfill that promise.

CHAPTER SEVENTEEN

SOPHIE'S STOMACH GRUMBLED. Lunch had been postponed because Beverly Baker had delivered on her promise. Three new foster people had arrived ten minutes after Sophie had returned to the Pampered Pooch from walking Ella to school that morning. Between the adoption paperwork, a mixed-up supply order and several spunky day-care dogs, her Monday morning had turned into late afternoon before she'd taken a seat behind the counter.

The reprieve had lasted a mere five minutes before Erin, her part-timer, had arrived, allowing Sophie to take Ella to her after-school appointment with her vision therapist.

Sophie wasn't needed at the doctor's during Ella's regular visit, so she headed for Kay's apartment to check on April. The ten-block walk only increased Sophie's appetite. She welcomed the discomfort, which gnawed through any thoughts of Brad. Work had been a welcome distraction, as well. She quickened her pace, stomping away the memory of Brad's words and his touch. Reminding herself last night was a blip and nothing more.

Kay's place was above the Sugar Beet Pantry. Sophie stepped inside the café for a bowl of fresh soup. She planned to eat while she visited with April until she had to pick up Ella.

Sophie lifted the stainless-steel lid on a pot of creamy tomato soup and inhaled the thick scent of basil. But the peppery odor only took her back to her kitchen and the intoxicating scents Brad had created last night. She dropped the lid too quickly and it rattled loudly. She'd been much the same since last night: rattled. Sunday-night surprise had delivered more of a surprise than she'd imagined possible. She had to stop these intrusions of thoughts of Brad. She lifted more soup lids, concentrating on her hunger. Finally she discovered the wild-mushroom soup and settled on her longtime favorite that carried no connection to Brad.

Sophie flattened a plastic lid on her soup and balanced several fresh breadsticks on top before grabbing a handful of crackers.

Pans crashing in the kitchen ensued before a woman strode through the swinging door, wiping her hands on a neon apron and moving behind the cash register.

Sophie set her food on the counter and smiled. "Is this your third new chef, Liv?"

"Fourth." Liv grimaced at the kitchen. She opened a paper bag and placed the food inside. "But I'll be looking for the fifth tonight."

"That bad?" Sophie leaned across the counter to peek into the kitchen at the disgruntled cook.

"I called the culinary school in Napa to inquire about private chef classes for myself." Liv punched the keys on the cash register.

Sophie picked up the bag. "Then you'd have to manage the storefront and the kitchen. You're just one person."

"That fact slaps me awake like a dirty dish towel to the face every night when I crawl into bed." Liv rolled her shoulders, slowly stretching. "You're understaffed, Sophie, and you make it work."

Barely. But Liv didn't need those details. And Sophie planned to do more than *barely* make it. She just had a few roadblocks to remove first. "You've been here less than two months. You'll find your rhythm soon. It'll work out."

Another crash echoed from the kitchen, the pinging of steel utensils hitting the tile floor. Liv's eyes narrowed. "I hope that magical rhythm finds me soon before my kitchen implodes."

Sophie patted her bag. "You've still got one of the best soup selections in the city."

"Thanks for the boost," Liv said. "I should get

back in there, but I'll see you at the gala in a few weeks. I wish I could've done more."

"You made donations to the auction and you're coming to the gala. That's quite a lot." Sophie understood too well the stress on Liv's small business. If only both Liv and Sophie had unlimited funds to support their business goals.

Liv reached under the counter and handed Sophie another small bag. "Hopefully, this helps April find her smile again."

"Has she been crying?" Sophie asked.

"Not in front of me." Liv watched the kitchen door. When only silence pressed back, she glanced at Sophie. "But there's sadness behind April's too-brief smiles. And she seems distracted or like she's retreating."

April had always been melancholy. "Maybe it's nerves."

"Probably," Liv said. "I can't imagine having one baby, let alone two. Hug April for me and let her know I'll be up after I close."

"Will do." Sophie hurried around the side of the building to the apartment entrance and let herself in with the emergency key Kay had given to her.

Sophie had seen April two nights ago. There hadn't been much laughing or time for giggling as they'd worked on the gala financials and silent-auction starting bids. April had seemed happy enough. Sophie had tried to ask about the babies, but April always deflected their conversation to the gala. Tonight they planned to finalize the starting bids for the silent auction items so Sophie could deliver the final version of the list to the printer before Wednesday.

Sophie set the food on April's nightstand and smiled. "I can eat this in the kitchen if the smell bothers you."

"Everything bothers me these days, even the scent of my own deodorant." April jammed her elbows into the pillows stuffed behind her and scooted higher up on the bed.

Sophie pointed at the bags on the nightstand. "Liv sent up something for you, too."

"I've got a drawer full," April muttered, and pulled open the nightstand drawer to reveal a pile of ginger lollipops.

"Look, we don't have to work tonight." Sophie sat on the edge of the bed. "We can play cards. Watch some TV. Talk about the babies' room."

"You need to get ready for the bash." April shoved the drawer closed. "I can't be the reason you aren't ready."

"You won't be." Sophie touched April's arm and drew the woman's attention to her. "I promise. If I'm not ready for the gala, it's my own fault. You've been a huge help already."

April nodded, but the motion seemed distracted, as if April were carrying on an internal argument with herself.

Sophie took in April's pale lips and rubbed her cold arm. Even April's copper curls had unraveled and dulled. Liv hadn't exaggerated the changes in April—her eyes looked as if they'd withdrawn into the deep, dark circles underneath. "Have you eaten today?"

April picked at a loose thread on her comforter. "A few crackers."

"Have my soup." Guilt had wiped out her appetite. She'd been so focused on her own problems she'd missed the downturn in April's health. "Let me do something for you first."

"You are doing something. You're letting me help with the gala planning."

That hardly seemed enough. The woman was pregnant with twins. About to be a mother soon. About to be responsible for two lives. Sophie knew firsthand how overwhelming and humbling that could be. April looked as if she hadn't quite gotten beyond the overwhelming part yet. Sophie'd eased into things. "What about tea or something?"

April nodded and shoved her limp curls behind her ear. "Liv gave me ginger tea. It helps my stomach."

Sophie smiled and quickly went into the kitchen to heat a pot of water. She'd lost her smile after one cup of ginger tea and April's resistance to discuss the babies. Finally she'd switched over to the pricing of the auction items, determined to talk babies while they worked. But April ignored Sophie's every attempt to chat about the twins. She'd even cut Sophie off when she started to ask April if she'd like some of Ella's old baby supplies.

Every time April moved, Sophie cringed. It was as if every adjustment in the bed encouraged April's argument against Sophie's price suggestions or the topic of the twins. They'd made not a lot of progress—on the bash or April's impending delivery.

But Sophie refused to cry defeat. She was here for April. She'd give the mom-to-be something to focus on other than the four walls in her tiny room.

"Find the starting bid for the Napa two-night getaway that we did the other night." April tossed off the blankets and rolled into a sitting position, her legs hanging over the side of the bed. "My price wasn't that low."

Sophie gaped at April's ankles, swollen with deep indents from the mattress like fingerprints mushed into a stale marshmallow. Worry tapped on Sophie's shoulder, but she forced herself to slow her words from a startled shout. "Where are you going?"

"The bathroom." April stood, and her puffy bare feet smacked against the floor like two flat bricks. She braced one hand on the nightstand and the other on her lower back.

Sophie sucked in a breath. There was pale, porcelain skin and then there was April's. Even Ella hadn't looked that translucent when she'd been born. "Can I help?"

"No," April snapped, and rubbed her back. "Sorry."

"Don't apologize." Sophie moved toward the doorway, within lunging distance on the chance that April's muscles and bones had become as paper-thin as her skin. "You're carrying twins and on bed rest. I'll get more tea." And check the time. Surely Kay would be coming home soon. Or Liv would be closing up. Surely someone was coming so April wouldn't be alone when Sophie left.

Sophie lifted the teapot and used her free hand to steady the swaying from the tremble in her arm. Something wasn't right, but Sophie wasn't qualified to offer good advice to a mom-to-be. Even her stomach had stopped rumbling, as if it too anticipated something bad.

"Sophie!" April's shout splintered through the apartment and cracked along Sophie's spine, releasing her inner terror.

Sophie dropped the teapot on the burner and

sprinted down the hall. April stood in the bathroom, clutching her stomach with one hand and bracing herself with the other. "There's blood. There isn't supposed to be so much blood."

Sophie rushed forward as April swayed, her legs buckling. Sophie wrapped her arm around the woman's waist and guided them both to the floor. A quick glance at the usually white bathroom tile confirmed April's words.

Bile rolled through Sophie's stomach and crawled up her throat. That was too much blood. Sophie pushed aside her panic. "I'll call for help."

April's head rolled to the side, her green eyes wide, her lips dry and her face ashen. Sophie flashed back to Tessa and those frightening moments in that damp basement, too petrified to do anything more than hold her sister's hand and too powerless to take the pain that stole her newborn niece's cry.

But April wasn't in labor. Sophie watched for contractions but none came. The look in April's eyes was the same as Tessa's, though—terrified.

"Don't leave me." Tension dominated April's whisper, making her voice brittle. "I can't die here alone. On the floor."

"No one is dying," Sophie shouted. "I have to call for help."

April refused to release Sophie's arm. Sophie's throat tightened against the fear. More blood seeped through April's nightshirt. "My phone's on the nightstand," April murmured.

Sophie stretched into the bedroom, clawing with her free hand toward her purse on the floor. "I won't let go. I just need my phone."

One small lunge and her fingers caught the purse strap. In seconds she had 911 alerted and an ambulance on the way. She squeezed April's arm. "I need to unlock the door."

April shook her head. "You can't leave me."

Sophie stretched again, catching the phone number on the front of the Sugar Beet Pantry bag sitting on the nightstand. But her fingers weren't steady. Meanwhile, April kept getting more and more pale, a color so light Sophie had never seen it before. But April never lost the strength in her grip on Sophie's arm. That remained steady, firm and constant, just like Tessa's grip all those years ago.

On the third try, Sophie finally entered the phone number correctly. At Liv's happy greeting, relief zipped through Sophie. She managed to get out what was happening, tossed her phone on the floor and wrapped her arms around April as she concentrated on the sound of the siren.

She heard sirens every day in the city, considered them backdrop noise, something she paid attention to before crossing the street. But for the second time in her life, the siren seemed too distant, too slow, too quiet. She willed the paramedics to hurry. Willed the siren to get louder. Willed April to stay with her.

Sophie closed her eyes and counted to one hundred, just like she'd done while waiting with her sister and newborn niece. Counted to keep the fear contained. Counted to keep herself breathing.

At her fifth time reaching a hundred, the siren blared outside the apartment building. Finally. Hearing noises nearby, she called out, "In the bathroom!"

Liv rushed in behind the paramedics. Sophie scooted aside to give the paramedics room to work. Secure on the gurney, April cried out for Sophie.

She used the toilet to push herself up and moved to the doorway. "I'm here, April." She grabbed April's hand. "I'm not leaving you."

April's head dropped against the pillow before her eyes closed.

Sophie looked at the paramedic, composed and young. "I'm riding with her."

The paramedic adjusted the oxygen tube beneath April's nose. "You'll need to release her hand for now or we won't get out of the apartment."

Sophie squeezed April's fingers. "I'm right here. I'll be with you the whole time."

Liv said, "I'll call Kay and take her to the hospital."

"Thanks." Sophie tipped her head toward the apartment. "It's a mess in there."

"I've got it." Liv nodded.

Sophie followed the paramedics into the hallway. The red lights from the ambulance flashed against the entryway.

The paramedics loaded April inside the emergency vehicle. Sophie got in and sat, twisting her hands, trying to keep control. Another ambulance ride. Another drive full of uncertainty. But April was still conscious. Tessa hadn't been at this point. April hadn't delivered her twins. Tessa had had Ella before she'd been carried from the basement. Sophie's arms were empty; she wasn't holding Ella's frail body this time. She wasn't deciding if she should ride in Ella's ambulance or her sister's.

Clearing her mind, Sophie hit her autopilot switch and held April's hand without shaking. Kept her tone soothing without a quiver in her voice. Buried the tears, the sobs and the fear. Emotions ricocheted through her and they'd bring her to her knees eventually, but that'd come later. Later she'd cry, scream and shake. When she was alone in her bedroom. Not now. There wasn't time to fall apart now.

AN HOUR LATER, Sophie stretched her legs, leaned against the stiff plastic chair and exhaled her first steady breath. The ER doctor rushed away, through the wide doors, already moving on to her next patient, leaving Sophie to gather herself. April and the twins were stable. No emergency delivery had been required. April might make it to term, but she'd do that under the care of the doctors and nurses at Bay Water Women's and Children's Hospital.

All Sophie was waiting for now was April's room number. The twins hadn't been moved to the neonatal intensive care unit and April hadn't been put in isolation like her niece and sister had been all those years ago.

Tubes and monitors of every kind had covered Ella's tiny body. She'd been more wires than skin and bones. The memory still made Sophie's breath stutter, even though it was almost ten years later.

Sophie checked the time. She had to pick up Ella from her therapy in less than twenty minutes. She'd promised to take Ella with her to Dr. Bradshaw's office to collect the kittens Brad had rescued. She scrolled through her contacts, clicked on Ruthie's number, then noticed the date on her phone screen. Ruthie and Matt had left that morning for a week in Napa to scout out potential wedding venues. Ruthie had already texted Sophie pictures of one hillside winery. Charlotte had been sick and absent from school that day. Sophie couldn't call Charlotte's mother to watch Ella. And Kay needed to get to the hospital, not the vet's office.

Ella's therapist would let her stay. She'd understand. She might even bring Ella to the hospital. Sophie watched another doctor approach an agitated man in his early thirties and an older couple. Not even a box of tissues seemed enough to contain their tears. No, Sophie wanted to believe everything would be fine with April and the twins. But what if it wasn't? She didn't want Ella there for that.

Sophie scrolled through her recent call list. Brad's name popped up more than once.

If she called Brad, she'd have to admit she trusted him. If she asked Brad to pick up Ella that meant she *did* trust him. She shouldn't trust him. She couldn't trust him. Not this soon. Not with something as important as Ella.

But she needed help. The PA system announced a code red. The ER staff scrambled. Sirens from other ambulances blared through the waiting room. Pages sounded for Dr. Morris stat. Dr. Reid stat. More rushing around the ER. And then the repeat: code red. Dr. Morris stat. Dr. Reid stat.

Sophie hit the call button.

CHAPTER EIGHTEEN

SOPHIE'S NAME FLASHED across the screen of Brad's phone, then disappeared. The call ended before it had even begun. Most likely a butt dial. He'd been known to accidentally make a few of those calls himself.

This was about the time Sophie usually visited April. She was probably racing from April's place to the Pampered Pooch with her phone unlocked and shoved in her back pocket. He put his phone down before the image made him smile. He'd vowed no more Sophie Callahan. "Sorry. Where were we?"

"You were picking my brain for places George and I traveled." Evie patted a Whisk and Whip Pastry Shop napkin against the corner of her mouth.

"Actually I was picking your brain for specific hotels you and George stayed at." Brad's phone lit up and Sophie's name filled the screen. Only once. Then nothing. If he did see Sophie again soon, he'd enjoy teasing her about so many crank calls. That wasn't happening—seeing Sophie—

anytime soon. The only Callahan he planned to see soon was George. He studied Evie. "You were evading the question."

Evie folded her napkin into a neat square. "It's not appropriate to reveal details about one's relationships."

"It's even more inappropriate to steal from one's girlfriend," Brad countered.

"It just feels…" Evie paused. "Awkward."

"I won't judge."

"But it's as if I'm sharing my personal life with my own son." Evie glanced at the pastry shop's menu posted on the wall and took a sip of water from her glass.

He noticed the slight pink staining her cheeks. That she thought of Brad as her own son made his cheeks slightly warmer. He hated prying, but he hated even more letting Evie down. Evie mattered too much for that. "You know I can keep secrets better than anyone in my family."

"I'm thankful for that every day."

Another call came through from Sophie. But this one didn't end. Her name remained on the screen. Brad frowned, then looked at Evie across the small round table. He wanted to send Sophie's call to voice mail, but hesitated. What if she needed him? What if these weren't accidental crank calls? "Sorry, I have to take this."

"Go on." Evie picked up her tea mug and

jumped up from her chair, her agile movement betraying her joy at the sudden reprieve. "I'll give you a moment and get more hot water."

"And then answer my questions." Brad picked up his phone.

"Take your call." Evie rushed to the counter.

Brad answered and was about to tease Sophie, but a page for a Dr. Reid stat blared through his phone, vibrating against his eardrum. He straightened and his legs tensed, lifting him partially out of the chair, as if that page had been for him. He plugged his free ear with his finger and spoke into the phone, no humor in his voice, everything focused on the woman on the other end of the call. "Sophie. Where are you? What's happened?"

"At Bay Water Women's and Children's Hospital. With April." Static and sirens mixed with her voice.

"Are you okay?" Brad asked.

A page for Dr. Morris covered her silence.

"Sophie?" he repeated.

"Fine. I'm fine." Again more static interrupted her words. "I shouldn't have bothered you."

He wanted to be bothered by Sophie. Anytime. He wanted to help her. Anytime. He wanted to matter to her. All the time. He shoved that last notion aside to revise later. "What do you need?"

"I'll handle it," Sophie said.

Evie returned and watched Brad. Concern drew her eyebrows down beneath her glasses. She really was like a mom to him. Evelyn knew his moods probably better than his own mother.

"Sophie. You called. You need help." Brad squeezed his phone as if that would be enough to force the doubt out of Sophie. "Let me help."

"It's Ella."

"Ella," Brad repeated. Another spike of panic shot him out of his chair. He bumped into the table, knocking his notepad to the ground and tried to steady the sudden rushing in his ears. "What happened?"

"Nothing, she's fine." Sophie paused, then rushed on. "She needs to be picked up from her vision therapist's office. And I promised her we'd get the kittens. It's okay. April is waiting on her room. I'll get Ella and come back here."

Brad grabbed his pen and several napkins. "Where is Ella?"

"I shouldn't have bothered you. You're busy."

"But you did call me." Brad clenched the pen and tried to dull the clipped edge in his tone. Why wouldn't the woman just listen? "And I'm not busy. Where is Ella's therapist?"

"Sun Tower Medical offices in the Heights. The therapist's name is Dr. Sanders."

"And the kittens?"

"I'll pick them up later."

"But you promised Ella." Brad wrote down Sanders on the napkin.

"It's not the first time I've disappointed her." Sophie cleared her voice. "I'll call the vet when April is in a room."

"What's the address?"

"It's Bay Water Women's and Children's Hospital in the Bay District."

"Not the hospital, Sophie. The vet."

"Dr. Bradshaw is over in the Sunset on 1st."

"What do I need to get Ella and the kittens?" Brad scribbled across another napkin. "Is there a password or code word?"

"Code word?" Sophie repeated.

Brad smashed the pen tip into the napkin wishing instead he could wrap Sophie in his arms and smash her cheek against his until she regained her focus. He'd never heard her so unsettled before. "Sophie, do I need permission to take Ella home from vision therapy?"

"I'll call Ella's therapist now and tell her you can pick up Ella. Bring ID. Dr. Bradshaw will be more than happy to give you the kittens. He refuses to be a kennel service."

But Sophie sounded less than happy to let Brad lend a hand. He didn't care. He was helping and she'd have to deal with it. "Got it. You concentrate on April. Ella and I will be just fine."

He ended the call before Sophie could argue or change her mind.

"What can I do?" Evie asked.

Brad checked the time on his phone, worried about whether he'd be able to get Ella and then get to the vet's office during regular business hours. Driving across town in afternoon traffic would be a challenge. "Do you mind heading to Dr. Bradshaw's office and bringing a litter of kittens to the Pampered Pooch? Sophie promised Ella they'd get the kittens this evening." Brad handed Evie the napkin with the vet's information. "I'll get Ella and meet you at Sophie's shop."

Brad slipped on his jacket, cleared their table and held the door for Evie. Outside on the sidewalk, Evie and Brad departed in opposite directions.

OVER AN HOUR LATER, Brad tossed his and Ella's Roadside Burger wrappers in the pet shop's garbage can and rubbed his stomach.

Ella finished off her last French fry with the last sip of her shake. "Maybe we should hide the wrappers in the outside trash can."

"It isn't our fault Roadside Burger is the best in town and we had a craving for burgers," Brad said. "We can't be held responsible."

Ella grinned and swung her legs, sitting on the

stool behind the counter. The bells chimed and Evie walked in sideways, carrying a cardboard cat box and smiling. "Made it to the vet's just in time. That Dr. Bradshaw is a force, but he'd never met the likes of me before."

Evie carried the box to the counter, set it down and turned her full attention on Ella.

Brad stepped behind the counter beside Ella's stool, close enough for her to take his arm if she needed. "Ella, this is Evelyn Davenport. Ms. Evie is like a second mom to me. She's known me since I was in diapers."

"Even changed a fair share of those diapers, too." Evie's laughter filled the air. "Pleasure to meet you, Ella."

"Brad, you have two moms, sort of like me." Ella pushed on her glasses and looked between Brad and Evie. "But if you changed his diapers then you've been around more than my one mom. But it's okay because my auntie makes up for it. She's the greatest mom."

"Your aunt certainly is. She called us to make sure we'd picked up the kittens." Evie moved the box in front of her. "Your aunt knew you wouldn't want them alone at Dr. Bradshaw's another night."

"The kittens are home." Ella clasped her hands together.

"There's only one problem," Evie said. "Brad and I don't have any clue what to do now."

Ella chewed on her bottom lip and pressed a button on her phone that announced the time. "We have to love them and cuddle with each one before we put them in their kennel for the night."

"I think we can handle that," Brad said.

"Except I have to shower," Ella said. "It's Monday and I have to stay on schedule. If I don't, then Auntie says our mornings are too feisty." Ella dropped her voice to a whisper. "I like school a lot. I just don't like getting up for school very much."

"I had the same problem." Brad chuckled. "What's our plan?"

"We can take the kittens upstairs," Ella suggested. The hope in her voice covered the sly edge in her tone. "I know how to shower. Auntie just likes to be within shouting distance, just in case."

"I'm not sure about bringing the kittens upstairs." Evie tapped her fingers against the box. "If one dives under the sofa, then Ella, you'll have to climb under there and help me. I'm afraid my old knees aren't quite the same as they used to be."

Ella tipped her head. "You don't sound very old, Ms. Evie."

"Aren't you sweet," Evie said. "Unfortunately, my body disagrees."

"My great-nana was old. She had a rusty voice and smelled like an old leather purse." Ella slid off the stool and used the counter as her guide to Evie. "You smell like spring in a rose garden and your voice sounds like you sprinkled it with bells."

"That's lovely, especially since one of my favorite places is my garden," Evie said. "I spend a lot of time gardening since my husband passed."

"Maybe my great-nana needed a garden," Ella said. "Auntie says Nana's heart broke when my great-papa went to heaven and it never got fixed. I think her voice was rusty because she cried out all her tears and had none left for any of us. Do you still cry?"

"Sometimes I do." Evie met Brad's gaze over Ella's head.

Evelyn Davenport rarely cried, or, at least Brad could count less than a handful of times he'd seen her cry. He'd been there for her most recent tears, in his office, when she'd recounted George Callahan's misdeeds.

"Maybe the kittens won't make you so sad." Ella grinned.

"Your aunt suggested I get a new pet," Evie said. "What do you think?"

Ella tapped her fingers at the holes in the top

of the box. "We'll have to talk about it. It's hard to decide between a dog and a cat. Can you have both?"

"Probably not right now," Evie said.

"We can talk while you braid my hair after my shower." Ella's fingers paused on the box like a child afraid to be discovered with their hand in the cookie jar. "Can you braid hair? My auntie can only do a regular braid. But that's okay because my friends' moms can only do that, too. But Ruthie, she can do all kinds of fancy braids."

"Ella, I'm not sure..." Brad started. The pair chatted as if they were long-lost family. His presence wasn't really required. And there was something in Evie's patient smile and in her soft voice that he hadn't heard or seen since she'd lost her husband. Something refreshing, like hope.

"Bradley Trent Harrington, just because I don't have any children of my own doesn't mean I haven't always had girlfriends." Evie's scolding voice drew out Ella's giggle. But Evie wasn't finished. "I learned to French braid before I learned to write my name."

Ella's mouth dropped open. "Then would you French braid my hair?"

"I'd love to." Evie frowned at Brad. "What should we do with the boy in our group? Boys can't braid hair."

"Brad needs to stay with the kittens." Ella

hugged the carrier box. "They can't be alone on their first night home."

"What should I do with them?" Brad crossed his arms over his chest.

"You play with them until they fall asleep and then you can put them in their kennel," Ella said. "But you need to make sure they have a litter box and water and a soft bed. Maybe a toy or two."

Evie looked at him over her glasses as if to ask him if he needed more detailed instructions than that.

Brad looked down at Ella. He'd bought her a burger, fries and her favorite shake. She was supposed to be on his side. "Anything else?"

Ella shook her head. "I'm sure Auntie will have more for you to do when she gets home."

"Don't you want to play with the kittens?" Brad asked.

"I can't." Ella pulled her phone out of her front pocket and pressed the time button. "It's a school night, remember? I have a schedule."

Convenient. Brad narrowed his gaze on the pair, wondering how he'd been so neatly outmaneuvered. "Then you two are good?"

"Yup," Ella said. "I'll take Ms. Evie upstairs."

"And I'll let the kittens out to play," Brad said.

"You should probably let the other ones out for a while. They've been alone all day, too." Ella opened her walking stick and started toward the back room.

"I have my orders." Brad moved in to get the carrier box. "It's play time, kittens."

"Thanks for dinner." Ella intercepted him and threw her arms around his waist. "You're the best."

Brad froze, trying to catch his breath. One precious child had certainly left him winded. He wrapped his arms around Ella and hugged her back. "Anytime."

The catch in his voice startled him. Then the realization that he meant it, that he'd help Ella anytime, upset his balance. Maybe he'd been more than winded.

Evelyn and Ella made their way through the kennel area and lingered for another twenty minutes, in spite of Ella's schedule, while the girl introduced Evie to each four-legged resident. Discussion and some cleanup complete, the pair finally headed up the back stairs. Brad watched until they'd disappeared into the apartment.

What had just happened? Worlds had just collided: Evie's and Sophie's. Now Brad couldn't erase the unease from his skin no matter how hard he rubbed his neck. He shouldn't have answered Sophie's phone call. He shouldn't have asked Evie to pick up the kittens. He definitely shouldn't have introduced Evie and Ella.

He should've stopped Ella from inviting Evie upstairs. He should've explained that Sophie wouldn't have minded if Ella's schedule changed for one night.

But he'd done nothing. Stood there like he'd lost his voice and listened to their conversation and let himself get taken in by two smart females. A stranger would've assumed they were grandmother and granddaughter with the ease of their conversation and comfort between them. It was as if they'd recognized instantly that each one needed the other.

Brad opened the box and lifted each kitten onto a towel he'd spread on the floor. But everything was wrong. This wasn't Evelyn Davenport's world. And Ella and Sophie had their thing—a good thing with just the two of them.

Seeing Evelyn with Ella should have tightened his focus on finding George Callahan. On ending this favor so everyone could return to their lives.

Yet watching Ella and Evie together, all he could think about was how finding George Callahan was going to ruin more lives than help them. But George had to be brought to justice and the truth had to be revealed. Would Sophie still need him after he exposed her father? That shouldn't matter. But Sophie needing him was starting to matter. A lot.

Brad lowered himself onto the floor beside the kittens. He worried the consequences of completing this particular favor might leave a mark, a painful one, that even he might not be able to remove.

CHAPTER NINETEEN

SOPHIE USUALLY RACED up the double staircase to their third-floor apartment. But tonight, each step seemed more exhausting than the last. And every time she looked up, the landing seemed farther away, as if she were caught in a recurring nightmare. A quick check of Ella and a thank-you to Brad, then she'd collapse on her bed. Bury herself under the comforter and hold herself together.

She was tired. So very tired. Of picking herself up and everyone around her. But that was only the exhaustion talking. If she could just get to her bed, everything would be right by morning.

Things were already on track to be better by then. April had eventually been moved to a room. Kay and Liv had arrived, prepared to divide the night shift at the hospital. Sophie had promised to return later to sit with April.

The Closed sign had been hung in the Pampered Pooch window and the storefront lights turned off. She could deal with the night's cash drawer in the morning before opening. She counted five more stairs and used the railing to pull herself along.

Only Ella's bedroom light glowed in the otherwise dark flat. Had Brad fallen asleep on the couch? She considered leaving him there to deal with in the morning, too. She wasn't herself. She'd probably embarrass them both and collapse in his arms, desperate for someone to hold her. But she hadn't asked him to help her because she needed him to hold her.

She padded down the hall, away from the family room and toward her reality. Ella lay asleep in her bed, an open book beneath one hand and a walkie-talkie clutched in the other. Her hair was pulled back in the neatest French braid Sophie had seen. Her therapist must have braided Ella's hair while they'd waited for Brad. Ella was forever conning someone into braiding her hair. One of these days, Sophie would watch the internet videos and teach herself to French braid like the other perfect aunts did.

She kissed Ella's forehead, put her book and walkie-talkie aside, and blamed her comparison to other moms on her exhaustion. She was too tired to even debate the aunt-versus-mom issue. One last task and she'd welcome sleep.

But only an empty couch and a cold kitchen greeted her. Brad wasn't in the apartment. But he wouldn't have left Ella. He'd texted hourly updates and Ella had texted her own version of the evening.

Sophie sighed and considered the back stairs leading to the yard and kennels. She could get down those stairs, but coming back up would be the challenge. She had to relieve Brad to put an end to this night.

Sophie stepped into the kennel area and pulled up short. Brad sat on the floor, his legs stretched out, his head resting against the wall. The white kitten slept on his lap, and the gray stretched out against his thigh, with the calico beside its sibling also asleep. The largest silver-and-black kitten batted at Brad's shoelace, while the tabby jumped at the feathers Brad swung over its head.

Her legs wobbled, along with her resolve not to open any part of her heart. But she wondered if Brad would open his arms and let her fall into his embrace. She'd seen Matt do that for Ruthie more than once, and Ruthie's sister and her new husband, even strangers on the street. When was the last time she'd just been held? Had she ever been held? She couldn't remember. Certainly not by her father.

Sophie crossed her arms over her chest, flattened her back against the wall and slid to the floor beside Brad.

"Welcome home. Ella is sleeping." Brad lifted

a walkie-talkie. "But we're connected. She fell asleep midchapter. I'm sitting here waiting to find out if the heroine saves her ice-queen sister."

"I know." Sophie wound her arms around her bent legs and set her cheek on her knees to hold herself together like she'd always done. Always would. "I went upstairs first. Ella was holding a book and her walkie-talkie. You've been here the whole time with the kittens?"

"Ella refused to allow them to be put in the kennels with the older cats." The white kitten stretched into Brad's gentle touch. "Evelyn refused to let them upstairs with Ella."

"Evelyn?" Sophie resisted the urge to set her head on his shoulder and curl into his side, seeking his warm touch.

"Evelyn Davenport." Brad edged the calico's paw off its sibling's face with his finger. "You met her at my mother's."

"You chopped up her flower garden." Sophie nudged her shoulder against Brad's. A light, friendly tap that left Sophie wanting more. Something more meaningful. Something lasting.

He winced. "I was four."

"And creative with scissors." The tabby dove for the feathers and landed on the gray kitten next to Brad's leg. The calico slapped at his brother, obviously irritated by the interruption, and rolled into the warm spot its sibling left beside Brad's leg. She'd have been irritated, too, if she'd had the pleasure of being curled up against Brad, then woken from the dream.

What happened to her quick good-night? A simple "thank you for your help, I owe you and goodbye." But the words failed to come and Sophie waited for Brad to continue. Waited for that something more.

"Evelyn was with me when you called." He picked up the tabby and the gray, then set the feather between them for a wrestling match. "She picked up the kittens, while I went to get Ella."

"Why would she do that?" Sophie cringed at the suspicion crowding out the surprise in her voice. She'd never quite learned to trust unsolicited kindness. There always seemed to be a price to pay.

"She likes to help. Evelyn is what Matt would call good people."

Sophie recognized good people all the time: the competent nurses and staff at Bay Water, the paramedics tonight and all those years ago. Her foster families. Accepting good people into her inner circle proved much more difficult. "I need to thank Evelyn for her help."

"She'll most likely visit again soon."

The fondness in his voice drew Sophie's gaze to him.

"She sort of lost herself with the cats. Cleaned the litter boxes, rinsed and filled the water bowls. Added new toys." Brad motioned toward the kennels. "All that after she'd met Ella."

Sophie smiled. She knew all too well about the Ella effect. The charm, laughter and sweetness were such a natural part of her niece. Nothing forced or fake or phony about her. Ella was definitely good people.

"It's possible they conspired to keep me down here while they kept Ella on her weekly schedule upstairs. Braiding hair, possibly painting nails. I hadn't noticed the glittery pink nail polish on Evie's fingers when she arrived from the vet."

"You're not feeling left out, are you?" Sophie pushed her voice into a light tease, trying to hide her own hurt. She felt left out and resented Evelyn's time with Ella and Brad. So many mean thoughts. Sophie surely wasn't good people.

But there was something lovely and comforting about sitting on the floor beside Brad, taking a reprieve from the big topics. Once again the urge to drop her head on his shoulder gripped her as if she had that right. As if there was more between them. Instead, she stretched out her legs and brushed her fingers over the white kitten's back, using the kitten as her excuse to scoot closer to Brad.

"Boys can wear some pink, too."

Sophie laughed. "Maybe next time. I'll put in a good word for you."

"How's April and the babies?" Brad unhooked the tabby's claws from his jeans.

The concern was there in his tone. Now she really wanted to lean on him. To let him shoulder her worries, her fears. But she'd never unloaded on anyone before. She wouldn't know how. But she kept her thigh pressed against his, building strength from the contact. "She's in the ICU with every monitor available and her mother. The doctors want her to get to thirty-two weeks before delivering."

"How far along is she?"

"A few days over thirty weeks," Sophie said. "She has twelve more days to go."

"It'll be a long time."

"Kay will be there. She'll help her through."

"And you'll be there."

"As much as I can." Between party planning, running the store, selling her grandmother's furniture, Ella's school and appointments, and finding her father. Resentment whispered through her, but she blew it away. April and Kay needed her. She'd be there. She lacked the ability to say no.

She also wouldn't whine about it. This was her life. She'd accepted that when she'd brought Ella and Tessa home from the hospital. She'd simply sleep away the overwhelming worry tonight and wake up ready to manage everything as usual. "Where's Erin?"

Brad glanced at her. "Erin had an exam and sprinted out as soon as we came in."

Sophie jerked back and tapped her head against the wall. It was Monday. Erin had classes on Monday and Wednesday afternoons and evenings. She'd forgotten. That was a bad sign. "Did you look after the store, too?"

"Until closing," Brad said. "I even rang up two sales. You need a new cash register."

She needed a new everything. "It's on the list."

Brad rubbed the white kitten under its chin. "You were right. She's deaf. Will someone want her?"

Someone had to. Being deaf didn't make the kitten unlovable. No one should feel unwanted. The kitten simply came with special considerations like Sophie and Ella for anyone interested in them. But none of them were any less because of that. "You could adopt her?" *But could you want me?*

"Not sure I'm the most appropriate fit."

But we could fit. We could work. If we reached out for each other. Together. At the same time. Then we wouldn't be alone. "It's not one or the other, you know?"

"What's not?"

Us. Me. Your freedom. "You don't have to be a dog person or a cat person only."

He shifted and looked at her, his gaze searching hers.

"She obviously really likes you," Sophie said. *I really like you.*

He leaned over, cupped Sophie's chin, and kissed her softly and gently. Just the simplest touch of tenderness before he pulled back to look into her eyes. "And I like you." He picked up the white kitten and set it on the towel. "Now, we need to get these little guys into their home for the evening because my entire backside has fallen asleep on this floor."

Brad switched gears before Sophie could slow the rush of adrenaline and find those padlocks for her heart. If only putting away her feelings for Brad was as easy as putting kittens into their kennel.

She locked the door behind Brad and made her way upstairs. But she knew before putting her head on the pillow that sleep would elude her. Brad's words, *I like you*, tumbled around her brain, tempting her with a different version of her future. If she slept though, she just might wake up to find she believed in a new dream.

CHAPTER TWENTY

"DON'T FORGET, WE can't be late getting home from school later." Ella hugged Sophie. "Ms. Evie promised to let me help with the doggy manicures this afternoon."

"We won't be late." Sophie adjusted Ella's stuffed backpack, surprised again that the child hadn't toppled backward from the weight. Sophie's backpack had been a suitcase when she was a kid, holding her few possessions. But Ella would never learn what it meant to live like that. Not under Sophie's care. "Are you sure you want to tackle dog manicures? You don't even like to file down your own nails."

"You don't like manicures," Ella corrected. "You always complain about the nail polish chipping off. I like my nails painted."

Like her mother. Tessa polished her nails every week as if the pearl pink sheen proved to the world that she had it all together. If only a coat of nail polish and a brush of a quick-dry clear coat was enough to instill order into Callahan lives. Sophie had sworn off polish. She didn't need chipped nails to amplify the dents in her world.

Ella stepped away, pulling her walking stick from the side pocket in her backpack. "Ms. Evie gave me a special nail buffer. It doesn't make those scratchy noises like the one you use. You should ask Ms. Evie to get you one, too."

"I'll do that." Sophie waved to a mother on the other side of the crosswalk. "Peyton and Audrey are racing over here."

Ella grinned and turned toward the shouts of her friends. "Perfect. I get to find out if they like the flower decorations Ms. Evie put on my nails. You should ask Ms. Evie to get you new nail polish, too. She found me scented nail polish. It's the best."

Sophie squeezed Ella's shoulders and kissed the top of her head. It'd been five days since Ella had met Ms. Evie, four days since Sophie had hired Evelyn Davenport to work at the Pampered Pooch, and already Ella had a book on the things Sophie needed to ask Evelyn for. Every day Ella added a new page to her Evelyn Knows Best notebook.

Evelyn had met Sophie outside the Pampered Pooch before she'd opened on Tuesday morning just like Brad had predicted the evening before. Brad hadn't predicted that Evelyn would offer her services. He hadn't predicted the basket of fresh-baked muffins and two thermoses: one with tea and the other with Evelyn's special Irish coffee to be shared after hours.

And Sophie hadn't predicted her own reaction to the older woman's generosity. She'd swung open the door to the Pampered Pooch and welcomed her newest employee into the family. Within twenty-four hours, Evelyn had filled the void April's absence had left. Within forty-eight hours, Evelyn had sprinkled her spirit into every corner of the building, inside and out. She'd created new Open and Closed signs in the form of giant paw prints. She'd organized the kennels, enlarging Ella's walkway and worked with Troy on a new doggy day care drop-off circuit. And yesterday, Evelyn earned her fairy-godmother wand when she'd brought Andrew Harrington to see Sophie. The donation from Brad's brother had saved the Paws and Bark Bash, reigniting Sophie's vision to make the gala more than an average affair.

Now, seventy-two hours later, Sophie breathed without pasting an everything-is-just-fine smile on her face. Everything seemed balanced. The illusion Brad had created several nights past hadn't burst, and she felt steady enough to believe in it, even tentatively. She liked what this world could be like for her and Ella. And she'd even dared to believe that her father would come through for her, after all. How could he not? Sophie's luck was obviously changing.

Sophie waited while Ella made her way up the school steps with her friends. Beside Sophie, a mother zipped up her son's jacket and promised to return with his lunch box, but vowed this would be the last time—next time he'd have to go hungry. A father fist-bumped his two sons before giving his daughter a bear hug. She wondered if Brad would fist-bump or hug. She knew he'd walk to school, push a stroller and wear one of those baby carriers. After all, he'd sat on the floor with five kittens, long after it'd been necessary. Ella wouldn't even have known that. He'd never hesitated when Sophie asked. Never left Ella. Brad would stay.

Sophie wanted to believe she would stay, too. In this new world Brad made her want to believe in.

She smiled at another father and waved to a mother sprinting toward the parking lot.

"Where did Ella get her curls?"

A pleasant male voice scattered the image of Brad beside her, pushing a baby stroller. She shook her head, not sure what had been in her coffee. She wasn't one to ever daydream. She preferred the truth. Then she never worried about getting swept away by her fantasies and falling face-first into a frozen pool of reality.

She glanced over her shoulder, expecting to see a parent, not her father's business associate. She turned and frowned at Teddy Gordon.

He tipped his chin at her in greeting before shifting his gaze toward the school entrance. "Her curls must have come from her grandmother."

"Why are you here?" Sophie wished Ella would move faster and cringed when the girls stopped on the landing to laugh while another friend hurried to catch up. Sophie willed them all inside with their teachers where it was safe.

"Your father hasn't contacted me."

"Get in line." Anger threaded through Sophie's tone. How dare he follow her to Ella's school. How dare he invade her personal space. How dare he intrude into her world again.

"My sister had long, straight hair. She always wanted what your niece has. So she paid for every kind of curl available." His head shook as if to dislodge a distasteful memory. "She never did get those natural curls like Ella."

Sophie remained rooted to the sidewalk, figuring she'd run inside if she needed help, past the numerous security cameras and right up to the guards. She told herself she could handle this, and yet that knowledge did little to take away the icy chill raising bumps across her skin. Nor could she deny that a big part of her wished her daydream about Brad walking to school with them had been real.

Finally, the school doors closed behind the last late student and the bell buzzed, signaling the start of the day.

"My sister wasted all that time and money on perms and still her hair always ended up straight. That was its nature." He examined his titanium bracelet as if searching for something inside the thick links. "If you're waiting for your father to change his nature, you're better off—"

"You didn't come here to talk about perms and human nature." Sophie stuffed her hands inside her jacket pockets and squeezed her phone. "You could've had that discussion with any of your other business associates."

"You'd be wise to consider my advice." He slipped on tinted sunglasses even though the overcast morning was anything but bright. He brushed her shoulder as he walked down the sidewalk.

Sophie hurried away in the opposite direction and avoided her usual route, wanting as much distance as possible between her and Teddy Gordon. Sophie'd sprint across the Bay Bridge and circle back if she had to in order to bypass another run-in with Teddy Gordon.

She'd only reached the potholed alley by the school's parking lot when Teddy called out to her.

Sophie slowed and looked back. He hadn't moved more than a few steps past where they'd been standing. He'd been watching her leave. That chill pushed more bumps along her skin, making her wonder if they'd be permanent.

"One last thought." He tipped his glasses down and stared at her over the rims.

Despite the distance, Sophie saw his hard expression and the ruthless predator he hid behind his false smiles and balance bracelet. Sophie clutched her hands together inside her sweatshirt pocket, trying to find some warmth. Somewhere.

"I'd regret having to ask you to repay your father's debt, but I will if pressed." He pushed his glasses up and grinned as if he'd enjoyed an impromptu meeting with a dear friend. "Until next time."

There wasn't going to be a next time. And if, by some unfortunate chance, there was a next time, Sophie intended it to be between Teddy Gordon and her father, not her.

Sophie stared as Teddy walked to the intersection and disappeared around the corner. She waited another five minutes and kept her eyes on that corner, willing the chill inside her to recede. A bike messenger sprinted across the intersection and flew past the school, squealing around an open car door, yet never slowing. A crowded city bus passed the stop across from her, leaving the waiting passengers to hope the next one wasn't full. And Sophie to hope she'd find warmth again.

The light at the intersection changed and the city moved around her. Sophie never moved. And Teddy Gordon never returned. Two more city buses, windows steamed from the bodies crammed inside, passed without pausing. The bus passengers waited and so did Sophie.

Another fifteen minutes clicked by before the bell inside Ella's school buzzed for the end of homeroom and Sophie ran back to her world. But that chill remained with her no matter how far she stretched out her stride or how much she pumped her arms.

Reality bit even harder. Served her right for daydreaming outside Ella's school. The last few days had been an illusion, a version of someone else's life. A life that didn't belong to Sophie. Her world contained fathers who ruined their daughters' lives.

Twenty years later, her father was poised for a repeat. Ruining everything she'd worked for and once again taking away her home. Every minute she stopped focusing on that, she put Ella and herself in danger.

She knew Brad would leave if she gave him her heart. She didn't know how soon, though. How soon before her heart wasn't enough for him. How soon before he wanted to leave. To move on. She knew better than to fall for some illusion.

Good thing she wasn't stupid and hadn't actually fallen for Brad already.

However, she needed Brad now.

Sophie slowed to a fast walk and found Brad's name in her list of contacts on her phone. She texted him to ask for his assistant's information. She had to sell her grandmother's furniture quickly. She might need that money to assuage the philosophical Teddy Gordon. Why couldn't her father have chosen a less astute business associate? And one less attuned to women's hairstyles.

She touched her familiar ponytail. Perhaps it was past time to schedule her own hair appointment at the Makeover Studio. Charlene Raye was a long shot to help locate her father, but the hairstylist was the only lead Sophie had. The clock had suddenly moved into overtime and Sophie'd wasted all of her time-outs.

CHAPTER TWENTY-ONE

BRAD FOLLOWED EVIE into the back room of the Pampered Pooch. He hadn't been to the store since Monday night. Issues with his boat had caused him to drive two hours up the coast to meet the Delta Craft staff on Tuesday and he'd stayed the night to catch up with a business contact in the area to discuss a computer-hacking case.

Once he hit the city again, network and cloud security problems had pulled him into the office for round-the-clock troubleshooting. He'd seen several of his staff circling his assistant's desk throughout the last two days. No doubt revising their bets on the office pool.

Evie tugged a trash can toward the cat kennels.

"What are you doing here?" Brad asked. She wore a Pampered Pooch polo shirt. When had Sophie started selling those? He'd only ever seen Sophie's employees wearing the familiar purple.

"I offered Sophie my services. Sophie offered

me a job." Evelyn frowned at him over an open kennel gate. She thrust two cats at him.

He knew from Ella that the older cats were brothers, surrendered when their owner had traded them for a pair of young kittens. Felix looked like a chain smoker had exhaled on him repeatedly. Milo rested his head on Brad's shoulder.

"Sophie needs help." Evie emptied the litter box and shook her head. "You didn't assist her like you promised."

Brad adjusted the cats in his arms, trying not to squeeze too hard. "I promised to help you find George and your money."

"And we agreed you'd help Sophie with her gala." Evelyn motioned for him to put the two brothers back inside their kennel. She opened the neighboring kennel and handed him a heavyset calico cat. "She's obviously nothing like her father. I'm not certain she knows how to put herself first."

"You intend to show her how to do that." The calico cat's ears flattened toward its head as if offended by the sarcasm in Brad's tone.

"I intend to ease her burden," Evelyn said.

"You're the reason I'm going to have her father arrested." A low growl vibrated through the calico, its ears plastered to its head. Brad could relate. When had Evelyn infiltrated Sophie's world and how did he stop this catastrophe?

"George has wronged his own daughter far more than me. He told me how he'd regretted leaving her as a child." Evelyn urged the calico back into its kennel and opened another one, handing a thin tuxedo cat to Brad. "That I'm certain was a lie. And I'm just as certain he lied to Sophie more."

"Those aren't criminal activities." Brad adjusted the frail cat in his arms and tried to sound calm. He wanted to shake some sense into Evie, but he didn't want to scare the cat.

She knocked the litter scooper against the trash can with more force than necessary. "Moral injustices are often worse."

"And yet Sophie loves her father." Brad handed Evie the frail cat and accepted a Persian, its nose punched in beneath thick layers of creamy-white fur.

"As did I," Evelyn said. "She needs us now, Bradley."

No, Sophie needed to have her gala. She needed to learn the truth about her father. But she didn't need them. They'd hurt her and Brad wouldn't be there to clean up the fallout. The thought of Sophie in pain made him feel as if he should be dumped on the side of the road.

Evie finished with the kennel and studied the

Persian in Brad's arms, muttering about scissors and mats. She returned with scissors and told Brad to hold the cat tight. As she finished trimming the fur around the cat's neck, the front bells chimed. Brad glanced into the store and swore.

Evie tsk-tsked before following his gaze. A grin spread across her face. "You can greet your brother when we finish with these mats."

"You called Drew, too." The cat's back claws pierced through Brad's sweater into his arm. Not that he cared much. He'd like claws of his own right now. How many of his family members had invaded Sophie's life?

Evelyn snipped at the cat's fur. "One of Drew's clients had a wedding with a service dog in the ceremony. Surely you remember. The wedding photos circulated through the news."

Did everyone remember that particular wedding but him? "Drew mentioned it the other day."

"The Wrights are a perfect fit for the gala." Evelyn pointed the scissors at him. "Although you should've thought of it sooner. Like you'd promised."

"Drew's client is a perfect sponsor for the gala," Brad clarified. That involved nothing more than mailing in a monetary donation and receiving top billing in the program.

Sophie stepped through the front door and

his brother lifted her into a bear hug and they chatted away like they were longtime friends. Chatted away with her without releasing her. Brad didn't bother dulling the edge in his voice. "Why is Drew here now?"

Evelyn turned the cat in his arms to clip its other side. "To offer his services, I suppose."

No. Nope. No way. "His services?" Brad asked. His brother was not offering anything but a sponsor's check. What was happening? Why were his friends and family bombarding Sophie's life? He had to stop this. Nothing good could come from this.

Of all the weeks to have a problem with his boat that couldn't be solved with a simple phone call, and for the office network to crash. He could've prevented this.

He noticed Drew setting Sophie down. His brother wasn't a hugger, never one to linger over any woman. He wasn't going to start now with Brad's Sophie.

The joy spreading across Sophie's face cut through Brad and scrambled his insides. Then she wiped her cheeks. Those could not be tears. Not for Andrew, his brother.

Brad glanced at the mangy cat in his arms. He suddenly felt as carved up as the cat's fur. He flatlined with the realization that Sophie had welcomed Evelyn and Drew into her life because she trusted Brad.

But that was all wrong. He was lying to her.

He should toss the Persian into the kennel, storm into the storefront and confess the truth. Right here. Right now.

Sophie's laughter, all the more animated with her beaming happiness, floated into the back room and surrounded him, soothing and mocking all at once. He strode toward the counter and glared at Drew and Sophie, their heads almost touching as they examined a leopard-print cat bed.

"What are you doing?" Brad asked his brother. He flexed his fingers into the Persian's still-too-thick coat and rubbed behind its ears.

"Adopting Felix and Milo." Drew frowned at the cat bed and pushed it aside. "Milo needs a more manly bed than that."

"You don't like cats," Brad said, trying to process the nightmare he'd walked into. Maybe if he raced to the kennel, tapped his heels three times and walked out again, then the world might have righted itself.

"Sophie needs to free up kennel space." Drew pointed at one of the two beds Sophie held up to him. "She has another litter and a surrender coming in this afternoon."

Brad glanced at Sophie. The Persian purred

beneath his touch, but the sound was weak, more like a mumble. "You told me you couldn't take in any more rescues."

Sophie shrugged and avoided looking at him. "I told you I shouldn't take in any more rescues."

And because he'd completely lost his footing in this world, he repeated himself. Because it needed repeating. And his world needed to be righted. "Drew doesn't like cats."

Drew leaned his hip against the counter and eyed the cat in Brad's arm. "You don't like cats."

"Actually, you shouldn't consider a cat because cats don't like water." Sophie stomped up to the counter.

Disappointment soaked her tone and seemed to make her lips drop into a deep frown. What had he done to her? He hadn't taken scissors to the Persian's mat and chopped up her coat like he had the flowers all those years ago. She needed to blame Evie for the bad grooming. Still, Sophie's displeasure stuck in his chest. "Cats don't like me."

Sophie rolled her eyes and eased the Persian from his arms. The cat protested its warm perch against his chest as if to expose his lie. Sophie strode into the back room. The door swung defiantly closed behind her.

A customer approached the counter. Evie

stepped up to the cash register while Drew pushed his items off to the side.

Brad followed his brother, cornering Drew beside the betta fish display and hamster supplies. "You can't be serious."

"Why not?" Drew lifted one of the plastic containers with a large betta inside.

"You like your privacy. Your space." Brad took the container and set it on the shelf, feeling Drew had poked his cage and made him puff up like the betta. "You wouldn't even let me crash on your couch until I left."

"I don't like people messing up my space."

"But you want cat hair and litter boxes and hair balls?" Brad challenged.

"I need to learn to share." Drew grinned at the attractive woman buying organic dog treats. "The cats are a good start."

Evie wished her customer a good day and turned on the brothers. "Don't you remember that Natasha broke up with Andrew because of his selfish ways?"

Drew tossed a plastic ball with a bell inside from one hand to the other. "It wasn't all me. Natasha hated being alone. And I like being alone too much."

"Now you don't want to be alone, so you adopt two cats?" Brad's gaze bounced between his brother and Evie.

"It's past time to expand my horizons." Drew added two more cat toys and juggled the plastic balls. "Try something new."

"Take a cruise," Brad suggested. But adopting cats from the Pampered Pooch was a nonstarter. He couldn't have his brother more intertwined with Sophie than he already was. "Hard to be lonely with the other five thousand passengers on the ship."

Drew caught all of the balls in one hand and eyed his brother as if he was considering pelting Brad. "What's your problem with me getting cats? I'm helping your Sophie. You should approve."

Evie nodded and stepped out to greet a customer in the dog-supply aisle.

His Sophie. When had she become *his*? And why did he like the idea so much? She wasn't his and he wasn't hers. But they could be. No, he wasn't treading into those forbidden waters. That way lay more problems than his brother adopting two cats. He shouldn't care if his brother adopted an entire litter of cats. But he did. Very much.

He should be the one to rescue Sophie. Not his brother. Not Evie. Just him. He scrubbed his hands over his face, surprised his skin was dry since he'd just belly flopped into those forbidden waters.

Sophie returned and diverted his brother's attention.

"You're still good dropping everything off tonight, right?" Drew asked Sophie.

Now she was making house calls. To his brother's place. At night.

Brad hadn't drowned in those waters yet. He wasn't claiming Sophie as his, though Sophie wasn't going over to his brother's place alone.

Drew handed Sophie his credit card and added, "Brad has a key to my place and a truck for all this stuff and the cats."

Sophie glanced at Brad. "Can you drive me over there?"

Absolutely. Heck, yes. He managed a stiff nod, not quite trusting his mouth not to spout off at his brother or suddenly shout out that Sophie was his. Already Drew was watching him intently, a sly grin on his face, fully aware he'd gotten to Brad like a dozen burrs under his bare feet.

"Perfect. The cats can settle in while we all have dinner." Drew slapped his hand on Brad's shoulder and squeezed hard. "Evie, you're welcome to join us."

"What can I bring?" Evie asked.

"Well, Sophie tried to hide the Irish coffee thermos when I walked in." Drew leaned over the counter. "I can almost reach it."

"I did not." Sophie kept him from grabbing

the thermos. Once again, her laughter spilled through the store. "I was making room on the counter for all your stuff."

"Nice cover story." Drew crossed his arms over his chest and tilted his head. "You really need to learn how to share better, Sophie. I can teach you."

"He'll teach you how to guard your dinner plate and steal all the rolls before the first course." Brad shoved his brother, falling into the easy harmony he'd always enjoyed with Drew. Falling into the fun. Falling into what he'd always known. And stepping away from what he couldn't have: Sophie. "That isn't sharing."

"Brad believes everyone likes to share their food from their own plate. He has this habit of eating off every plate at the table," Drew said. "It's very barbaric."

"That's how I survived since you ate all the food when we were kids," Brad said.

Drew straightened his shoulders and grinned. "I had to keep up my strength for my extended growth spurt."

"I'm less than an inch shorter than you," Brad countered.

"Still shorter." Drew patted Brad's head. Brad knocked his shoulder into Drew, shoving him away.

"Take it outside, boys," Evie chided.

"Got time for a game before dinner?" Brad asked. He might need more than a basketball game to find his center, but he'd take what he could get.

Drew checked his phone. "Meeting until five. Then I'm good."

"See you on the court. I'll call Patrick."

"I'm sure Knox will want in, too." Drew waved to Evie and Sophie. "See you ladies tonight. Don't forget the Irish coffee and chocolate lava cakes, Evie."

"When did we agree on chocolate lava cakes?" Evie looked between Drew and Brad.

Brad didn't answer, but rubbed his stomach and nodded his agreement.

"When I promised you chicken piccata." Drew blew her a kiss as he backed up toward the front door. "It's still your favorite, isn't it?"

Evie chuckled. "And chocolate lava cakes are still your favorite, I presume."

"You really are the mother of my heart, Evie." Drew tapped his chest and left.

Evie pointed at Sophie. "Harrington boys are—"

"Are what?" Brad asked.

"Trouble," Evie said, gesturing at him. "A whole lot of trouble."

"But fun to love," Brad added.

Evie hugged him. "Impossible not to love."

She shooed him away. "Now go warm up or something before your game with Andrew. The women have a successful business to run here."

Brad laughed and grabbed the door handle.

Sophie's voice stopped him. "Do you have plans now, besides warming up?"

He'd wanted to check in with Patrick on the hacking case and follow up with his tech staff about the software upgrade and any issues they'd encountered. But the hesitant hope in Sophie's voice made him linger. "I was just heading over to the office. Nothing that can't wait."

"I wanted to talk to you about that furniture. Ella's school is sort of on your way. Want to walk with me over there?" she asked. To Evie, she said, "I promised not to be late so Ella can help with the doggy manicures this afternoon."

"I better get Troy to help me get everything ready for us." Evie disappeared into the back room.

Sophie pointed at the security camera. "I never did thank you for adding the bell that rings in the back room. Now we can work there and still know when someone enters the store."

Brad held the door for Sophie and followed her outside. He wouldn't have been shocked to discover Sophie's street had tilted while he'd been inside and become the steepest in the city. He suddenly felt off-kilter. Again.

Tempted to reach for Sophie's hand to settle himself, like it had before, he shoved his hands in his front pockets and added space between them on the sidewalk. Telling himself she wasn't his and this wasn't that kind of walk. The kind of walk that married couples or new lovers or first dates took. "You changed your hair."

"I had it cut earlier today." Sophie grabbed her ponytail swinging against her hood. "I didn't think anyone would be able to tell."

Of course he could tell. Her hair looked like the color of warm honey now. And he'd had a weakness for honey ever since he'd snuck into his mother's bruncheon when he was six and stolen a piece of homemade country bread with whipped honey butter on it. He'd snuck back in and swiped the whole loaf and the dish of butter, then blamed the dogs. "You came in without your hat on."

Yeah, he'd noticed that, too.

Sophie jammed her hands into her sweatshirt pocket as if she wanted to hide from him now. But her elbow brushed against his arm. "I need to find my father. He's in Reno."

"You can't wait until he returns?"

"This can't wait. He has my money."

She tucked into herself, but she never eased fully away from his side. Curious about how much she'd willingly divulge, he asked, "Did he borrow the money or take it?"

"It doesn't matter. I need it for my loan." Sophie pulled a quarter from her back pocket and dropped it into an expired meter.

The woman was always rescuing or helping or assisting. It was just in her genetic makeup. Did she understand how rare that trait was? How precious? He waited at the intersection while she dropped two more quarters into two other expired meters, a bit awed and humbled by her. She was better than him in so many ways and she deserved more than he could give. He frowned at the thought of someone else giving her everything. Someone else making her smile. Someone else holding her hand.

"Fine." She stepped up beside him and tugged on her ponytail. "My father took the money, but he has plans to give it back—with interest. Although the bank won't wait on him."

Brad assumed from her clipped words and frustrated tone that she'd read his expression wrong.

She charged across the intersection, her words tumbling out. "He hasn't returned my calls, which I'm certain has more to do with his habit of always misplacing his phone charger than not wanting to speak to me."

Thankfully, Brad crossed the intersection

before she opened up that pothole. Her father's habit was lies. George Callahan wasn't returning the money or his daughter's calls anytime soon. Yet Sophie made excuses for his behavior. But the nauseous feeling in his stomach came from the hope in her voice. That desperate hope that her father would come through for his daughter. Just one time. That desperate hope gutted him almost as much as the knowledge that he'd become like her father with his own lies.

But he'd never set out to hurt her. He wanted to set her free with the truth. Set her free from the wasted, useless hope she held for her derelict father.

Brad would hurt her. He understood that now. His hands fisted inside his pockets. "So what's your plan?"

He had a revised plan. Get to Reno, find George Callahan and have a one-on-one conversation with the man. Without Sophie. If he'd been doing his job and not arguing with his brother and Evie about cats or helping his employees, he might've gotten to George first. Too late for him to discuss the should-haves. He needed to deal with the now. Maybe he could still salvage this whole mess. Maybe a sinkhole would swallow him.

"Go to Reno as fast as I can and find my father." Sophie nodded with her chin toward a group of parents lingering outside the school.

"You expect him to have your money in his hotel-room safe?" Brad asked. "How much money are we talking about anyway?"

"Too much." She moved closer to the other parents and kicked a rock across the sidewalk. "Life changing."

"What makes you think he still has it?" Brad asked.

"He promised."

"And he's never broken a promise before?"

"My father has broken every promise." Sophie tugged on his arm to shift them out of the way of the wheelchair ramp that sloped from the side of the school entrance. "But it's different this time."

"Different how?"

The school bell buzzed. Less than ten seconds later, the school doors swung wide and students spilled out like ants from a kicked-in hill.

"This time my father will hurt someone other than just me." Sophie rolled onto the balls of her feet, her attention on the children.

Brad watched the kids, his gaze skipping over the dark brown hair, the long black hair and two redheads. Finally a familiar blond head emerged, a bright smile and even brighter laugh announcing Ella's arrival.

"I have to try to find my father. I have to do

that in Reno." Sophie looked at him. "I have to go because I have to save Ella."

Brad cursed under his breath. How was he supposed to deny her now? He watched Ella extend her walking stick and weave her way down the ramp, her friends chattering away beside her. Ella and her friends could possibly wear out his mother and her Myna Bird crew. He'd like to put the two groups together, but he wasn't sure his eardrums would survive.

Ella rounded the last corner and made it to the end of the ramp. Brad wanted to cheer. Ella was his ticket to keeping Sophie safe in the city. She needed to watch Ella, and she couldn't bring the little girl with them to Reno. He'd have his chance for his sit-down with George Callahan, alone, after all.

CHAPTER TWENTY-TWO

BRAD STOOD AT the floor-to-ceiling windows in his brother's loft looking at the city skyline and the car headlights streaming over the Bay Bridge. His headlights would join the others within the hour if he could just end this evening. Every bite of chicken piccata had been devoured. Ella and Drew had shared the last lava cake so that cake wouldn't be lonely.

The kitchen had been cleaned and his after-dinner drink declined. Now Ella, Sophie, Evie and Drew debated the ideal location for Milo's and Felix's beds. He'd have thought Drew's apartment was over eight thousand square feet, not the open-concept space, given the way the foursome were considering every corner and possible complication. They huddled in the guest bedroom, continuing their discussion.

He looked at Felix curled up on the plush charcoal throw draped over the sofa, eyeing Brad as if asking what all the fuss was about. Brad shrugged and picked up Milo, who'd been weaving through his legs, rubbing on his ankles with each complete circle. The brothers had clearly settled in better than their new owner.

The lock on the front door clicked and Brad spun around. Three people had keys to Drew's place: Brad and their parents. He adjusted Milo in his arms and walked toward the kitchen, watching the door the same way Felix had watched him.

His father held the door open and ushered his mother inside.

"Dad." Brad raised his voice, letting it carry throughout the loft. "Mom."

"You won't return my calls. So I have to resort to subterfuge to see my own son." His mother ran her hand over Milo's back. "And I need to meet my new grandsons, as it appears the only kind I'm ever going to have are four-legged."

She moved on, smiling wide. Brad twisted to see the cat-bed quartet lined up together like a receiving line, Ella flanked by Sophie and Evie with Drew loitering nearby. He began to wonder if his world would ever right itself. His mother had never mentioned grandchildren before as if she expected her sons to deliver her grandchildren. And now she hugged Sophie. *Hugged* her.

"Sophie, lovely to see you here, too." His mother bent toward Ella. "This must be your niece."

Sophie placed her hand on Ella's shoulder.

"Ella, this is Drew and Brad's mother, Mayor Harrington."

"That sounds a bit too formal for girls who share a love of all things pink and wear the same fur boots. My sons' friends used to call me Mrs. H," his mother said. "But that's for the boys."

Ella grinned. "Maybe Mayor H."

"How about Ms. Nancy," his mother suggested, and looked over her shoulder at Brad. "For now."

No, his friends had never called her Mrs. H or Mayor H—or anything but Mrs. Harrington. Ever. What happened? Where was his mother? And why had she added that cryptic *for now*? Brad glanced at Milo to make sure the cat hadn't morphed into a fox.

His mother returned to Ella. "We should discuss what other items you have with sheep lining, like gloves or a scarf or hat?"

"I just have boots." Ella chewed on her lip. "The gloves must feel like pillows around each finger."

"Well, we'll have to find you a pair so you can decide for yourself."

"You can do that?" Ella asked.

"If you can do something for me."

"What if I can't do it?" Ella's voice carried a mixture of suspicion and doubt with a dash of curiosity.

Brad had enough skepticism regarding his mother for everyone in the room. But he matched Ella's curiosity with a pinch of his own.

"Can you tell me what happens to Princess Noel? Does she find true love with the Sentinel or the Duke? If you can tell me, then I'll search for a pair of special gloves just for you."

"You've read *The Ten Summers* series?" Ella gripped Sophie's hand, her excitement radiating through the room.

"More than once, although that's between you and me." His mother stepped toward the sofa. "And I'm still not happy about the rumor that the dragonling, Bunny, won't be in the movie."

Sophie and Evie chimed in with several rumors they'd heard. Ella needed no more encouragement as she launched into her list of complaints regarding the upcoming release. The women settled on the couch, Ella wedged between Evie and Brad's mother. Sophie picked up Felix and settled in the chaise longue across from the trio, joining their lively discussion.

Brad petted Milo, drawing out his purr, the only sure thing he understood in the room. He followed his brother and father into the kitchen. "Mom read a children's book series?"

"There are sides to your mother I'm still discovering." His father pulled a highball glass from the cabinet and tipped it at Brad. "I've learned that women are in a constant state of evolving and you should never question it."

"But Mom, as in Mayor Harrington, the cutthroat politician who exposed the truth about every childhood fantasy before I was five... She read a series with warlocks, magic and dragonlings?"

"Apparently so." Drew slapped him on the shoulder. "Need something to drink?"

He wanted a double of whatever Drew had to offer. But he was driving to Reno soon. "Water works. I'm afraid to add anything stronger, given the evening. I might discover Mom has a secret talent for karaoke."

His father shook his head. "She won't ever possess a musical talent."

Still, Brad wondered what had happened with the real Mayor Harrington. Evie was quoting from one of the books, and the others joined in. Brad groaned. "Not Evie, too."

"I've promised to see the movies with your mother." His father tapped his glass against Brad's water.

Drew laughed and clinked his glass with theirs in toast. "I might need to get in on this. Dragonlings could be cool."

Brad set Milo down and watched the cat scamper into the laundry area toward his covered litter box. He wanted to hide in there, too.

Brad's mother walked into the kitchen with a palm covering each ear. "I didn't want to hear the spoiler for Book Five. Ella and Evie have read all six books already."

Sophie followed and accepted a glass of wine from Brad's father. "I've only finished the first one, so you won't get any spoilers from me."

Brad lifted up his hands, palms out. He wasn't certain now if his glass contained water or something more mind-bending. "Don't look at me for information."

"You need to read more than those sports and car magazines, Bradley," his mother chided. "Expand your horizons."

Something the Harringtons seemed to be doing quite a lot lately. And here he thought he was the only one about to expand his horizons on the *Freedom Seeker.* Drew adopting cats and his mother... He didn't know this woman who looked like his mother, but wasn't.

His mother sat on one of the bar stools and picked up her wineglass. "Everything ready with the gala?"

"Yes, thanks to Drew's assistance with a few last-minute sponsors." Sophie scooted out the bar stool beside his mother and sat.

"Splendid." His mother clinked her glass against Sophie's. "I'm looking forward to it. I've invited several acquaintances that could benefit from owning a pet to soften their edges and sever their selfish tendencies."

Brad forced his sip of water to dribble down his tight throat rather than spit all over Drew's granite counter. His mother had made a career out of selfish tendencies. He and Drew were the product of her selfish tendencies. But then Drew had admitted to adopting Milo and Felix to learn to share. His mother had rescued greyhounds since he'd been a toddler and yet the dogs hadn't softened her.

Brad moved to the refrigerator and refilled his water glass. Maybe if he fully hydrated he'd see everything clearly.

Not long after, his headlights still not crossing the Bay Bridge, his confusion still twisting him up, Brad held the door for his parents' departure. Evie and Sophie kept to their stools at the kitchen island. Ella slept stretched out on the couch, Milo curled up next to her and Felix guarding her from the sofa.

"Your father is lovely." Sophie smiled at Brad. "Thanks for letting us meet him."

Sadness lingered in Sophie's eyes, tugging at Brad. "He found you and Ella to be equally lovely."

"He seems to be everything a father should be." Sophie swirled the wine around in her glass. "Everything a father is supposed to be."

And Sophie was everything a mother should be. "He's a good man. He balanced out our mother."

Drew laughed and Sophie scowled at them. "Your mother is wonderful, too."

"In her own peculiar way," Drew added and turned to Brad. "Did Mom actually mention grandchildren when she walked in?"

Brad closed his eyes. He'd blocked out certain portions of the evening.

"She most certainly did," Evie said. "There's nothing wrong with a parent wanting to spend time with their grandchildren."

"We don't have children." Drew stretched his arms out wide. "No kid stuff. No grandchildren to entertain."

"I have the complete opposite problem." Sophie spun her stool toward the living room. "There's a sweet child. And her grandparent refuses to spend time with her." She pressed her lips together and pushed her wineglass across the counter as if that might stop her confessing.

Pink stained her cheeks and she wouldn't look at him when she spun back to face the counter.

"You told me your father has business to finish up. I'm sure he'll spend time with Ella once that's resolved." Evie rubbed Sophie's shoulder and also refused to look at Brad. "But what I'd really like is for your father's business associate to stop frequenting the store. Twice this week already. That's too much, but at least you weren't there."

"It doesn't matter," Sophie muttered, and swallowed the last of her wine. "He still found me this morning at Ella's school."

"Who found you?" Brad asked before glancing at Drew. His brother straightened and approached, his attention on Sophie. Why hadn't Brad been told before now? If they were being harassed, he should know. He should've been informed. How was he supposed to protect her?

"He's no one." Sophie waved her hand as if swatting away his pestering question and his protection. "It's handled, or will be once I find my father."

"He was nice looking to start with." Evie finished her wine and walked around the island to rinse out her glass. "But then he came up to the counter to ask for Sophie and I wanted him to leave. Something unfriendly in his eyes."

Brad looked at Sophie. "And he talked to you at Ella's school?"

"He must have followed you." Evie dried her hands on the dish towel and frowned. "I'm not certain I like that."

"I need to get Ella home." Sophie jumped up and rubbed her hands on her legs as if she was warming herself up for a long run.

She wasn't running anywhere without him. "And you need to pack," Brad said. "We'll leave for Reno within the hour as long as you're okay with Evie staying with Ella."

"You're coming with me?" Sophie asked.

He nodded and watched the relief roll through her. But the quiver in her lips snagged at his heart. Didn't she know he'd always protect her? Always help her? Of course not. He'd only just made that discovery. He pressed on his chest, trying to put everything inside him back in place.

"We talked about it earlier." Sophie wrapped her arm around Evie's waist. "She's practically a second mother to you and Drew. You trust her and so do I."

But Sophie shouldn't trust anyone, especially the ones standing around Drew's kitchen. But he liked that she trusted him. He liked that too much. Without trust, there'd never be love. And he needed Sophie to love him. He needed her to love him because he loved her.

Every rational thought he had suddenly evaporated. Why did he have to fall in love? Of all the irresponsible and irrational and stupid things he could've done, this captured the number-one spot. But that didn't mean he had to do anything about it. So he loved Sophie. What would that change? Nothing, unless he allowed it to. And he wasn't letting anything change. He ground his fingers into his chest, digging between his ribs. Even his skin seemed to have shrunk on his frame, and everything seemed too tight, too closed in.

Sophie's soft voice broke into his scrambled thoughts. "You still want to watch Ella, right, Evie?"

"More than anything." Evie hugged Sophie back.

"Thank you both." Sophie rushed around the island and launched herself into Brad's arms.

Everything inside Brad uncoiled. Her touch brought him focus. He seemed to always be coming back to her. He held on a little longer than necessary and a little tighter than decent, stealing the moment, uncertain if he'd have a chance for more. Or even if he'd take the risk again.

She pulled away enough to look into his eyes. "Thank you for helping me find my father."

And there was that hope again in her voice. And that spark in her gaze. And he saw that little girl she was once—the one who'd wanted to believe with all her heart and strength that her father was good. The little girl who struggled to still believe.

For once, he wanted to be wrong about someone more than he wanted anything in his life, even his freedom. He wanted George Callahan to prove him wrong with a desperation that bordered on the ridiculous. And he wanted Sophie not to ever lose her hope. If he could give her that, it'd be worth anything. "I can pick you up in thirty minutes. Can you be ready that soon?"

SOPHIE STUFFED SEVERAL pairs of underwear, jeans and two sweaters into a duffel bag. She pulled only from the pile of clean laundry stacked on top of her dresser, not bothering to match anything. This wasn't a vacation or surprise getaway with her boyfriend. This road trip wasn't for fun or relaxation or entertainment. She had only one goal. She might not look color coordinated when she located her father, but she'd certainly have clean underwear on when she returned her money to her bank account to cover the loan payment that was due in two weeks.

Zipping up the duffel, she strode into the family room and looked at Ella and Evie perched beside each other on the couch like coconspirators. "Where was I? Did we go over the bedtime routine?"

"That was part of section two on your list, I believe." Evie tucked a touch pad between them, trying to hide it from Sophie.

Ella nodded and grinned, her elbow nudging

into Evie's side as if to give the older woman a silent high five.

"And you've been here for the shower routine." Sophie walked across the hall toward the bathroom to grab her essentials—toothbrush, toothpaste and hairbrush. Makeup wasn't needed on a father hunt. "You just need to be in shouting range in case Ella needs something."

Evie's loud whisper carried into the hall, but Sophie couldn't quite make out the words. She paused in the hallway, listening as Ella responded, "That might make her start again from the beginning of the list."

The dread in Ella's tone made Sophie smile.

"I'll wait until she goes into the kitchen," Evie suggested.

"We can't move," Ella said. "Or she'll find us making popcorn and assume we never listened to anything."

"And she'll start all over," Evie added.

"Yup." Ella sighed. The sound heavy and dense as if launched from a heat blaster. "I find it's best to let her get it all out."

Ella's voice sounded wise and old and sage like a philosopher on a lost mountain who knew all the world's secrets.

"Does she do this with all of your sitters?" Evie asked.

Definitely not. She'd never allowed just anyone to stay with Ella overnight. That would be irresponsible. Besides, wherever Sophie wanted to go, she wanted Ella to be with her.

"I don't have any," Ella said. "Just Ruthie and now you. But she does this with Ruthie every time. Ruthie can recite the list. She's really smart and she's known me since I was born."

"Your aunt loves you." Evie's voice was earnest and kind and soft.

Sophie loved Ella more than the child could ever know.

"She loves me like a mom should," Ella said.

Sophie pressed her fist against her mouth.

Ella continued, "And she loves her instructions."

The distress in Ella's tone stirred the laughter in Sophie's chest, forcing a smile against her fist.

"They're her way of protecting you," Evie said.

"And she promised she'd always protect me," Ella said.

Always. And forever. She hadn't broken that vow yet. And she didn't intend to start now.

"So we listen to her list from beginning to end," Evie said.

"Every time," Ella said. "It's the right thing to do."

Sophie's eyebrows lowered in tandem with her shoulders as the tension receded. She was doing the right thing going to Reno. She was saving her family. She walked into the living room, her gaze jumping from Ella to Evie. Neither had moved, only Ella's one foot swung up to tap the coffee table and then drop down on repeat. Sophie twisted her toothbrush in her hand and looked at the older woman who'd come to mean so much to her in such a short time. "Ella gave you the list already, didn't she?"

"She might've mentioned some things." Evie grinned, almost secretive, but understanding flashed in her pale blue gaze.

And Sophie knew like she knew the sun rose in the east that Evie wouldn't let anything happen to Ella. She stepped around the coffee table, reached for Ella and pressed a kiss on her forehead. "Ella can recite my whole list with my warnings and tones. She's that bright and talented."

Ella's smile lightened Sophie like the cathedral bells ringing on Sunday.

Ella stood and wrapped her arms around Sophie's waist. She rested her cheek over Sophie's heart and patted Sophie's forearm. "It's your list, Auntie, you really should tell it."

Sophie brushed her hand over Ella's forehead and kissed her again before tightening her hug. She'd been holding her niece close and tight since she'd been an infant.

But when Ella hugged her back, it was like an embrace from the sun, whole and strong. The warmth left no room for shadows, worry or doubt. Sophie cherished these moments. "I need to tell it. For me."

"So when you leave, you know I'm protected." Ella loosened her arms, but never let go.

Sophie never wanted her to let go. Everything she did was to look after this precious child, her family. "Exactly."

Ella lifted her head. "And I double the protection because I know the list, too."

"Now I know it, as well." Evie rose and walked over to them, putting her hand on Ella's back. "I can't replace your aunt, but I can make sure you stay safe, too."

Ella opened one arm to invite Evie into their hug.

Sophie couldn't recall the last group hug she'd been a part of. But she welcomed Evie's ready embrace. Sophie's inner circle was growing. But she wasn't afraid. For the first time in too long to remember, Sophie felt something other than fear.

CHAPTER TWENTY-THREE

THREE HOURS OF the journey had Sophie dedicated to tracking down her father's hotel. Poor cell reception, thanks to the continuous snowfall; a bathroom break during their one gas-station stop; and at least fifteen minutes to rein in her frustration and temper with every dead-end call to an inn, hotel or motel filled the remainder of the drive.

Brad remained silent and stoic, only butting in twice: once to suggest inns not on her printed list and once to tug the phone from her stiff fingers and place a bag of chocolate candy in her hand, telling her to breathe and snack.

He didn't offer false encouragement or empty promises that they'd definitely find her father. Nor did he blame her for taking him on some wild-goose chase through a snowstorm. He just drove—a competent, confident presence beside her as if he'd already understood her need to do this her way, before he'd even stuck the key in the ignition to start his truck.

He pulled into the entrance to the Grand Desert Casino Hotel, the only place she'd called that hadn't offered another dead end. The pleasant Grand Desert concierge had thanked Sophie for calling the hotel before connecting her to George Callahan's guest suite. Four rings and the phone had been answered. She'd managed to squeak out the word *Dad* before the dial tone echoed in her ear. That had been less than an hour ago.

Brad parked and opened his door to hand his keys to the valet. Sophie stepped off the running board into the snow and drew in as deep a breath of the frigid air as she dared. They'd passed under the famous sign welcoming visitors to Reno and she prayed this city proved to be little just like the sign claimed.

But the hotel looked to be a small city unto itself with its two massive towers and wings that spanned the length of several blocks. Lights flashed on the casino sign and guests rushed inside from the unrelenting cold. Sophie wiped her boots on the carpet and crossed the massive marble floors in the lobby to the check-in counter. Her pace much less anxious, much less excited than the other guests swarming her, their suitcases bouncing along with their joy.

Sophie stepped up to the high counter and requested to be connected to George Callahan's room.

The woman smiled, tugged on her blazer and

typed on a keyboard Sophie couldn't see. "We don't have a guest by that name."

Sophie tried not to wilt against the check-in counter and slide down to the shiny marble floor. "But I was connected to George Callahan's room about forty minutes ago."

The polished hotel clerk stared at her screen and shook her head. "I'm sorry, we no longer show a guest under the name of George Callahan."

"But you had a guest registered as George Callahan," Sophie challenged.

The woman's hands paused as she pushed a kind look onto her face. "I'm sorry. Unless you're part of George Callahan's party or registered to the guest's room, I cannot release that information."

Sophie refused to let her head drop. *Always keep your chin up, so you can duck when reality tries to knock you down.* Not the best time for Grandmother Callahan wisdom. "Could you connect me to Cal Henry's room, then? He's my uncle." The lie lifted her chin higher as if she was prepping for the sucker punch about to crack her jaw.

If her father used an alias like the ones in the articles she'd discovered in the attic, then he'd need false identification and credit cards. It would mean her father would be more than a liar—he'd be a fraud. And she'd be the fool for ever believing in the man.

The woman glanced up from her screen. "I'm sorry we don't show Cal Henry registered with us. But I'd be more than happy to check you in to your room?"

Brad set his arm on Sophie's waist. "We're sorry to bother you. Her grandmother is ill and we need to bring the gentleman home."

"Oh, I'm sorry to hear that." The desk clerk lifted her arm to motion for the next guest to step up to the counter.

Brad led her toward the leather lounge chairs and glass tables gathered around a massive fireplace on the other side of the lobby. Sophie leaned into him for only a moment before pulling away. "My grandmother is dead."

Brad remained silent. Sophie skirted past the lounge and followed the signs leading to the casino. A Friday night close to midnight was early by casino standards. And the snow outside hampered travel. If her father had vacated his room, he'd hang out in the casino, the temptation too much to avoid.

Sophie scanned the crowded slot machines, even though she knew the return was too low for her father on those machines. She wove through the gaming tables, stopping to search the bodies pressed up against a craps table, then pausing to watch the ball settle into red five at the roulette wheel. Cheers and claps echoed over the muffled groans of the losers. Her father wasn't among either group. Sophie moved on, dismissing the crowded dance floor covered with a smoky haze. The dance floor offered no viable return for George Callahan. And he lacked the patience for poker, so she only skimmed her gaze over the numerous tables in that section.

Brad remained beside her, silent and patient, letting her search for her father. Never pulling her aside to make her stop. Never once suggesting the whole thing was futile. Never once calling her out for wasting his time.

Sophie entered the sports-betting area and watched a gentleman at the cashier station. He was too tall to be her father and his hair too gray, but still, she waited until she could see more than the man's profile. The gentleman finally turned, counting a large stack of bills in his hands. The stranger had too much money to be her father. Sophie skipped her gaze over the multiple high-def TVs lining one wall. Basketballs dropped through hoops, cars squealed around tracks, horses lunged from the starting gates, pucks cracked against the boards and defeat cracked through Sophie. "He isn't here, is he?"

"No," Brad said, close enough to touch.

The single word dropped like a steel door slamming in her face. The certainty in his voice set her off. Sophie rounded on Brad. "You're a private investigator. Can't you investigate?"

He pushed away from the pillar he'd been leaning against and stilled, everything in him quiet, even his wide eyes, no unnecessary blinks to disrupt his stillness. The only active part of him was the gaze that searched her face. "Do you want me to investigate your father, Sophie?"

His voice was low, but jolted through her.

"No. Yes. Maybe." Sophie threw up her hands. "I don't know what I want anymore."

She wanted something not to be complicated. For once. She wanted something to be easy. What did it even matter what she wanted?

He stepped forward and reached for her.

Sophie spun toward the lobby sign, away from him and the emotions he tangled up inside her. There was nothing simple or straightforward about her feelings for Brad. But this wasn't the time or place to dig into those truths now. She waited until he fell in step beside her and said, "I know I don't want to stay in Reno another minute."

"It's after midnight," he said. "We can get a room and leave early in the morning."

"I need to go home." *Now.* She needed to polish the furniture to sell. Maybe she could use the proceeds to extend her loan or for first month's rent at a new location. A shiver expanded from her core and extended over her whole body as if she'd collapsed inside a twenty-foot snowbank.

She had to find a new home for her and Ella. She had to find homes for all of her fosters. She couldn't rely on the gala for the adoptions. That left her only a week. Seven days until the event and ten days until the balloon payment was due.

Sophie slowed as if that snow weighed her down with each step. But her mind, frantic and overloaded, scratched out a massive to-do list. Sophie struggled to move, although she knew that avalanche was about to suffocate her if she didn't keep going. If she didn't keep believing.

Her father might return with her money. But could she sit around and plan her future and Ella's on that possibility? She tripped and stumbled. Nothing except her foolishness blocked her path.

Brad's arm circled her waist. Sophie sagged into him, but kept her shoulders stiff and her head held high. She wasn't falling apart. Not in the warm comfort of Brad's embrace. Not now. Not ever.

He stopped and pulled her fully against him. She dropped her forehead against his chest, but kept her arms at her sides. He wouldn't break her. She wouldn't break. She squeezed her eyes closed, willing the tears to stop. There wasn't time for crying.

Her tears dampened Brad's shirt. Sophie curled her fingers into her palms, digging her nails into her skin. Brad's arms tightened around her. Sophie held herself together.

Then his hand smoothed up her back and his lips dropped onto her head. His kiss poured through her. His silent acceptance rocked her and his tender strength undid her.

Sophie wrapped her arms around him and clutched at his jacket. "I'm not crying over my father."

He rested his chin on her head and rubbed her back.

"I stopped crying over him when I was ten," she mumbled into his shoulder. "I'd have to be a fool to let him hurt me again."

His hands continued to loosen all the tension from her muscles. His embrace continued to comfort all those lonely places inside her.

"I'm not a fool." At least, she wasn't supposed to be a fool. Her grandmother had raised her better than that. She lifted her head and swiped her palms over her wet cheeks. "Besides, my dad might be on his way back to San Francisco with my money."

Brad's eyebrows lifted into his hairline and his mouth opened, but only silence escaped.

Sophie closed her eyes. "I said *might*. It's not like I really believe it."

But heaven help her, how she wanted to. How she wanted to believe her father would keep this promise that would change her and Ella's lives. Her father had to come through, so that Sophie knew risking her heart wouldn't always mean pain.

Her grandmother had failed after all. Sophie was a fool.

Only a fool believed in derelict fathers.

Only a fool strove to change her roots.

Only a fool lost her heart to Brad.

Sophie opened her eyes to find him watching her. Weariness darkened the skin under his eyes and his gaze had dimmed. She'd made him drive through a snowstorm on a wild-goose chase. He had to be tired from the journey and from her. "I never thanked you for driving me up here. I owe you."

He rubbed his thumb across her cheek, removing the last of her tears. "I like seats behind first base or the home team dugout, hiking in the foothills and a double with extra cheese from Roadside Burgers."

A laugh gurgled through her tears. "That's all back in the city."

"Should we get going?"

She searched his face. That he was willing to

drive home after their useless trip without complaint made her heart tumble over itself. "In the morning."

She was a fool, but not stupid. The snow had increased and her weather app showed it wasn't letting up soon. Who knew what the road conditions were now. She wouldn't be able to sleep with all of her racing thoughts. But Brad could.

Twenty minutes later, Sophie slipped her nightshirt over her head, tucked her toothbrush inside her bag and flipped off the bathroom light. Brad stretched out on top of the comforter, still in his clothes, pillows jammed behind his head, the TV remote aimed at the flat screen. Only king rooms had remained when they'd returned to the concierge desk.

Sophie hadn't hesitated and accepted the room key. She wanted to be close to Brad. For one night. It could be the only one they ever shared and, besides, she wasn't ready to rely on her own arms to hold her.

She crawled under the covers and scooted closer to Brad. He lifted his arm and invited her to curl up beside him. Her head rested on his chest, his arm curved around her back. The feather comforter divided them, but she was next to Brad. It was more than she'd dared to wish for. More than she'd dared to want.

He clicked through the TV channels and

stopped on a show with a couple buying their own private island and squeezed her. "You could sail away with me to any island we wanted."

"I have too many responsibilities in the city. I can't just leave like you." Sophie yawned, long and deep. "I don't have your freedom."

She rubbed her cheek against his chest, let out another yawn and fell asleep dreaming about sailing away.

CHAPTER TWENTY-FOUR

BRAD LOCKED HIS truck and crossed toward the dock. The sun peeked out from behind the clouds, but failed to remove the chill from the air. He rubbed his hands together. He hadn't been warm since Saturday morning when he'd woken with Sophie in his arms.

It'd been four days since the call had come on their drive home from Reno, telling him that his boat was ready when he was. A gulf had opened between him and Sophie inside his truck as if she had been gathering herself together like pieces of a jigsaw puzzle and putting everything back in the box. Everything besides him.

He wasn't part of her life. She wasn't part of his. And he'd been insane to even suggest she join him. Maybe that's why he'd offered. To prove to them both that it could never work. That they were on two different paths and those paths weren't meant to converge. Not now. Not ever. So he could tell himself he'd at least tried. With a halfhearted offer. An offer he'd known she couldn't and wouldn't ever accept. He shoved on his sunglasses to block out the sun and his own foolishness.

Brad stopped at boat slip 118 and stared at the cursive writing on the vessel's stern. The *Freedom Seeker* was waiting. The updated master stateroom with the redesigned head and down-filled duvet-covered king bed, the stainless-steel appliances in the open-concept kitchen that flowed into a media room with an L-shaped leather couch and fifty-inch flat-screen TV, and computerized cockpit with leather captain chairs beckoned him aboard. Beckoned him to unpack his clothes and fill the cedar-lined drawers. Beckoned him to stock the refrigerator and light the grill on the sundeck. Beckoned him to pull into the bay and ultimately seek his freedom.

Yet he remained on the dock, arms crossed over his chest, boots planted as if he'd suddenly lost his sea legs. As if he'd never gain his sea legs.

A low whistle drifted by before Drew's deep voice called out to him. "Freedom awaits. Can't think of a better way to leave town."

Brad couldn't, either. Everything he'd envisioned at the start of the restoration floated before him, from the special-order hand railings to the teak stairs to the custom swim platform. It was all aboard, ready to welcome him.

Except he hadn't envisioned everything. He hadn't envisioned a certain honey blonde or her adorable curly-haired sidekick. "Why are you here?"

Drew slapped a folder against Brad's arms still crossed over his chest. "Called in a few favors. If it's information you don't already have, then you're going to owe me."

Brad had promised several favors the last few days himself. Favors he'd need to deliver on before he set sail or his word would mean nothing when he returned. Now he might owe his brother's contacts or Drew's reputation would suffer and he wouldn't be the cause of that.

A boat motored out into the bay. The dock swayed from the wake, the motion rocking up through Brad's legs. He questioned if it was all worth it. His heart strapped on a life jacket and shouted a definitive yes. But he'd never listened to his heart before. Why was he now? "Thanks. Let me know what I can do for your contacts and I'll see that it gets done."

"From your cockpit or sundeck?" Drew asked.

"I haven't left yet." Brad flipped through a timeline and several photos of Teddy Gordon—George Callahan's business associate and Sophie's unwanted customer.

"About that," Drew said. "When do we crack

the champagne against the bow and bid you bon voyage?"

"Soon."

"Soon as in this week or soon as in within the next month?" Drew nudged him in the side with his elbow.

Brad turned away from his boat and his brother and strode down the dock toward the parking lot.

Drew caught up and matched Brad's quick pace. "So I'm guessing not this week."

"I've got to finish up a few things first."

"Things like Sophie Callahan?"

Brad stopped and faced his brother. "Sophie isn't a thing. She's…" He stopped himself before he said *everything*. And there was nothing finished about them. "What are you getting at?"

"I'm getting at your single-minded, absurd resolve to sail away on that boat. Alone." Drew pointed toward the *Freedom Seeker*. His voice dropped, becoming serious and stern. "To leave behind your family. Your business. And possibly the only woman you've ever really loved."

"Harringtons don't do love." Brad slapped the folder against his leg.

Drew scratched the back of his neck and studied Brad, his mouth opening and closing like a beached fish. The same expression Drew had when they'd been kids and Brad had suggested they jump from the roof like stuntmen, or light firecrackers in the garbage can. Only Brad could make his brother more bewildered than a hung jury on a defenseless trial. "Of course we do love. Everything Mom has ever done has come from her love for her family."

Brad's tight grip pinched the folder. "Let me revise that. The Harringtons don't do love well." His family distorted love, twisted it inside out and manipulated those they loved for their own selfish gain. Sophie deserved better than that.

"You haven't ever loved someone. How do you know if you're not good at it or not?" Drew tipped his head and put both hands on his waist. "Wait, this isn't about the Bureau and Marlene, is it?"

Brad had sworn to personally protect his witness, but had in the end deferred to his superiors' order to let the US Marshals do their job.

Brad looked away, walking toward the parking lot again. He'd confided in his brother when he'd resigned from the Bureau. The only outsider who knew the full details of that fatal error. "That's in the past."

"But not dealt with." Drew paced him.

Mandated therapy sessions had forced Brad to deal with that part of his past. However, there was still the present, and that he'd not dealt with.

His disloyalty to Evie when he'd ruined her husband, ensured Richard's electoral defeat in favor of his mother's success. He'd even held Evie's hand at her husband's funeral three weeks later. And then he'd failed to protect Evie from the likes of George Callahan. All the while he loved Evelyn Davenport as if she were his family. "When did you become a psychologist?"

"When did you let fear convince you to run away?" his brother countered.

"I'm tired of the manipulation," Brad said. "When I sail away, then my life will be on my terms."

"You can have a life on your terms here."

If he had a life on his terms here he wouldn't still be lying to Sophie. It sounded nice, but it was impossible. "It doesn't matter. When Sophie finds out the truth, she'll bolt just like Marlene."

"If Marlene had really trusted you, she wouldn't have run away that night. She would have believed in the future you'd promised. You have to trust in Sophie's love for you."

Evie trusted him and look where that'd gotten her. But Sophie wouldn't trust him when she discovered he'd been lying to her from the start. And Brad wasn't certain he could ever trust anyone with his heart. "I need to find Teddy Gordon and then meet Lydia at the office at five to see what else she's found."

"Then this concludes our therapy session." Drew gave a quick nod. "I'll forward my bill to your office. When would you like to schedule the next one? I tend to book up fast."

Brad laughed. Once again thankful for Drew's natural ability to diffuse situations. "Is never available?"

"That's a low blow for how insightful I was." Drew clutched his stomach as if Brad had punched him. "I even impressed myself."

Brad stopped beside his truck. "It's not that difficult. How about we discuss your tendency to place work above social interaction? Or your tendency to forget your girlfriend's birthday or date night because you slept at the office for the third night in a row? Or your unwillingness to eat in public while preparing for a trial?"

Drew backed away, his arms spread wide. "I'm an open book and today wasn't about me."

"Scared to open the door and see your skeletons?" Brad taunted.

"I adopted Felix and Milo." Drew opened his car door and smiled over the hood. "I've dressed my skeletons and invited them outside to play."

"We'll chat when you finally meet the woman that makes you hear your heart." Brad knocked his fist on the truck's roof.

"Is that what Sophie's done to you?"

Not that he'd ever admit it. And not that it

mattered once she learned the truth. He shook his head, the movement small and tight and fast. "Not yet."

CHAPTER TWENTY-FIVE

SOPHIE WALKED THE length of the ballroom and checked on the items in the silent auction, manned by Erin and her sorority sisters. She'd created a text message tree for everyone to communicate. Thumbs-up images popped on her phone screen from the check-in desk and the two public-relations majors emceeing the runway show for dogs that would begin in less than fifteen minutes.

All of the college kids had asked to return next year to work the event. Not wanting to disappoint them with the news that this would be the first and last Paws and Bark Bash, Sophie had smiled and agreed.

Evie, Olivia and Ruthie volunteered to handle the staging area where the dogs relaxed until their turn on the runway. She'd gotten a dozen requests from guests asking about how to put their dogs on the runway next year. One guest even inquired about the price to walk the runway. Sophie cursed herself for missing the potential revenue. Her foster families prepped their charges for the runway and hopefully adoptions.

Troy and his partner manned the kitty kennels and were helping people complete the adoption paperwork. She'd only brought in the four kitten litters and photos of her older cats. But the boys had a tablet with guests interested in several other cats and animals. Sophie prayed those guests would still be interested tomorrow when she called them personally.

Ruthie's fiancé, Matt, circulated the room with Brad and Drew beside him. Mayor Harrington was doing the same on the other side, with Mr. Harrington holding her hand.

Kay would've loved their salesmanship, but she was at the hospital, waiting on the birth of her grandchildren. She'd been assisting with the setup for the silent auction when the call came from Bay Water Hospital. Sophie was still in awe of Kay and Evie's swift and easy friendship. Evie had even promised to head to the hospital after the event so Kay wouldn't have to wait alone. Thanks to Mayor Harrington, Evie and Kay, only ten seats hadn't been purchased. She was thankful for the women's ability to rally so many of their friends to this cause.

Sophie heard Brad's laughter and turned toward the brothers. Brad toasted her with his glass from across the room. He was handsome when he was in jeans and a T-shirt, but now he was second-glance worthy in his suit and tie. She congratulated herself for controlling her emotions and wrangling the lock back in place around her heart. No silly heart flip-flopping or one-sided yearning for her.

More thumbs-ups flashed on her screen from Ruthie and Troy. Sophie had everything in hand.

"I knew you'd pull this off. Never discount a Callahan."

A warm hand slipped around Sophie's waist. She twisted as her father dropped a kiss on her cheek. "Dad?"

"I returned like I promised." He adjusted the knot on his tie and tugged his white shirt cuffs out of the sleeves of his pin-striped suit jacket. "The girls let mc in when I told them I was your proud father."

He smiled over Sophie's shoulder. She turned to see an older woman touching her necklace and grinning back. Grabbing her father's elbow, Sophie steered him toward the back of the ballroom. "Where have you been?"

"Plenty of time to talk about that later." He scanned the silent-auction tables running the length of the wall. "Is this a couples' event or are there singles here, too?"

His voice was too pleasant and the speculation in his tone and scheming in the narrowing of his eyes made Sophie tighten her grip on his arm. "You can't just show up here."

As if he'd been invited. As if he belonged. As if he'd assisted in her success, not her potential downfall. Sophie pushed out a wide smile for the couple discussing one of the pet spa baskets and guided her father away from the auction items.

"I got a voice mail reminder about your event. I had to support my daughter." He pulled free with a quick twist and soft pat to Sophie's fingers, and eased beside an elegant woman reading the information card about a weekend wine getaway. Her father whispered in the woman's ear, drawing out a cultured laugh before she bid. He returned to Sophie and nudged her in the side. "See that. She's paying the buy-it-now price. I can be very persuasive and very helpful."

"Helpful would be giving me my money back," Sophie muttered.

Suddenly her father grabbed her arm and towed her backward toward the door. "Tell me that isn't Evelyn Davenport by the stage?"

Sophie spotted Evelyn stepping from behind the black stage curtain. She approached the emcees. Her black skirt flowing and the black feather motif embroidered on the sleeveless white top made the older woman look classic and timeless. Sophie wanted to steal a pinch of Evie's poise for herself. Sophie smiled at her father. "That's Evie. How do you know her?"

"It's not important." He adjusted the silver tie at his neck and stretched his shoulders. "You know, you're right, honey. I shouldn't be here. I didn't buy a ticket and this is your event. Walk me out, we need to talk."

Her father spun and sprinted into the hall. Sophie paused, but no one shouted an SOS and only thumbs-up images flashed on her phone screen. She looked at Brad and saw him with his cell phone to his ear, his expression dark and angry.

But she could only deal with one crisis at a time. She hurried into the hall after her father, trying not to seem frantic or uncoordinated in hccls she never wore and in a gown she didn't own. She'd risk a ripped seam and blisters before she'd let her father walk away. "This is the part where you return my money, right?"

"I haven't forgotten what I owe you." Her father stuffed his hands in his pants pockets and rocked back and forth in his polished dress shoes. "I just need a loan and then I can bring us all even."

"A loan?" Sophie stuttered and pinched her hips, trying to loosen the vise of her sheath gown. The sequins became like chain mail, no longer shimmering and elegant.

"Not a big one." Her father tugged on his jacket sleeves and rubbed his hands together. "I've got a real good plan. Something's already in the works."

"Have you forgotten what you owe me?" a woman demanded from behind Sophie.

Sophie peeked over her shoulder and caught Evie's steady approach, the older woman's gaze fixed on her father. Sophie looked to him. He was holding a hand up as if a spotlight blinded his view. Then she went back to Evie and noted her set face, anger thinning her mouth. Sophie's gown contracted another inch, slowing her movements; otherwise, she'd have whiplash jumping back and forth between the pair.

Sophie lowered her voice, trying to hide the slow-burning accusation. "Dad, how do you know Evie?"

"You remember I mentioned E.D. I tried to introduce you last fall." Her father swiped his hand over his mouth as if to slow his words.

But he failed to temper his panic. Sophie heard his dismay in the way his words tripped over each other. "That was Edie, not Evie."

"Evelyn Davenport. I called her E.D. for short." He lifted his hands toward Sophie and shrugged. "Simple and easy like Soda-Pop."

Only roosters lived simple and easy, never laying an egg or ending up on the dinner table.

More Grandmother Callahan wisdom. Sophie dropped her chin and stared at the black sequins on her gown: dull and somber and grim like the betrayal and shame that consumed her.

Why hadn't Evie told her? How could her father have fleeced a wonderful woman like Evie? Did Evie pity her?

"Sophie?"

Brad's voice reached her like an escape route in a dungeon. Sophie moved toward him, seeking the safe shelter she'd only ever discovered in Brad's arms.

Two police officers flanked Brad, who nodded and said, "That's George Callahan."

One of the officers pulled out a pair of handcuffs as he read her father his rights.

Those iron bars slammed shut, making her a prisoner in that dungeon. That shelter only an illusion. Always an illusion. Always a lie. Sophie swayed on her heels, fighting against the weight of her gown dragging her lower. "What did you do?"

"What I asked him to do." Evie stepped forward. "Find George Callahan, the man responsible for stealing my retirement fund."

Sophie pitched forward, forcing her words out in a blast of distaste and disgust. "Is that true?"

Her father winced. "I borrowed it."

The only strength left inside Sophie lashed

through her voice like a whip. "Like you borrowed the money in my savings account?"

"That was *our* savings account, Soda-Pop." His eyebrows pulled together and his chin stiffened. "I had every right to it."

"You had no right," Sophie shouted. Her father looked at his dress shoes and straightened the pleat on his pant leg. Always more worried about his appearance than the truth. Sophie's gaze narrowed on her father, remembering his landlord's rant. Bile crawled up the back of her throat. "What have you done? Evelyn and I aren't the only ones you've stolen from, are we?"

"It was all gifts." Her father jerked his gaze to her, but his head shook and his focus slid off her face like tires on black ice. "And E.D. has property in the city. A place in Pacific Hills. She has more money."

Desperation infused his words again. Sophie countered, "But it wasn't your money!"

"Would've been once we married." Resentment scratched up his attempt at a smooth, placating tone.

Evie coughed.

Sophie didn't need to look at the older woman. "But Evelyn refused you."

"She needed more time to make our arrangement permanent," he said.

"But you didn't have any more time." Sophie's

bank account, her father's distracted phone calls, the intrusion of his world into hers: everything clicked into place like the magnetic ends on a black titanium balance bracelet. "You never called Teddy Gordon, by the way."

"He'll wait. He stands to double the money he loaned me." Her father stretched his hand toward her and slowed his words into a plea. "If you'd just spot me, Soda-Pop."

"There's no more money."

"You're wearing that fancy dress for this fancy ball with your new fancy friends. You got your store." He shook his finger at her as if ratcheting up his anger. As if she'd insulted him. "You've got access to money. If you'd only listen to my plan."

She'd borrowed her fancy dress from Ruthie's twin sister, Becca. The clutch purse belonged to Evie. The heels belonged to Ruthie. Kay had lent her the jewelry. She might have begged and borrowed, but she'd never stolen like her father. "No, you need to listen. I have no money."

"None that you'll share." His mouth dipped into a pout worthy of any toddler denied his favorite toy. "I just want to make us whole like I promised. Everything I've done is for Ella."

Sophie's stomach dropped. She struggled to draw a breath as if something or someone had seized her scream. How dare her father blame his granddaughter. Sophie swallowed, searching for her voice, searching for strength, searching for a reason not to vomit. She looked at the officers. "You can take him now."

"I'll call you, Soda-Pop. We need to talk more." Her father walked with the officers as if he believed everything would still work out in his favor.

Sophie turned her back on him. Turned her back on the fantasy family she'd dreamed about as a child. Turned her back on the past. But she didn't move from her spot. Hurt should consume her, but only emptiness poured in.

"Sophie?"

The familiar voice dislodged her numbness and made her ache. She hurt, after all. Now there was someone else she needed to relegate to her past.

Sophie stiffened her shoulders, yanking her spine into place to block out Brad's soft voice trying to lead her in another direction. A hand landed on her waist, the warm touch jarring through the cold seizing her. She jerked away and rounded on Brad, digging her heels like spikes into the concrete floor, anchoring her knees and her resolve.

"We need to talk," he said.

It was way too late for that. "I love you."

Brad rocked back as if she'd pierced him with

a knife. Her revelation shocked them both. She'd heard the accusation and threat in her tone, the lack of warmth and friendship. But there was just too much pain for her heart not to be involved. And the hurt wasn't for her father. George Callahan had broken her heart years ago and had yet to repair that damage. No, this pain was new, fresh and all Brad's fault. "But those words don't matter."

He grabbed her hand and held her in place. "It matters."

"I trusted you." That cracking in her voice matched the splintering in her heart. The heart she'd locked away. The heart she'd sworn no man would ever break like her father had. What a liar she'd turned out to be.

"I'm sorry." He wrapped her hand inside both of his and squeezed. "We can still make us work."

She stared at her hand cradled in his, protected and safe. But a chill blew through her as if the cold breath of reality sighed against her bare neck. She jerked her hand free and stepped away from another illusion. "I need to see to my guests and volunteers."

"That's it." He reached for her, his arms stretching toward her, his bewildered voice circling her. "You tell me 'I love you' and then walk away."

"It's not enough." The pieces of her shattered heart pinged against the concrete like crystals from a broken necklace. Wasn't that enough?

"It's everything," he said. "But you're too scared to trust your heart."

The truth in his words stung.

He attacked again, his next words pricking even deeper. "You're too scared to trust in love. In our love."

She notched her chin up and pressed her lips together as if that would cut off his words. As if that would crush the sting.

"Just like you're too scared to be called Mom." He hadn't softened his attack, never restrained the ruthless edge to his tone, never concealed his anguish. "But you aren't your sister or your mother. When are you going to see that?"

She couldn't see through the hurt, the emptiness or the lies. So many lies, she'd lost the truth. "I have to go."

"Don't walk away, Sophie." Brad shook his head and focused on her. "Don't deny us."

"I can't do this."

"You're not a runner." His gaze narrowed on her as his voice lowered. "You don't quit because it's a little too hard. A little too overwhelming. A little too much."

"But you are a runner." She sealed her arms against her sides, as if that was enough to insulate her from any more pain. "You are still sailing away on your boat, right?"

He quit reaching for her and squeezed the back of his neck. Everything inside Sophie squeezed as if she hadn't shattered enough already.

"I have to." He tried smiling, but his smile was too small, too weak to push through the guarded look in his eyes. "You and Ella could come with me."

He offered the impossible. But he never offered to stay. "That's not the life I've chosen." She'd made a life in the city. A home for her and Ella. "That's not the life I promised Ella. My niece won't become a runner like the rest of her family."

"You can't make the loan payment," he lashed out. "What do you really have here?"

"What will you have alone on a boat?" She kept her arms plastered to her sides, refusing to rub her bare skin. Refusing to reveal the cuts his words caused. She had to end this verbal duel that sliced deeper than any blade. "You're not willing to give up anything, while I lose everything. Safe travels, Brad."

"Don't walk away, Sophie." The plea in his voice pushed against her, all the more forceful in its softness.

Sophie stormed off, stuffed away useless wishes, then stopped abruptly beside Evie. The older woman's familiar jasmine and honeysuckle perfume swirled through Sophie's shallow breaths, linking her to those might-have-beens and what-ifs. "I don't know what to say to you. *I'm sorry* feels empty and useless."

"We say nothing tonight." Evie touched Sophie's arm. "And tomorrow or when you're ready, we'll talk."

Sophie blinked against the tears in her eyes, refusing to break down in the lobby of her gala or anywhere in public. Her gown morphed into armor, holding her together inside its rigid, unforgiving sheath.

Ruthie appeared in the doorway, her eyes widening and her mouth thinning. One stiff head shake brought Ruthie to Sophie's side. One stuttered inhale and Ruthie hooked her arm determinedly through Sophie's. No words required. Just the reinforcement of a best friend.

Ruthie escorted Sophie into the ballroom. Liv appeared just inside the entryway and stood next to Sophie on her other side. Sophie inhaled and forced herself to smile. She'd survive the evening with these strong women beside her. She knew without asking that they wouldn't leave her. She knew because that was what real family did: never left you.

BRAD PACED THE hallway. The DJ's music pulsed against the closed ballroom doors, each beat pounding like a fist to his chest. He considered storming inside and tossing Sophie over his shoulder and leaving with her. But that wouldn't be right, either.

Storming inside and kissing her senseless held appeal. A lot of appeal. If he showed her what was between them without words, then she might believe. Then she might take a risk.

But she'd accused him of making her a runner like her family. Of turning her into everything she never wanted to become. But she wasn't like her family. Sophie stayed. No matter what life threw at her, she stuck by those she loved. And he wanted her by his side. He needed her to stick with him.

But that wasn't happening now. She'd told him she loved him with loathing in her tone, blame in her voice as if love had betrayed her.

Brad strode toward the hotel's main entrance and stopped a foot from the exit, unable or, perhaps, unwilling to leave yet. If he pushed on into the night, he became the runner Sophie had accused him of being. But he couldn't stay. Staying was never in his plans.

The music's volume swelled before the ballroom door swung shut, blocking him out once again. There wasn't enough music to sweep away the emptiness building inside him. He couldn't recall ever feeling this alone. But he wanted to be alone, didn't he?

"Why did you tell Sophie's father about the event?"

Brad faced the tinted glass windows overlooking the hotel's circular drive. The city lights and traffic blurred against the tint, washing through his reflection and that of his mother. Nothing could wash out his misery, though. He removed the doubt from his voice, and said, "She had to learn the truth about him."

"You could have simply told her." His mother stepped up beside him, her expensive jeweled necklace glittering in the tinted glass.

His mother only reached his shoulder in her heels, but they shared the same hair color and eye color. He'd always considered his mother's eyes to be shrewd and wondered if Sophie thought the same about him now. "Sophie needed to hear the truth from her father."

"And this was the only place you could've arranged that conversation?"

His mother's vanilla scent clogged his throat. She offered no reassurance. No soothing words. No validation that he'd done the right thing. "George Callahan was desperate enough to choose to come here. I'm not responsible for his choices."

"No, but you're responsible for your own."

He knew that only too well. The choices he'd made at the Bureau had been costly for so many. And then there was Evie. Now with Sophie. "I wanted Sophie to stop letting her father hurt her. I wanted to end her pain." Brad had hurt her more.

Evie walked up behind them. Two very different women and yet so fiercely united.

"Would you do it all again, Evie?" His mother spoke to her friend, but kept her gaze fixed on Brad in the window.

"Would I give you what you'd need to ensure my husband's defeat in the election again?" Evie grabbed Brad's hand and squeezed. "Yes, without question."

"You knew?" Brad asked. He'd brought down her husband and she'd known. She'd wanted it to happen. He looked at his mother. "Why didn't you tell me?"

"You wouldn't have listened. You accused me of only ever speaking lies," his mother said.

Brad pinched his eyebrows together with his fingers as if that would make him see everything clearly. "Evie, why did you do it?"

"Because I loved my husband, always, and I was desperate," she said. "He was reckless in the pursuit of his political goals despite his declining health. He refused to pull out of the mayor's race and seek treatments for his cancer."

Brad crossed his arms over his chest and faced his mother and her best friend. "So you made the choice for him? You let me ruin him?"

"I made a choice to try to save someone I loved." Evie lifted her chin, her gaze unwavering, her belief in her decision absolute. "I never once thought that when Richard lost the primary he'd simply give up on life."

"Sophie suffered tonight," his mother said.

"She won't give up," he said.

"But will you? I wouldn't have thought Richard would give up after his defeat. I never imagined that politics was more important to him than me. Than us. But I was wrong." Evie grabbed his shoulders and pressed her cheek against his. "But I would do it all again. Would you?"

Evie hugged his mother and returned to the ballroom.

"Perhaps now you understand some of my choices. Why I've done what I've done for you and to you," his mother said.

He faced her and pulled back at the fierce protectiveness in her gaze. The shrewd, cunning politician replaced by a mother who willed her son to understand. She'd brought him home after he'd left the Bureau, given him purpose and focus, all to ease his own suffering. She'd stood by her friend's decisions to try to ease her pain.

"You might resent my methods and doubt me,"

she said. "But never doubt my love for you and my family. I've only ever wanted to shield my family from any hurt or misfortune or slight. I won't apologize for loving you enough to watch over you."

"When you love someone, aren't you supposed to set that person free? Isn't that how it goes?" He'd set Sophie free. That should be enough.

She placed her hand on his cheek. "Sometimes there's more freedom in belonging than in solitude."

"Do you consider yourself free?" He didn't bother to conceal the disbelief and scorn in his tone. His mother was handcuffed to her agenda. Nothing appealing or freeing about that.

"I don't want to be free." She cupped his jaw and drew his gaze down to her, clearly to make him listen. "I want to belong to a political party that institutes positive change, to a marriage that gives me security and unconditional love, to a family that loves despite our faults. And to a cause like Sophie's that supports ordinary people doing extraordinary things for a community that needs them."

He would not second-guess his decisions. Not now. "Sounds like a political speech for the campaign trail."

She smiled, but sadness seemed to weaken it as her hands dropped to her sides. "I wish I knew the day you stopped seeing me as your mother and only saw the politician."

"Why?" he asked. She'd always wanted him to be like her, like the politician.

"That'd be the day I'd go back to and change," she said. "You've only ever seen the politician. Until Sophie. When you're with her, you treated me more like your mother and less like your enemy."

She made them enemies with her interference. "You like Sophie because she advances your platform. She's good for your agenda."

"It's true I can help Sophie with her cause as much as she can help my political goals." She set her palm on his chest, covering the hollow place where his heart used to be. "But that's not why I like her. I like her because she reached your heart and gave you balance—light to soften the dark."

"I misled her. Lied to her," he said. "Betrayed her trust."

"Did you stop loving me when I did the very same things to you?"

"No, you're my mother." But he'd planned to leave town and not look back.

"And what is Sophie?"

"The only woman I'll ever love."

"Don't you think you should tell her that?" She kissed his cheek, then went over to his father, took his hand and together they left as a team. Always together. By each other's side. Never alone.

CHAPTER TWENTY-SIX

ELLA SLEPT SPRAWLED across her mattress, arms spread wide as if prepared to wake up and hug the world. She even smiled in her sleep. Ella's pretty dress, back on its hanger, no doubt thanks to Ruthie, hung on the closet door with her silver sparkle sandals facing the hallway as if ready to dance into the morning.

Sophie had sent Ella home with Ruthie once the DJ had ended his second thirty-minute encore. Sophie, her sorority volunteers and foster families had loaded the kennels and ensured every animal made it home. Tomorrow the families arrived for the adoptions. Sophie hoped the families hadn't just been caught up in the music and the fun. But that worry slipped lower on her list—below finding a new apartment, closing the Pampered Pooch and telling Ella.

Sophie tugged Ella's comforter from the floor and covered her niece. The thought of breaking the news to the little girl terrified and angered her. She never wanted to be the one to cause Ella to lose her smile. Tomorrow, after the adoptions, when it was quiet and they could celebrate the animals finding forever homes, then she'd tell Ella this wasn't their forever home, like she'd once promised.

Her phone vibrated in the clutch purse she'd borrowed from Evie. Stepping out into the hall, she answered, wondering if it was the venue calling to tell her she'd forgotten something. But she'd triple checked and accounted for all the supplies, decorations and animals. Yawning, she said, "Hello, this is Sophie."

"The credit card was denied."

Tessa's frantic voice crackled through the static. Sophie walked into her bedroom, closed the door and stepped out of the strappy four-inch heels. "There's no more money."

"What do you mean no money?" Censure coated Tessa's voice, displacing any concern.

"It's gone." She'd used the credit card tonight for the DJ and then to close out the bill with the Pavilion at the Reserve. There'd been a few extra overages for audio equipment she hadn't known about until this evening.

"But I need to pay the spa." Tessa's tone was demanding. "You promised to pay for my extended stay here."

Sophie had promised Pacific Bank and Trust she'd pay the mortgage. She'd promised to pay her vendors. She'd promised to keep a roof over Ella's head.

"Sophie? Did you hear me?"

"Yes, but I don't think you heard me, Tess." Sophie dropped onto the bed in her gown, her legs too tired to hold her up. But this wasn't the tired that came from dancing too many hours in a crowded ballroom. This tired was the soul-deep kind that spread into every bone, every muscle. Nothing pleasant about this tired. "There's no money."

"What am I supposed to do?" Tessa whined.

What was Sophie supposed to do? Plant a money tree and hope it grew in twenty-four hours? If only Olivia sold Jack's magic beans in her café. Taking on a giant for a bag of gold sounded much easier than dealing with her sister and father. Her body sank deeper into the bed. Lifting her free arm to massage her forehead where an ache throbbed required too much energy. She could at least still talk. "You're going to do what I've done for the past decade…figure it out."

"What did you do with all our money?"

The thorns in Tessa's voice needled into Sophie. When had her bank account become the Callahan community checking account? Her sister had never made a deposit. Never lifted a finger in the store. Never contributed to the family's welfare. "You'll have to ask Dad about the money. But I believe the jail limits him to one phone call."

"Jail?" Tessa screeched. "What are you talking about now?"

"Sorry, Tessa, I have to go." Exhaustion had consumed her and mustering the strength or the patience or the encouragement to continue the conversation had left her. Just one time, Sophie wanted someone to ask about her. Someone *had* asked about her, cared about her: Brad. No, she wasn't going there tonight. Closing her eyes, she said, "I love you, Tessa, but I have a life to figure out."

Sophie ended the call and dropped the phone on the bed. The phone vibrated immediately. Apparently Tessa had more than one call, unlike their father. Sophie's voice mail chimed before the phone vibrated again, followed quickly by the jingle of a new text message. Next, the video-chat ringer hummed.

Sophie picked up her phone and looked at her sister's smiling picture filling the screen. Tessa never asked about Ella. Never asked about Sophie. Never considered what they might be up against without money. Everything was always about her sister.

Except now. Now it was about Ella and Sophie.

Sophie turned off her phone, turned off the past and threw it across the room. The phone bounced off the wall and smacked against her dresser. Something banged inside Sophie—perhaps it was the power of saying no. The freedom in simply saying no more. The crack of the phone on the hardwood floor released her smile as if her new backbone had tested its strength and won.

She pulled the throw blanket over her and shut her eyes. She needed a few hours to sleep, enough to face tomorrow and design their new life.

MONDAY MORNING, SOPHIE sat in the leather chair across from Beth Perkins at Pacific Bank and Trust. Sunlight streamed into the window behind Beth, the only shadows the ones created by the pigeons flying up and down to the sidewalk in search of their breakfast. The same floral tissue box squatted on the desk between the women.

"We have bank regulations and complicated federal laws to follow. I want to shake your hand and tell you that will be more than enough to extend your loan." Beth broke form and yanked a tissue from the box. She dabbed the tissue underneath her glasses. "There are days I hate my job. And I can tell you that today is one of those days."

Sophie clung to the purple folder in her lap.

"It's my fault that I don't have the funds to pay off the loan."

"I was really pulling for you." Beth removed her glasses and wiped her eyes fully. "Really wanting you to shove a check across my desk this morning."

Sophie had been pulling for herself, too. Unfortunately, too many other people had been pulling against her and she'd lost the tug-of-war. "How much time will I have to move our things out?"

"I have quite a bit of paperwork in the queue and most likely won't be able to start the foreclosure process until the end of this week or next." Beth tossed the tissue in the trash bin, replaced her glasses and her reserved, professional tone. "Could you be out by the end of the month?"

Sophie sagged into the leather chair. Three weeks was like a stay of execution and Sophie wanted to reach for the tissue box at the unexpected surprise. They wouldn't be homeless tonight or even that week, and for that she was so very grateful. Sophie straightened in her chair and assumed a more businesslike tone. "The end of the month won't be a problem."

"If you need a reference on a new apartment, I'd be happy to give one," Beth added.

"I'm not sure a foreclosure is something a new

landlord wants to see on a tenant's application." Sophie bent the edge of the folder.

"There isn't a foreclosure yet. And up until this point, you haven't missed or been late on any of your mortgage payments." Beth looked at Sophie and smiled. "Send me the paperwork when you have it and I'll give you that reference."

Beth dropped her buttoned-up persona and gave her an open, natural smile. One given to a friend, not a negligent customer. The kind that offered no judgment, only support. The kind that reminded Sophie good existed and extended even to her. Overwhelmed, Sophie managed to nod a silent thank-you.

She started to stand and noticed a newly framed photo of a little girl holding two kittens. Now Sophie could return one kindness for another. "As it turns out, I've several boxes of kitten food that can't be returned to the vendor. I could drop it off later this week."

"I'd appreciate that." Beth grinned at the picture. "The food definitely won't go to waste, given the two new additions at my daughter's birthday party this past Saturday."

"Then I'll see you later this week with the food." Sophie stood.

"And your reference paperwork." Beth pulled out her keyboard.

Sophie checked the time on her phone as she

strode through the bank's lobby. Now, Sophie had her own birthday surprise to orchestrate.

Outside, she ran across the intersection to catch the bus headed for downtown. She preferred walking to her destinations, but this errand was too important. She didn't know if there'd be lines or extended lunch hours at the courthouse. She opened the purple folder and confirmed Tessa's signature and date on the paperwork terminating her rights as a mother.

Sophie hopped off the bus and ran up the stairs to the courthouse entrance. Turned out she was a runner after all. But she ran toward her future, not away. Toward a commitment that she'd made in her heart ten years ago. A commitment that she wanted the world to recognize. Today she began the process for permanent guardianship and when funds permitted, she'd begin the formal adoption paperwork.

Today she became Ella's mother.

CHAPTER TWENTY-SEVEN

"You're going to forgive Callahan's loan." Brad leaned against the granite counter in his galley and stared down the man seated at the table. He'd chosen to have this discussion on the boat for privacy and a lack of recording devices, aside from his own. "We'll consider it a measure of goodwill."

Teddy tipped his chair back, crossed his arms over his chest and met Brad's gaze. "Don't believe in goodwill."

"Then how about this? I know what you did to Leo Baxter." Brad tossed a stack of documents on the table.

The front chair legs rapped against the floor. "No one knows nothing."

"I wouldn't be so sure of that." Brad tipped his chin toward the papers. "I imagine it'd be bad for business if word got out that you snitched on your associates to help out your detective cousin in Texas."

"Don't know nothing about Texas." Teddy lifted out of the chair. "Besides, every copper in this town who's tried to pin something on me has failed. You don't even have a badge. You got less than nothing."

"Take a look, Teddy." Brad shoved away from the counter and pressed his fists into the table. Better than planting his fist in Teddy's nose. "Depositions. Police reports. See what the guy without the badge knows about you."

Teddy slammed back into the chair as if he'd slammed into Brad's fury. Teddy flipped through several pages before he pushed them aside. "This is more like extortion. I could have you arrested."

Brad noted the calculating gleam in Teddy's stare as if the man were running through potential scenarios to gain the upper hand. But this was Brad's meeting. Brad's rules. And the deck belonged to Brad and he'd decide when to deal Teddy in.

"I'd be very careful right now. These aren't the only copies." Brad slid his cell phone out of his pocket. "And I've got several of your local business contacts on speed dial."

Teddy ran his palms smoothly over the armrests. His fingers never twitched, his shoulders never sagged. But defeat was there in the way he avoided looking Brad in the eyes. "I've always considered myself a forgiving man. We'll consider Callahan's loan a gift."

"The gift, Teddy, is me letting you walk out of here, instead of getting into a police car. Don't ever threaten or harass Sophie and Ella again. You ever try to collect again from any Callahan and I'll arrange a tell-all across the entire West Coast. I'll ensure you have no place to run." Brad flexed his fingers, but never stepped away from the table.

"I get it. You can stop." Teddy raised his hand. "What am I supposed to do now?"

"Go about your business, whatever that is, and try not to get arrested," Brad said.

Teddy pushed out of his chair, glanced into the media room and rubbed his chin. "Think the owner will mind if I conduct some business out here?"

"Do you want to get arrested for trespassing?" Brad asked.

"Never seen a boat this pretty." Teddy shrugged, but his tone remained pensive and almost sad. "Makes me want to set sail and never look back."

"That was the owner's intention."

Teddy followed Brad out onto the main deck and asked, "What happened?"

"He looked back."

Brad escorted Teddy Gordon down the dock, through the gate and into the parking lot. He waited until Teddy drove away before returning to the boat and locking up. He still wanted to punch the guy for scaring Sophie, but his heart wouldn't be in it. Not today. Unfortunately, Brad didn't foresee that feeling dissipating anytime soon.

One last check on the windows and locks and Brad headed to his truck for his next appointment. Teddy Gordon was a warm-up for this upcoming meeting. And all bets were off when it came to him retaining the upper hand.

Two energy drinks and a three-car fender bender that extended his drive past the usual twenty-minute commute, Brad finally entered his mother's office.

Nothing had changed. The air was starched. The furniture stiff and formal. The chairs too delicate. The vanilla candles flickered on the mantel. Everything was as it should be in his mother's domain.

But for the first time, he could breathe inside the space. He didn't want to race outside to the patio and inhale a few cleansing breaths.

He strolled behind his mother's desk and studied the framed pictures lined up in perfect symmetry. But that's where the staging ended. The largest photo contained the staid family portraits. But the smaller frames captured candid moments: an action shot of him on the rugby field, Drew passing on the forty-yard line, cotton candy–stained smiles from the state fair and the brothers asleep on the dog beds with the greyhounds.

He'd only ever glared at that fake family portrait and never looked closer. Never approached his mother's desk or walked behind it. When had he started seeing his mother as only a politician?

He turned around and noticed several pens with chewed caps like the ones inside his own desk drawer and a dozen or so candy wrappers in the trash. A ceramic bowl filled with hard caramel candies sat next to her monitor.

The candy surprised Brad. He'd never known his mother to indulge her sweet tooth. But the particular candy dish stunned him. He picked up the dish and studied the muddy-brown-and-green-glazed bowl. His mother and Evie walked into the office. "Did I make this?"

"Discovered her secret stash, I see." Evie's laughter filled the room.

His mother stepped up to him and eyed the candy as if counting to see if he took one or two. "Third-grade art class. A duck bowl you gave me for Mother's Day."

Brad lifted the bowl higher. He'd like to think he possessed a little more talent, even in grade school. "Duck bowl?"

"It's shaped just like a duck." His mother smiled. "Can't you see it?"

"It looks like a rotten potato." He tried to frown, but failed as he was too absurdly pleased his mother had kept his artwork after all these years and chose to hide her favorite candy inside. Not that he was sentimental. Or at least he hadn't been until a certain pet-shop owner invaded his life. "Are you sure Drew didn't make this?"

His mother leaned around him and tapped a flat panel on one of her built-in shelves. The panel swung open. He'd never known that was a door. So many hidden secrets that he'd never paid attention to until today. He peeked over her shoulder and felt his eyebrows stretch into his hairline. It was her personal curio cabinet filled with child-drawn artwork, more ceramics and what looked to be stick art. She chose a piece and shut the door before he could get a good look. She placed the ceramic piece on her open palm. "Your brother created this."

Evie leaned over his shoulder. "I remember that one. We passed it around at bruncheon one morning. Adorable."

Brad frowned at the thin green ceramic that extended from his mother's palm to the tips of her fingers. Clearly, his brother lacked an artist's DNA, too. "What is it?"

Evie nudged his arm with her elbow. "That's the fun. No one knows."

"It depends on your mood and imagination."

His mother shrugged, a grin spreading across her face. "Whatever it is, it always makes me smile, then and now." She covered it with her other hand as if she was protecting a priceless artwork from the elements, and returned it to her secret curio cabinet. Taking the candy dish from him, she shooed him out from behind her desk. "We'll sit by the fireplace. I've been behind this desk too much lately. And you didn't drive out here to discuss childhood memories."

Brad shifted in the squat antique chair, tried stretching out one leg for balance. The fragile chair seemed even more narrow, or perhaps his sudden unease took up too much space. "It's about the boat."

Evie and his mother shared a look before his mother raised an eyebrow at him. "You've decided on a date to set sail, then?"

"Not exactly." He glanced at Evie, but she remained quiet and attentive beside his mother, not even offering a smile of encouragement. "Evie called me earlier this week to tell me about her plans to relocate to the city." He knew his mother was already aware of the details. The women had been best friends for too long and Evie would've sought Nancy Harrington's advice before making any kind of big decision such as this.

"Richard always wanted to move into the

city," his mother said. "Now Evie gets to do things on her terms. Her way."

"And I want to help," he said.

"I'd expect nothing less." His mother touched Evie's arm. "There's a lot to be done and Evie cannot be expected to handle it without us."

Brad leaned forward, held his mother's gaze and considered grabbing her hand to make sure she heard him. "I want to do more than move plants in my pickup truck. I want to invest."

His mother looked at Evie. "You never mentioned this part."

"It wasn't my part to tell," Evie said. "But I support his decision."

His mother turned to him. "How am I involved in this?" she asked.

Brad gripped the armrests and ripped off the proverbial Band-Aid. "I want you and dad to buy the boat from me."

"You want us to buy the *Freedom Seeker*?" Surprise and confusion pulled her eyebrows together before she composed herself. "What would we do with it?"

"Sail away on it when you retire at the end of your term," he said. "Use it to take Dad around the world. Spend time on it with Dad alone. Just the two of you. You don't even need to leave the dock."

"And you'll do what?" His mother studied

him, her gaze probing for an angle and coming up empty.

"Use the funds to invest in Evie's venture in the city." And if all went as Evie planned, he'd invest in his new life. Not the one spent alone on the open ocean, but the one he hadn't known he'd needed until he lost it at a dog gala five nights ago.

"You have other savings." His mother continued to search his face.

"Nothing that I can easily access. I used most of my savings on the boat's restoration." And the money needed to come from the boat. He needed to make this choice to prove himself. To prove he was serious about his commitment. To prove he didn't want to run. That he was ready to give up one dream for the reality of a new one.

His mother walked to her desk, picked up her candy bowl and returned to her chair. "When do you need to know?"

She offered a candy to Evie as if in celebration, and he sensed victory. But he had to make certain. Too much depended on her decision. He launched his final shot. "As soon as possible. Otherwise, I have to look for another buyer. But since it was Grandfather's boat, I thought it might be nice to keep it in the family."

His mother's hand paused inside the candy

dish, just a second, just a small flinch. He'd hit his mark.

She recovered quickly, unwrapping a candy as if it were diamonds, not caramel. "Have you spoken to your father?"

"Not yet. He'll defer to you since it was your dad's boat." Brad rose and checked his phone, leaned down to kiss his mother's cheek, then Evie's. "I have a meeting at the office. I'll call you later."

Brad stepped into the hallway, but didn't close the door.

His mother's voice carried into the hallway. "My son isn't leaving."

Brad smiled and popped the candy he'd swiped from his mother's hand into his mouth. Surprise tinged her slow words.

Evie chortled. "It doesn't appear so."

"Our family will stay together," his mother added.

Her voice crinkled like one of her candy wrappers and Brad rubbed at his chest. He understood the importance of staying together. He understood the strength that came from belonging.

"It's what we wanted." Evie's voice soothed.

Brad exhaled, all too grateful that Evie belonged in his family, too.

"And we've wanted it to grow for some

time now." Again that crinkled catch laced his mother's voice.

"If he doesn't mess this up, that just might happen."

The grim warning in Evie's tone almost had Brad choking on the hard candy in his mouth.

"Do you think he needs our help?" His mother's soft laugh was muffled as if she spoke behind her hand or a tissue.

"Most definitely," Evie said. "But he'll have to do this one thing all on his own."

The confidence in Evie's voice restored his smile and his determination as Brad exited the front door, taking his family's support with him. He'd have to do this next thing on his own.

But for the first time in too long, he saw more than shadows and darkness. For the first time in too long, he muted his inner cynic. For the first time in too long, he listened to his heart.

CHAPTER TWENTY-EIGHT

ONE WEEK. SEVEN DAYS. One hundred and sixty-eight hours. That was all it took to dismantle Sophie's business. Her life. And her heart. She'd vowed not to live in the past. She'd vowed to keep her focus on the future. She'd vowed to keep moving forward, even if it was only a small shuffle at a time.

Unfortunately, she could roller-skate through the storefront now. The three-day flash sale with bottomed-out prices had cleared off every shelf. The only remaining inventory—four plush dog toys, a handful of cat balls with bells, one petite navy dog leash, one extralarge heavy-duty pink leash and a pair of betta fish.

Even the old, dented metal shelves bowed without any product. Without any purpose. Without anything to hold.

Sophie wrapped her arms around Erin and Troy, holding on to the group hug longer than necessary. She wouldn't apologize for that. These two meant the world to her. "I'm really sorry we have to close down."

"I'm really going to miss working here." Erin wiped her eyes with her sweatshirt sleeve.

"If you open a new place, you'll call us?" Troy asked. "You promised, remember?"

"You'll be the first on my list." Sophie pressed her lips together and swallowed past the emotion caught in her throat.

"Are you sure we can't help anymore?" Troy remained in the doorway to the kennel area as if ready to hold up the archway if Sophie asked.

"You've done more than enough." Sophie piled the unwanted inventory into her laundry basket and considered climbing inside herself. "Handling all those adoptions the last few days while I searched for apartments." And filled out job applications. Over a dozen applications for receptionist or cashier or bag girl. Anything to make the rent and give Ella a home.

"We still have two more weeks here." Erin kicked the edge of the counter with her running shoe.

Sophie kicked herself. Regret and sadness would only defeat her will and her resolve to be positive. She'd given notice to her customers about the closure. She'd given notice to her employees. Nothing had been as bad as giving the truth to Ella and watching the child's smile disappear.

But not permanently. Not forever. Only a night.

Ella had climbed into Sophie's bed, wrapped her thin arms around Sophie and hugged her with all the strength and hope and love she possessed. She'd hugged her until she heard Sophie's laughter. Until she felt Sophie's smile. Until Sophie matched her joy.

Together they'd worked everything out. Picked the families for each foster animal and even continued to laugh. The laughter kept the sadness contained. Sophie set her arm around Erin's shoulders and guided her out from behind the counter, dragging a lightness into her tone. "You both need to go home, have dinner and study. I know Troy mentioned a psychology test tomorrow. And I thought I heard something about statistics."

"That's mine." Erin groaned, but squeezed Sophie one last time before joining Troy.

Troy dropped his arm around Erin's waist. "Let's pick up sweet-and-sour pork on our way home. It's your favorite."

"Okay, but I'll buy." Erin pulled out her wallet while Troy dialed the takeout number. One last round of goodbye waves and the bells chimed signaling the pair's departure.

Sophie picked up a bottle of disinfectant to clean out the kennels and to hopefully distract herself from dwelling on how few chimes the bells had left.

She peeked into the only occupied kennel. The white kitten was curled up on an extraplush pink bed, both an apology and birthday present to Ella. Sophie hadn't been able to give the kitten up for adoption and decided she'd put a bell around its neck so Ella knew where the kitten was. At least she'd still have a bell chiming inside their apartment.

Sophie walked the length of the empty yard. As much as she'd wanted every foster to find its forever home, she liked the animals' company. She loved having the space busy, inside and out. It was never quiet. Never empty. And she was never truly alone. Her life was full. But like the vacant kennels, she now had a void to fill. But she wasn't useless or unnecessary.

She opened a kennel and sprayed it with disinfectant, hoping she might discover her new purpose in the polished stainless steel. Four kennels later and no enlightenment, Sophie listened to the bells chiming again. She kept her head inside the kennel and asked, "What did you guys forget?"

"It seems we've forgotten to have that chat."

Sophie straightened and closed the kennel door. All of her scrubbing hadn't revealed this encounter. She moved to look at Evelyn Davenport. "I've been meaning to call to set up lunch or dinner, but with the adoptions and everything…"

Evie held up her hand. "Don't apologize. I don't imagine there's a book out there on the proper etiquette for this type of situation."

"You mean, how do you apologize to the woman your own father fleeced?" Sophie crumpled up the paper towel in her fist.

"Or how do you apologize to the daughter of the man you're responsible for putting in jail?"

Sophie set down the disinfectant bottle, tossed the paper towel and her shame in the wastebasket. "Should we have to apologize for a man we don't and can't control?"

Evie loosened the scarf wrapped around her neck as if she'd anticipated a cold reception but now felt too warm. "I don't believe so, but there's this pressure to say something."

"You brought my father in. The other women he'd stolen from are making sure he stays in prison. Only time will tell if it's the best or worst place for him." Sophie hadn't resolved her feelings for her father and accepted that the process would be a long one. But she wanted more for this woman who still meant so much to her. For this woman who'd brought so much joy into her world. Sophie washed her hands in the cold water, wishing it was as easy to make things right with Evelyn. "I wish I could give you back your money."

"I know. And that means a lot to me." Evie walked around the barren storage area. "Where's Ella?"

"A sleepover with Ruthie." Sophie dried her hands and avoided looking at the empty kennels. Only her reflection waited to greet her in the polished steel. "Ella didn't want to be here and have to say goodbye to all the fosters."

"I understand. I'm going to miss that creamy Persian. I hope you sent the cat to its new home with a sharpened pair of scissors and grooming instructions."

Sophie laughed. "I might've suggested a dedicated pair of shears for felines only."

Evie pulled out her car keys and studied Sophie. "Do you have time to take a ride with me? I have something I want to show you."

Sophie glanced around. How was it possible for the space to become any more forlorn and deserted? Yet with each goodbye, it was as if the loneliness seeped right into the cinder-block walls and concrete floor. She needed the distraction if she wanted to regain her optimism. "Let me grab my coat and keys."

Ten minutes and a quiet cab ride later, Sophie and Evie stood across the street from the Sugar Beet Pantry. Sophie gestured to the organic café and market. "Olivia serves one of the best bowls of wild-mushroom soup in the city."

Evie glanced around as if seeing the street for the first time. "I've never been inside."

"Everything is farm to market and organic. And she sells hard-to-find spices and herbs. Anything her customers request." Sophie smiled. Olivia and Ruthie's support had extended beyond the night of the bash. A delivery boy had dropped off a container of wild-mushroom soup for Sophie that afternoon. "On the house," he'd told her when she'd tried to pay. She'd tallied up her friends' favors, and when the time came, she'd be there for her friends in return. "It's one of my favorite places to get dinner when I stop in to visit Kay and April. Kay's apartment is on the second floor."

"That's an even better surprise." Evie clapped her hands together and pointed down the street. "What about the local bar down on the left?"

"I haven't been inside in quite a while. I don't have much of a nightlife these days."

"I've spoken to the owner. He's quite a handsome young man." Evie nudged her shoulder, directing Sophie to turn around.

Sophie stared at a vacant storefront with a bay window and roll-up garage door. There were two floors on top of the storefront and from the absence of light, she assumed those were empty, too. A tree outside added shade and some greenery.

"What do you think?" Evie asked.

"I'm not sure I could afford the rent." Disappointment washed through her, but she ignored the whisper that she needed to return to her empty store. Solutions to her apartment hunt wouldn't be found in the stainless steel no matter how hard she scrubbed.

"That won't be a problem." Evie reached into her purse, pulled out a set of keys and walked to the wrought-iron gate protecting the storefront.

Sophie followed Evie, but her father's assertion about Evie owning property echoed in her head. Had she scrubbed a magic genie lamp? "This isn't your place, is it?"

"My husband invested years ago with several friends, Mr. Harrington being one." Evie slid in the key, opened the gate and motioned Sophie inside. "I never really understood the appeal, but he insisted on buying out his partners a few years back. He'd wanted us to retire in the city and run a flower shop." Evie shook her head. "I'd always indulged him. Can you imagine me running a flower shop?"

Sophie could imagine Evelyn Davenport doing whatever she wanted. She walked to the bay window, took in the lightly tinted glass and the angles. A perfect spot for vases of flower arrangements or a collection of books or… She stopped herself before she imagined more than she dared. She must have inhaled too many cleaning fumes. "This is lovely."

"I'm glad you think so. I was thinking it would be an adorable place to put a litter of kittens or several puppies for sale."

Sophie spun and stared at the older woman. Surely Evie would laugh or retract her words, or something to extinguish that wisp of hope curling inside Sophie. "What do you mean?"

"I find I'm restless in my empty house in Pacific Hills. I thought to put this building up for sale, but then I remembered Richard's retirement plan." Evie strolled around the space and opened her arms. "It isn't a floral shop, but I thought the Pampered Pooch might fit nicely in here. We'd have to do some remodeling, but if we connected the garage to the backyard, we'd have an indoor and outdoor space for the doggy day care."

Hope soared through her, threatening to buckle her legs. Sophie reached for the wall and slid down until she hit the edge of the bay window. "You want to move the Pampered Pooch here?"

"There'd be certain conditions, of course." Evie held up her hand. "Three, to be exact."

Sophie nodded. It was all she could manage

as tears formed and gratitude jammed her voice. She'd found her future—and Ella's.

"You'd have to pay rent for the space and the second-floor apartment." Evie waved her hands as if Sophie'd argue or complain. "Nothing extravagant, but enough to help us fund the improvements."

Sophie's head only bobbed up and down. Each strike of her chin toward her chest filled her with joy like a working pump on a well after a long drought.

Evie rushed on. "And I'll be the second tenant in the top-floor unit."

Sophie discovered her voice, although the high pitch extended into more of a squeal. "You're going to live here, too?"

"I see the appeal now." Evie stilled and watched Sophie. "I like being with you and Ella, if you'll have me."

"Yes." Evie belonged with them. They belonged with her.

"Also, I want to work at the Pooch." Evie set her hands on her hips as if preparing to defend her demands. "You gave me a purpose when you hired me, Sophie. I needed that more than I knew. More than a retirement fund."

"We needed you more." Sophie let the tears run down her cheeks, unchecked and free. This was more than she could have wished for. More than she'd ever expected.

"Then we might make this work?" Evie asked. "It won't be easy. And I fear we might have to do a lot of the renovating ourselves to cut down on cost. Eventually I'll sell the house in Pacific Hills, but it'll take a while and these renovations need to be done soon, so the pet store can open as quickly as possible."

"Yes. Yes. And yes." Sophie jumped up from the bay window and wrapped her arms around Evie. "We can do this. We can make it work for all of us."

"That's important because we haven't discussed the third condition." Evie hugged Sophie, squeezing as if she wanted to bolster her.

Sophie stepped away. A spiral of nerves curved around her hope and dimmed her brightness. But whatever the third condition was, she'd deal with it. She'd meant what she'd said. She'd make this work, no matter what it took.

Evie ran her hands down the front of her coat. "There's a silent partner we need to consider."

A partner? She'd been expecting something like more tenants in the building. Or a leaky roof. Or faulty electrical. Or cranky neighbors who hated animals. But a partner? Someone else to interfere? "Who?"

"Me." Brad stepped into the room from a back door.

Sophie wanted to stumble, but held her ground. Her gaze detailed every part of him and her heart pounded. "Why?"

"Because I need you. I need to be a part of your life," he said. "You make my world better. You make me better."

"So you're going to buy your way into my life?" Sophie struggled to tighten those chains around her heart.

"It's more of an investment into our life." He stepped closer, but not near enough to touch her. "The one I want to build with you."

"After you sail around the world."

"That will be hard to do without a boat."

"What happened to it?"

"I traded it in for a chance at a different life."

"You traded your boat and a life of freedom for me?" That wasn't possible. He'd told her he had to leave. Like everyone in her family.

"I don't have a life if you're not a part of it. My life is empty without you," he said. "You told me you loved me the other night."

Her life was empty without him, too. He'd left a void she knew she'd never fill.

"I never said the words back to you," he said. "That was my fault. I'm sorry for that and not telling you the truth about investigating your father."

"There can't be any more lies between us."

"Then let me say this, I love you, Sophie Callahan. I choose you."

His words poured through her, filled that void, washed away the pain and the distrust and the hurt. Her father had only ever made promises. But he'd never told Sophie he loved her. He'd never chosen his family first.

But Brad chose her. And three simple words had made those locks burst open with joy. Now she understood Ruthie's giddy grin and belief in fairy tales. Because standing in this empty, dusty storefront, she found herself believing in the power of love for the first time ever.

Sophie rushed toward Brad, nothing to stumble over like doubt or fear or uncertainty. "There's a weird echo off these blank walls. Can you say that again?"

"I love you," he shouted, and opened his arms, welcoming her into his embrace. Welcoming her into his heart. Welcoming her home.

Sophie framed his face in her hands and held his gaze. "I love you, too."

He pulled her tighter against him and kissed her until the fairy tale felt real, magic winding their hearts together.

Brad pulled away, pressed a soft kiss on her

lips, then looked around the space. "What do you think? Ready to make this our forever home?"

Sophie nodded and rested her cheek over Brad's heart. Her forever home wasn't a place after all. It was their love. And as long as they had that, they had everything.

EPILOGUE

One week later...

SOPHIE SCOOTED A bouquet of balloons up onto the coffee table, away from the curious paws of their newest family member, Stormy Cloud. The kitten climbed onto the sofa, her bell jingling as she gathered her courage to make the leap onto the table and capture her prize. Sophie picked up the bouquet before the kitten's leap and strode into the kitchen.

Only the blue sky remained from the oversize rainbow birthday cake that Kay had dropped off before she'd rushed back to the hospital to hold the twins and sit with April. More than a dozen sketches covered the kitchen table. Once Ella's school friends had departed, the discussion had shifted from favorite movie lines to design, specifically the best design for the new Pampered Pooch space, for Ella's bedroom and for updating the kitchen. Pencils, paper and opinions had flown around.

Mr. Harrington requested a comfortable recliner for when he and the mayor visited—those times when they were not in the mansion or on the sea. Ruthie and Matt designed the passageway from the garage to the outdoor play yard, complete with turf grass to protect the dogs' sensitive paws. Drew modernized both Sophie's and Evie's kitchens, while Evie sketched a new layout for the storefront with Erin's and Troy's input. Sophie searched through the sketches, looking for Evie's drawing. The thoughtful, practical and efficient design by her employees would guide the renovations.

Brad and Ella had ignored the pandemonium and escaped. For over an hour, they huddled together on the couch and designed Ella's new room. Nothing had interrupted their focus until the call had come in from one of Sophie's recent adoptions and they'd left with Evie on their rescue mission.

Sophie had packed up to-go boxes for her other guests while they'd added the final details to their sketches. Another successful birthday to add to their memory book. Only one present remained for Ella. Sophie wandered around the kitchen, then picked up Stormy Cloud rather than check the clock for the fifteenth time.

Laughter filtered up the staircase before the front door slammed shut. More laughter and the steady smack of boots on wood announced the trio's return. Ella walked into the family room first, her face bright and her smile wide. Evie's and Brad's voices collided and bounced down the hall.

"What's happening?" Sophie asked.

Ella pressed her finger over her lips to quiet Sophie and settled herself on the couch.

Sophie leaned down and whispered, "Do I need to get involved?"

Ella giggled and shook her head.

"Can you hold Stormy just in case?" Sophie asked.

Ella smoothed the throw blanket over her legs before Sophie placed Stormy on her lap. The kitten's purr vibrated through her whole body at Ella's soft touch.

Brad strode in, kissed Sophie and set down a pink cat carrier.

Evie followed him and picked up the carrier. "You already have one."

"That one belongs to Ella." Brad pointed to the kitten curled up on Ella's lap. "And you get too scissor-happy around cats."

"That was one time." Evie stepped away from him when he reached for the cat carrier.

Sophie dropped her hand on Brad's arm, drawing his focus to her. "What's going on?"

"Turned out one of the younger Harper kids

was allergic to the cat." Brad set his hands on his hips. "And now Evie is making a claim on Chai."

"Chai," Sophie repeated.

"She's a girl. A creamy, elegant Persian." Evie pushed the carrier behind her legs. "Her name is Guinevere."

"The last time you had her, you gave her a bad haircut. She probably hasn't recovered yet," Brad argued. "She should live with us and you can visit on weekends after a scissor check."

Ella laughed. "Tell him, Auntie?"

"Tell him what?" Sophie asked.

"The rules," she said.

Sophie wrapped her arm around Brad's waist and kissed his cheek. "I love you. But you can't keep all the fosters."

"I don't want all the fosters." He kissed her on the lips. "I just want the one Evie has."

"This one's mine, Bradley Harrington." Evie gripped the cat carrier and stared down Brad. "The old ladies need to stick together. You have to find your own."

Evie walked over to Ella and pressed her cheek against the little girl's. "Happy birthday, precious. And I've got vanilla ice cream, hot fudge and two spoons waiting at my place for our own private celebration tomorrow night."

"I've got the nail polish already packed," Ella said.

"I'll see you then for girls' night. We can get Guinevere settled in." Evie hugged Sophie. "He's becoming a bit territorial about the fosters. You're going to have to keep Brad in check or we'll have a zoo at our new place."

Brad hugged Evie. "I'll be by to check on Chai."

"I'll be expecting you." Evie left, promising Guinevere she'd love her new home.

"You really wanted to keep Guinevere?" Sophie asked.

"She needs us." Brad squeezed onto the couch beside Ella and Stormy.

"She has Evie, and that means she has us, too," Ella said.

Sophie sat on the other side of Ella. "Speaking of us, I have something else to share with you."

"Another kitten?" Ella asked.

"Let's see how we do with one and then we'll talk about it," Sophie said.

"At least she didn't say no right away." Ella nudged Brad. "There's still a chance you could get your own cat, too."

Brad reached behind Ella's head and grabbed Sophie's hand. "I've got everything I want right here. Right now."

"Did all your birthday wishes come true, Ella?" Sophie asked. "I know you wanted to spend your birthday with your mother."

Ella shifted toward Sophie and set her hand over Sophie's heart. "I did spend my birthday with my mom."

Sophie placed her hand over Ella's. "I filed the paperwork to become your permanent guardian. To become your mother according to the law. It means I'll be your mom."

Ella leaned forward and wrapped her arms around Sophie. "It means we're a forever family."

Sophie squeezed Ella, then opened her arms to include Brad. She held on tight to everything she'd ever wanted. To everything she loved with all of her heart—her forever family.

* * * * *

Be sure to check out Cari Lynn Webb's special Valentine's novella,
THE MATCHMAKER WORE SKATES,
in MAKE ME A MATCH.
Available now from www.Harlequin.com!

Get 2 Free Books,
Plus 2 Free Gifts—
just for trying the
Reader Service!

Get 2 Free Books,
Plus 2 Free Gifts—
just for trying the Reader Service!

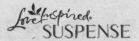